THE
DARK TIDE

Adrien English Mysteries

JOSH LANYON

mlrpress

MLR PRESS AUTHORS

Featuring a roll call of some of the best writers of gay erotica and mysteries today!

M. Jules Aedin	Drewey Wayne Gunn
Maura Anderson	Samantha Kane
Victor J. Banis	Kiernan Kelly
Jeanne Barrack	J.L. Langley
Laura Baumbach	Josh Lanyon
Alex Beecroft	Clare London
Sarah Black	William Maltese
Ally Blue	Gary Martine
J.P. Bowie	Z.A. Maxfield
Michael Breyette	Patric Michael
P..A. Brown	Jet Mykles
Brenda Bryce	Willa Okati
Jade Buchanan	L. Picaro
James Buchanan	Neil Plakcy
Charlie Cochrane	Jordan Castillo Price
Gary Cramer	Luisa Prieto
Kirby Crow	Rick R. Reed
Dick D.	A.M. Riley
Ethan Day	George Seaton
Jason Edding	Jardonn Smith
Angela Fiddler	Caro Soles
Dakota Flint	JoAnne Soper-Cook
S.J. Frost	Richard Stevenson
Kimberly Gardner	Clare Thompson
Storm Grant	Lex Valentine
Amber Green	Stevie Woods
LB Gregg	

Check out titles, both available and forthcoming, at
www.mlrpress.com

THE
DARK TIDE

Adrien English Mysteries

JOSH LANYON

mlrpress

Published by
MLR Press, LLC
3052 Gaines Waterport Rd.
Albion, NY 14411

Visit ManLoveRomance Press, LLC on the Internet:
www.mlrpress.com

Editing by Judith David
Printed in the United States of America.

ISBN# 978-1-60820-123-5

2010 Edition

To Lisabea

To say goodbye is to die a little.
Raymond Chandler, *The Long Goodbye*

CHAPTER ONE

It began, as a lot of things do, in bed.

Or to be precise, on the living-room sofa where I was uncomfortably dozing.

Somewhere in the distance of a very weird dream about me and a certain ex-LAPD police lieutenant came a faint, persistent scratching. The scratching worked itself into my dream, and I deduced with the vague logic of the unconscious that the cat was sharpening his claws on the antique half-moon table in the hall. Again.

Except…that boneless ball of heat on my abdomen was the cat. And he was sound asleep…

I opened my eyes. It was dark, and it took me a second or two to place myself. Moonlight outlined the pirate bookends on the bookshelf. From where I lay, I could barely make out the motion of the draperies in the warm July breeze in the front room of the flat above Cloak and Dagger Books.

I was home.

There had been a time when I'd thought I would never see home again. But here I was. I had a furry heating pad on my belly, a crick in my neck, and — apparently — a midnight visitor.

My first thought was that Lisa had called Guy, my ex, to look in on me. That furtive scraping wasn't the sound of a key; it was more like someone trying to…well, pick the lock.

I rolled off the sofa, dislodging the sleeping cat, and staggered to my feet, fighting the dizziness that had dogged me since my heart surgery three weeks earlier. I'd been staying at my mother's home in the Chatsworth Hills, but I'd checked myself out of the lunatic asylum that afternoon.

If Guy had dropped by, he'd have turned on the light in the shop below. There was no band of light beneath the door. No, what there was, was the occasional flash of illumination as though someone was trying to balance a flashlight.

I wasn't dreaming. Someone was trying to break in.

I felt my way across the darkened room to the entrance hall. My heart was already beating way too hard and too fast, and I felt a spark of anxiety — the anxiety that was getting to be familiar since my surgery. Was my healing heart up to this kind of strain? Even as I was calculating whether I could get to the Webley in the bedroom closet and load it before the intruder got the door open or whether my best bet was to lock myself in the bedroom and phone the cops, the decision was made for me.

The lock mechanism turned over, the door handle rotated, and the door silently inched out of the frame.

I reacted instinctively, grabbing the rush-bottomed chair in the hall and throwing it with all my strength. "Get the fuck out of here," I yelled over the racket of the chair clattering into the door and hitting the floor.

And — surprisingly — the intruder did get the fuck out.

Not a dream. Not a misreading of the situation. Someone had tried to break in to my living quarters.

I heard the heavy *thud* of footsteps pounding down the staircase back to the shop, heard something crash below, heard another crash, and, as I tottered to the wall light switch, the slam of a distant door.

What door? Not the side entrance of the shop below, because I knew that particular bang very well, and certainly not the front door behind the security gate. No, it had to have been from the adjacent structure. The bookstore took up one half of a subdivided building that had originally, back in the thirties, housed a small hotel. The other half of the building had gone through a variety of commercial incarnations, none of which had survived more than a year or so, until I'd finally been in a position to buy it myself the previous spring. It was currently in the expensive and noisy process of being renovated, the two halves divided by a wall of thick plastic.

Not thick enough, clearly.

The contractor had assured me the perimeter doors were guarded by "construction locks," and that it was as safe as it had ever been. Obviously he wasn't familiar with my history, let alone the history of the building.

I leaned back against the wall, trying to catch my breath and listening. Somewhere down the street I heard an engine roaring into life. Not necessarily my intruder's getaway car fleeing the scene. This was a nonresidential part of Pasadena, and at night it was very quiet and surprisingly isolated.

There was a time when I'd have intrepidly, Mr. Boy Detective, gone downstairs to see what the damage was. That that was four murder investigations, one shooting, and one heart surgery ago. Instead I got the gun from the bedroom closet, loaded it, returned to the front room, where the windows offered a better vantage point, and picked up the phone. The streetlamps cast leopard spots on the empty sidewalk, accentuated the deep shadows between the old buildings. Nothing moved. I recalled a line by Raymond Chandler: "The streets were dark with something more than night."

Reaction hit me, and I slid down the wall and dialed 911.

I was having trouble catching my breath as I waited — and waited — for the 911 operator, and I hoped to hell I wasn't having a heart attack. My heart had been damaged by rheumatic fever when I was sixteen. A recent bout of pneumonia had worsened my condition, and I'd been in line for surgery even before getting shot three weeks earlier. Everything was under control now, and according to my cardiologist, I was making terrific progress. The ironic thing about the surgery and the news that I was evidently going to make old bones after all was that I felt mortal in a way that I hadn't for the last fifteen years.

Tomkins pussyfooted up to delicately head-butt me.

"Hi," I said.

He blinked his wide, almond-shaped, green-gold eyes at me and *meowed*. He had a surprisingly quiet meow. Not as annoying as most cats. Not that I was an expert — nor did I plan on becoming one. I was only loaning a fellow bachelor my pad. The cat — kitten, really — was also convalescing. *He'd* been mauled by a dog three weeks ago. His bounce back was better than mine.

I stroked him absently as he wriggled around and tried to bite my fingers. I guessed there was truth to the wisdom about petting a cat to lower your blood pressure, because I could feel my heart rate slowing, calming — which was pretty good, considering how pissed off I was getting at being kept on hold in the middle of an emergency.

Granted, it wasn't much of an emergency at this point. My intruder was surely long gone.

I chewed my lip, listened once more to the message advising me to stay on the line and help would soon be with me. Assuming I'd still be alive to take that call.

I hung up and dialed another number. A number I had memorized long ago. A number that seemingly would require acid wash to remove from the memory cells of my brain.

As the phone rang on the other end, I glanced across at the clock on the bookshelf. Three oh three in the morning. Well, here was a test of true friendship.

"Riordan," Jake managed in a voice like raked gravel.

"Uh…hey."

"Hey." I could feel him making the effort to push through the fog of sleep. He rasped, "How are you?"

Pretty civil given the fact that I hadn't spoken to him for nearly two weeks and was choosing three in the morning to reopen the lines of communication.

I found myself instinctively straining to hear the silence behind him; was someone there with him? I couldn't hear over the rustle of bed linens.

"I'm okay. Something happened just now. I think someone tried to break in."

"You *think?*" And he was completely alert. I could hear the covers tossed back, the squeak of bedsprings.

"Someone did try to break in. He took off, but —"

"You're back at the bookstore?"

"Yeah. I got home late this afternoon."

"You're there alone?"

Thank God he didn't say it like everyone else had. *Alone?* As though it was out of the question. As though I was far too ill and helpless to be left to my own devices. Jake simply looked at it from a security perspective.

"Yeah."

"Did the security alarm go off?"

"No."

"Did you call it in?"

"I called nine-one-one. They put me on hold."

"At three o'clock in the morning?" He was definitely on his feet and moving, dressing, it sounded like, and I felt a wave of guilty relief. Regardless of how complicated our relationship was — and it was pretty complicated — there was no one I knew who was better at dealing with this kind of thing. Whatever this kind of thing was.

Which I guessed said more than I realized right there.

Jake's voice was crisp. "Hang up and call nine-one-one again. Stay on the line with them. I'll be there in ten minutes."

I said gruffly, "Thanks, Jake."

Just like that. I had called, and he was coming to the rescue. Unexpectedly, a wave of emotion — reaction — hit me. One of the weird aftereffects of my surgery. I struggled with it as he said, "I'm on my way," and disconnected.

♪ ♪ ♪

I went down to meet him, taking the stairs slowly, taking my time. From above, I had a bird's-eye view of the book floor. The register looked undisturbed. I could see where the bargain-book table had been toppled. Otherwise everything looked pretty much as normal: same comfortable leather club chairs, same wooden fake fireplace, same tall matching walnut bookshelves — strictly mystery and crime novels — same secretive smiles on the pale faces of the Kabuki masks on the back wall.

I unlocked the door, pushed open the security gate, which he'd knelt to examine. "You didn't have to come down. I'd have gone around to the s —" Jake broke off. He rose and said oddly, "Déjà vu."

I didn't get it for a second, and then I did. Echoes of the first time we'd met; although *met* was kind of a polite word for turning up as a suspect in someone's murder investigation.

Uncombed, unshaven, I was even dressed the same: jeans and bare feet. I'd thrown a leather jacket on partly because, despite the warmth of a July night, I felt chilled, and partly because I didn't want to treat him to the vision of the seam down the middle of my chest from open heart surgery. Not that Jake hadn't seen it when he visited me in the hospital, but it looked different out of context. The bullet hole in my shoulder was ugly enough; the incision from the base of my collarbone down through my breastbone was shocking. I found it shocking, anyway.

I said awkwardly, "Thanks again for coming."

He nodded.

We stared at each other. These last weeks couldn't have been easy on Jake, and not because I'd asked him to give me a little time, a little space before we tried to figure out where we stood. He'd resigned from LAPD, come out to his family, and asked his wife for a divorce. But he looked unchanged. Reassuringly unchanged. I think I'd feared… Well, I'm not sure. That he'd be harrowed by regret. For his entire adult life he'd fought to defend that closet he inhabited. Been willing to sacrifice almost everything to protect it. I couldn't help thinking he'd take to being out like a fish to desert sand.

He looked okay. No, be honest. He looked a lot better than okay. He looked…fine. *Fine*, as in get the Chiffons over here to sing a chorus. Big, blond, ruggedly handsome in a trial-by-fire way. He was very lean, all hard muscle and powerful bone. Maybe there was more silver at his temples, but there was a calm in his tawny eyes that I'd never seen before.

Under that light, steady gaze I felt unnervingly self-conscious. It was weird to think that for the first time in all the time I'd known him there was nothing to keep us from being together except the question of whether we both really wanted it.

He asked matter-of-factly, "Why didn't the alarm go off?"

"It wasn't set."

A quick drawing of his dark brows. He opened his mouth. I beat him to it. "We haven't been setting it while the construction has been going on next door."

"Tell me you're kidding."

He already knew I wasn't. "The city threatened to fine me because we had too many false alarms. The construction crew usually arrives before we open the shop, and they kept triggering it. So I thought…until the construction was completed…"

His silence said it all — good thing, because I was pretty sure if Jake got started, we'd be there all night.

"I think he must have come in from the side." I turned to lead the way.

He followed me across the front of the tall aisles. I pointed out where an endcap had been knocked over. "Only the emergency lights were on, and he crashed into that." I nodded to the fallen bargain table, the landslide of spilled books. "And there."

We reached the clear plastic wall dividing Cloak and Dagger Books from the gutted other half of the building. Staring from one side to the other was like peering through murky water. I could barely make out the ladders and scaffolds like the ribs of a mythological beast. I directed Jake's attention to the long five-foot slit through the plastic near the wall.

"Good call." He sounded grim.

I'd have happily been wrong. "The contractor told me that that side of the building would be secured with special locks. Construction locks."

He was already shaking his head. "Look at this." He stooped, pushing through the slit in the plastic, and I followed him into the darkened other side of the building. It smelled chilly and weird on that side. A mixture of fresh plaster, new wood, and dust. We picked our way through the hurdles of drop cloths and wooden horses and cement mixers to the door on the far wall. It swung open at his touch.

"Great," I said bitterly.

"Yep." He showed me the core in the center of the exterior handle. I discerned that it was painted, though I couldn't make out a color. "See that?"

I nodded.

"It's a construction core. That's a temporary lock used by contractors on construction sites. They're all combinated the same, or mostly the same, which means that if someone gets hold of a key, they've got a key to pretty much every construction core in the city."

"Better and better."

He shut the door and relocked it. "As security goes, this is one step above leaving the door standing wide open."

I swallowed. Nodded.

"Whoever broke in may have been watching the place and knew no one's been here at night."

I said, "It doesn't look like they touched the register."

"It might have been kids prowling around." Jake didn't sound convinced, and I knew why.

"Trying to break in to my flat was —"

"Pretty aggressive," he agreed. "Again, I think that probably gets back to the mistaken belief that no one was home. No one has been staying here at night for three weeks, right? So it was a reasonable assumption."

I absorbed that. "This might not have been the first time he was prowling around in here."

"True."

"I don't know that Natalie would notice the slice in the plastic wall. Hell, if Warren were hanging around, I don't know if she'd notice the Tasmanian Devil bursting through."

Sort of unfair to Natalie; Jake snorted, grimly amused.

All at once I was exhausted. Mentally and physically and emotionally drained dry. I didn't seem to have much in the way of physical resources these days, and this break-in felt like way more than I could begin to handle.

Jake opened his mouth but stopped. Through the dirty glass of the bay window, we watched a squad car pull up, lights flashing, though there was no siren.

Better late than never, I guess.

After a second or two, Jake looked at me. "You okay? You're shaking."

"Adrenaline."

"And heart surgery." He glanced back at the black-and-white. Drew a deep breath. "Why don't you head upstairs? I'll take care of this."

There it was again. That weird new emotionalism. The smallest things seemed to choke me up. Like this. Jake offering to talk to the cops for me.

Except this wasn't a small thing. Jake, who had hid his sexuality from his brother officers for nearly twenty years, who had been unwilling for people to even know we were friends, who had very nearly succumbed to blackmail and more to keep that secret, was offering to stand here in my place and talk to these cops — and let them think whatever they chose to about us and our relationship.

I'm not sure what was stranger: the fact that he was making the offer or that I was ready to start crying over it.

"I can handle it."

He met my gaze. "I know you can. I'd like to do this for you."

Hell. He did it again. It had to be that I was overtired and still shaken by the break-in. I worked to keep my face and voice from showing anything I was feeling, managing a brusque nod.

The cops, a man and a woman in uniform, were getting out of their car. I turned and started back through ladders and wooden horses and scaffolds.

∫ ∫ ∫ ∫

I was sitting on the sofa sleeping with the cat on my lap when Jake let himself into the flat.

I must have been snoring, because the *snick* of the door shutting seemed to come like a clap of thunder in the wake of a windstorm. The cat sprang from my lap. I straighted, closed my mouth, wiped my eyes, and when I blearily opened them, Jake stood over me, looking unfairly alert for four in the morning.

"Was that a cat I saw running into your bedroom?"

I cleared my throat. "Was it?"

"It looked like it." He sat down on the sofa next to me — all that size and heat and energy — and every muscle in my body immediately clenched tight in nervous reaction. I didn't feel ready for…whatever this was liable to be.

I said lightly, "Maybe the building is haunted."

"Could be." He seemed to study my face with unusual attention. "Your burglary complaint is filed. Tomorrow, first thing, you need to tell that contractor to get real locks on those doors. In fact, I'd advise you to change all the locks on both sides of the building."

I nodded wearily. "I've been trying to think what he was after."

"The usual things."

"Then why not break in to the cash register?"

"An empty cash register? Why?"

Good point. No point robbing the till after the day's bank drop had been made. I must be more tired than I thought. Maybe Jake had the same idea, because he said, "I thought you'd be in bed by now."

"I'm on my way. But I wanted to thank you…"

He said gravely, "Don't mention it. I'm glad you called me. I've been wondering how you're doing."

My gaze fell. "I'm all right." There was so much to say, and yet I couldn't seem to think of anything. "I'm getting there. The worst part is being tired all the time."

"Yeah." I could feel him watching me — seeing right through me.

"Jake…"

When I didn't continue, he said, "I know. I know it's a lot to ask. Probably too much, although I won't pretend I'm not hoping."

Forgiveness. That's what he was talking about. Forgiveness for any number of things, I guessed. I was talking about something completely different.

I shook my head. "It isn't — I don't know how to explain this. It's not you, though. It's me."

He waited with that new calm, that new certainty in his eyes. He was expecting me to drop the ax on him. I could see that. He had been expecting it since the last time we spoke in the hospital and I'd asked him to give me time. That's what he had expected when he answered my cry for help tonight — what he still expected — but he had come anyway.

Was that love or guilt or civic responsibility? He was the best friend I'd ever had — and the worst.

I said, "This isn't going to make sense to you, because it doesn't make sense to me. I know how lucky I am. I do. I know I'm getting a second chance, and even though I feel like utter *shit*, I know I'm getting well and I'm going to be okay. Better than okay. That's what my doctors keep telling me, and I know that I should be really happy and really relieved. But…I-I can't seem to feel anything right now."

Nothing from Jake. Not that I blamed him. What was he supposed to make of that speech?

I concluded lamely, "I don't know what's wrong with me."

"You feel what you feel. You're allowed."

It was getting harder to go on. I felt I had to be honest with him. "I was happy enough with Guy, but I don't want Guy. I don't want…anyone. Right now."

There was another pause after he heard me out. He said, "Okay."

It was that easy. I wasn't sure if what I felt was relief or disappointment.

I heard myself say, awkwardly, "I felt like I should —"

"Got it." Was there an edge to his tone? He still looked calm. Actually, he looked concerned. He said, "Why don't you go to bed, Adrien? I've seen snowmen with more color in their faces. You need sleep. So do I. In fact, I'm going to spend what's left of the night on your couch."

I said, despite my instant relief, "You don't have to do that."

"I know, Greta. You vant to be alone. But unless your need for space prohibits a friend crashing on the sofa, that's what I'm doing."

I didn't have the energy to argue with him — or myself. I nodded, pushed off the sofa, and headed for the bedroom. "There are blankets in the linen cupboard."

"I remember."

A thought occurred to me. I paused in the doorway, turning back to him.

"Jake?"

He was in the process of tugging off a boot. He glanced up. "Yeah?"

"Downstairs. With the cops. Was it okay?"

It seemed to take him a second to understand my concern. He smiled — the first real smile I'd seen from him in a very long time.

"Yes," he said. "It was okay."

CHAPTER TWO

I woke to the knowledge that a cat was licking my hair.

"Ugh," I muttered. "Don't *do* that."

"*Meow*," Tomkins replied through a mouthful of hair.

I reached up to push him aside, but he was so damned soft, so nice to touch — even if he did start licking my fingers with that rough little tongue. I stroked and tickled him for a second or two. I remembered that Jake was sleeping on my sofa.

I swung my legs over the side of the bed, gave myself a couple of seconds, and went to the door. The living-room sofa was vacant, blankets neatly folded on the foot.

I stood listening, sorting through the sounds of construction next door, the faint music from the shop below, thinking Jake might be in the kitchen; but after a second or two, I knew that the apartment was empty.

And that's exactly the way I wanted it, right?

Sure it was.

I went back in the bedroom, glanced at the clock. Ten thirty on a Tuesday morning. *Holy hell.* Granted, I was still convalescent, and it wasn't like I'd had a night's undisturbed rest, though last night's was the longest stretch of sleep I'd had since I'd regained consciousness in the hospital. Even at the Dautens' I hadn't been able to completely relax. Too many years of living on my own, I guessed.

Anyway, it was another day. The first day of the rest of my life, as the greeting-card people and physical therapists were so fond of observing. Time to get on with it.

I weighed myself on the bathroom scale. The good news was I hadn't lost any more weight. The bad news was I still hadn't gained any. I took my temperature: absolutely normal. Took my blood pressure and heart rate as I'd been taught to do in cardiac rehab. Good and good. I checked the incision in my chest. Healing nicely. There was an unattractive lump at the top of the incision; supposedly this would go away in time. Otherwise it looked perfectly normal — if you were a cadaver or related to Frankenstein's monster.

I studied my reflection in the bathroom mirror. Good thing I wasn't interested in being with anyone, because I couldn't imagine anyone, with the possible exception of body snatchers, finding me remotely appealing.

Still, there were things to be grateful for — beyond the fact that I was still alive and kicking. High on that list was no longer having to wear the white support hose prescribed after my surgery. Take it from me; support hosiery is not comfortable. And anyone who finds white support hose sexy needs to check in with the nearest sex-offender outpost.

Also in the plus column: the weird clicking noise in my chest that only I could hear had stopped. Either I was getting better or the slide into madness had slowed.

I did a very cautious and very short session of tai chi, showered, shaved, dressed, took my meds, fed the cat, and drank a protein shake, which was all I could manage in the mornings right now, and I did feel better. Simply being home made me feel better: stronger, more in control again.

And although I felt guilty for calling him, I couldn't deny it felt good that Jake had showed up when I needed him. Maybe there had been a fear in the back of my mind that if we weren't going to be more than friends, he wouldn't want to have anything to do with me.

It wouldn't have been the first time.

I drained the last of the strawberry-banana shake — now there's a flavor combo Mother Nature never intended — and started calling locksmiths until I found one willing to come by the shop that afternoon.

Mission accomplished, I headed downstairs.

I spotted Natalie, my stepsister, in conversation with an elderly man in a blue Hawaiian shirt. He had sparse jet-black hair, a pencil-thin mustache, and a camera around his neck. Tourists. We get a lot of them in this historic part of town. They don't tend to buy a lot of books.

"Oh I don't know," Natalie was apologizing. "Maybe Adrien would know. He's the owner. He's lived here about ten years, I think." She caught sight of me coming down the stairs and brightened. "Good morning!"

She's the physical type Hollywood producers cast to play ambitious young DAs in TV crime dramas: tall and blonde and very pretty. No one would cast her as a bookstore clerk. I'd hired her after Angus, my previous bookstore *associate* (as Natalie preferred to be called), had departed under the proverbial cloud. I have to admit I'd resisted hiring her pretty vigorously, but it turned out to have been one of my better business decisions.

To be honest, the whole stepfamily thing wasn't nearly as trying as I'd originally anticipated two years ago when my mother had unexpectedly decided to marry Councilman Bill Dauten. With Dauten had come three lovely and charming daughters: Lauren, Natalie, and Emma. Emma was the exact kid sister I'd have chosen if kid sisters were something you could purchase in a pet store.

Then again I didn't even buy my pets in pet stores, as indicated by the slip of a feline doing his best to send me tumbling to my death on my way down the staircase.

"Morning," I replied, grabbing at the banister in time to save my neck.

"Adrien, this gentleman —"

"Harrison. Henry Harrison," the tourist supplied.

"Mr. Harrison was asking about the history of the building—"

"That's right," Harrison interrupted enthusiastically. "You might not be aware of this, but the facade of this structure is one of the finest remaining examples of art deco in the city. That black tile out front — what's left of it — and those leaded glass transoms above the second-story windows and the grapevine design on the wrought-iron gates and window bars — aces."

Aces?

"Are you visiting from out of town?" I asked, safely reaching the bottom level and joining them at the large mahogany front desk.

"That's right. How'd you guess? I'm from Milwaukee. Old buildings are my hobby." He looked around the crowded main room of the bookstore affectionately. "Yes sirree, Bob. If these old places could talk."

"I hate to disappoint you. I don't know a whole lot about the history. The place was built back in the 1930s. Originally it was a hotel called the Huntsman's Lodge. This section and next door were all one building."

"I was interested in the murder."

I threw an uneasy look at Natalie. She was all pleased interest. "*Murder?* Really?"

"It was a long, long time ago." I kept an eye on the other customers wandering about.

Harrison said, "That's right. Took place back in the fifties."

"You never said anything about it, Adrien."

"It's not like it's preying on my mind," I told her.

"But that's a great angle. A mystery bookstore in a place where there really was a murder. We could really do something with this."

I smiled weakly, glanced at our visitor. Harrison had those dark, smile-crinkled Roy Rogers eyes. I got the feeling he was enjoying himself.

"So who was murdered?" Natalie persisted.

Harrison said to me, "I take it you own the other side of the building now?"

"That's right."

"How long has the renovation being going on?"

"Since May."

"*Who* was murdered?" Natalie, like all the Dauten women, did not take kindly to being ignored. "Did they ever catch the killer?"

"It was a rumor," I said. "I don't think they ever found a body."

"They didn't find the body, but I bet you there was a murder, all right." Harrison offered a quick flash of perfect dentures. "Like I said, I'm a history buff. Where there's smoke, there's fire."

"What is the story?" Natalie asked him.

"Young fella by the name of Jay Stevens was staying here. He played clarinet in a jazz band called the Moonglows or some damned thing. Anyhoo, one night back in fifty nine, I think, he disappeared out of his room." He shook his head. "There were a few drops of blood on the floor, but no Jay Stevens."

Natalie gave a delighted shudder. "And they never found him?"

"I don't think so."

"Nope," Harrison said.

"Maybe someone hit him over the head and he got amnesia and wandered away."

"Stranger things have happened," Harrison said, though personally I'd have had trouble coming up with many. I'd always thought there was a good chance Stevens had simply skipped out on his creditors. A musician living in a fleabag hotel was bound to have creditors after him. And possibly music critics.

"Why do people think he was murdered? What was the motive?" Natalie spoke like a true mystery buff. I was sort of proud of her, in between wishing she'd drop it and go reorganize the best-seller-paperback rack.

The door opened with a cheerful jangle of bells, and Mel Davis walked in.

Mel. My ex. My other ex. My first ex.

My first thought was that I was having a really weird dream. I'd had pretty bizarre dreams in the hospital, so why not? Or maybe this was Mel's doppelgänger? Maybe hallucinations were the latest — and most unnerving — manifestation of my surgery? But Mel smiled that wide, warm smile, and I realized that it was quite true. It was Mel. Brought to me in living color.

"Hi," I said, taking a few sleepwalker steps to meet him.

"Adrien English." He was across the floor in three big steps, and we hugged. I suspected he might have recracked my sternum.

I got enough breath to gasp with a semblance of cordiality. "Mel." It might have sounded like protest. It felt vaguely like protest.

We let go of each other self-consciously. Seven years later he still looked pretty much like he'd just stepped out to get a pack of antacids. Medium height, square shoulders, curly, dark hair, neatly groomed Vandyke, and cocoa brown eyes; maybe he was heavier; otherwise he hadn't changed.

He must have read something in my face. His expression changed. "You didn't get my e-mail."

"E-mail?" I sounded like I was a stranger to the age of newfangled technology.

"I sent you an e-mail a few days ago and said I'd be down this way and maybe we could get together. For lunch or dinner."

I nearly laughed at that awkward amendment, though it wasn't really funny. "I've been…away."

"Dad's having heart surgery this week."

"Sorry to hear it." I didn't know the old bastard had a heart; unsurprising it would need repair work.

"I flew down from Berkeley. I thought since I was here —" He interrupted himself to say, "It's *so* good to see you, man."

"Great to see you too."

Mel laughed the deep, husky laugh I remembered so well, held my gaze a few seconds too long, then looked away, staring around the bookstore. "I can't believe what you've done with the place. It's like... I wouldn't have recognized it. Do you own the other side of the building now?"

I nodded. His grin widened. "At last. You've been coveting that square footage since the day we signed the escrow papers."

I smiled despite the unexpected wrench of that memory. Why the hell hadn't I checked my e-mail when I got home last night, so I could have had warning?

I looked around for help. Henry Harrison had moved away and was studying the bargain-book table. Natalie was clearly waiting for an introduction.

"Mel, this is my — This is Natalie Dauten. Natalie, Mel Davis." I took a deep breath and said, "Natalie's my —"

"Sister," Natalie supplied.

They shook hands as Mel echoed disbelievingly, "Your *sister*?"

"Stepsister," Natalie admitted almost grudgingly.

"Lisa remarried a couple of years ago."

"Whoa." His shrewd gaze was warm with concern and understanding, though it wasn't necessary. I'd got over any hangups there long ago, and I was pretty fond of my overextended family — from a safe distance.

"And you work here?" Mel asked, eyeing the smiling-cat name badge that Natalie insisted on wearing.

"Adrien's last assistant had to flee the country after he was arrested for murder. Angus was arrested, I mean. Not Adrien. Not yet anyway."

Mel looked slightly bemused. I said, "Isn't it about your lunchtime, Natalie?"

"No," she said. "Actually, it's *your* lunchtime. You're not supposed to be here at all, remember?"

The look I gave her must have been suitably murderous, because her cheeks got very pink. Her jaw, however, took on a pugnacious jut eerily reminiscent of her old man's.

"Is it your lunchtime?" Mel asked quickly. "Because if it is, and if you don't have plans, I'd love to take you to lunch."

I hesitated. But what the hell. The only plans I had were my morning nap — which, granted, I was about ready for. I was going to have to deal with Mel sooner or later; why not make it sooner and get it over with? God knew enough time had passed. I was long over any lingering romantic feelings for him, even if I were currently in the market for that kind of thing, which I wasn't.

Right?

Right.

"I'd love to," I said. "Let me speak to my associate."

Mel nodded, and I gestured to Natalie to follow me.

"So *that's* the legendary Mel?" she whispered as we edged past customers busily reshelving books in the wrong slots.

"That's right," I whispered back. "Johnny Appleseed, Sasquatch, and Mel. And don't let anyone tell you that Sasquatch isn't one heck of a dancer."

"He's shorter than I imagined."

I let that go. We came to a stop in front of the hard-boiled shelf: tough guys grimacing, meaty fists brandishing pistols or clenched in fury. "Listen, Nat, I don't want you to freak out or anything. Someone tried to break in to the store last night."

"*What?* Oh *no.*"

"It's okay," I hastened to add. "It doesn't look like there was any real damage done. I don't even think anything was taken, although you'd better have a look yourself."

"My gosh, you could have been *killed.*"

Something I had strenuously avoided considering — and I didn't want her reporting that theory in the wrong quarters, so I said quickly, "No. I'm sure the burglar had no idea anyone was here. The place has been deserted nights for nearly a month."

"You never know," she objected. "You've probably made a lot of enemies through the years."

I think she intended it as a compliment to my sleuthing abilities. I said, "Uh…yeah. Either way, I've reported it to the police, but we need to get the locks changed. I've called a locksmith, and he'll be here around two." Not that I anticipated lunch with Mel lasting anything like that long — especially since I'd be wanting my afternoon siesta before long. Yet another annoying side effect of my surgery was the fact that I couldn't seem to get through the day without one or two naps.

I showed Natalie where the plastic wall between the two sides of the building had been breached. She lost color. "You mean he could have been hiding in here after the bookstore was closed?"

"I don't think so," I reassured. "I think the construction crew would have noticed anyone loitering around the place."

I sounded more confident than I felt. For one thing, I wasn't sure the burglar wasn't part of the construction crew, and when I got back from lunch, I was going to have a word with Fernando, the foreman. I knew what Natalie was thinking, and I didn't blame her for being freaked. The construction crew next door usually knocked off at about three o'clock, so it was possible someone could have slipped inside before Natalie had locked up for the evening and started counting out the day's cash.

She nodded, her blue eyes dark with worry. Crime was so much more fun when it happened to other people.

"Have you noticed anything weird lately?"

She shook her head.

"Anything weird in the last couple of weeks?"

"You mean, aside from you getting shot by that homicidal maniac?"

The guy who'd shot me had been a business acquaintance who had turned out to be an ex-lover of Jake's — although that wasn't why he'd shot me. At least I didn't think it was. Although I'd hate to think I was shot on general principle.

"Yes. Besides that. Any indication that someone's been sneaking in here after hours? Anything out of place? Are we missing any inventory?"

She slowly shook her head.

"Maybe it was a bum looking for a place to spend the night." I didn't really believe that, though.

"Or kids?" she suggested hopefully.

"Maybe." I didn't believe that either. I guessed I had a jaded impression of the younger generation. I couldn't help believing kids and vandalism went hand in hand. At the very least I'd expect wall graffiti or to be short an erotic mystery or two.

If it wasn't kids, surely the motive had to be theft. So why wasn't anything missing?

Or was it simply that last night had been the intruder's first visit, and he'd been caught in the middle of breaking in to my living quarters? That was the most reasonable explanation. That was what Jake thought, and Jake was the expert.

Natalie shivered at her own thoughts. I said, "Look, don't worry. I'm going to talk to the contractor and tell him to keep a sharp eye out for trespassers. We'll get these locks changed today. That should be the end of it."

"Famous last words," she said.

§ § § §

"*Cat* name badges?" Mel teased.

We were having lunch on the crowded rooftop patio at Café Santorini in Old Pasadena. I'd steered us away from any of our old favorites. I was already feeling way too nostalgic listening to Mel talk about his family and work. He taught film studies at UC Berkeley, and he loved his job. He always had. Something we'd had in common. One of many things.

I said gravely, "You bet. Mine says 'Top Cat.'"

He burst out laughing. I laughed too, though I realized with a twinge that I was being disloyal to my hardworking stepsis.

I said, "In fairness to Natalie, she's been great for the bookstore. She's not nearly the ditz she appears to be."

"She can't be, because you'd never put up with her. I can't see you with siblings. Let alone a sister. Let alone *three* of them." He was still chuckling. "To be honest, I can't believe Lisa finally remarried."

"Yeah. Well." I forked through the seared Pacific seafood salad, looking for the good bits. There didn't seem to be any. Granted, I'd only had breakfast an hour earlier.

"I've been monopolizing the conversation, haven't I?" Mel said ruefully.

I offered a quick smile. "No way. I'm enjoying myself."

And I was, although I couldn't seem to get past the weirdness of it. The weirdness that we were sitting here having lunch. The weirdness that Mel had turned up out of the blue at all. My stars were obviously aligning in a freaky configuration.

"But I want to hear about you," Mel said, all at once serious. "What's this about your last assistant being arrested for murder?"

"It's kind of a long story."

His warm brown eyes smiled into mine. "Are you in a hurry?"

It was unexpectedly hard to look away. "No."

"I remember when there wasn't enough bookstore traffic to keep *you* busy all day."

"Me too. Thank God those days are past."

"You've done really well, Adrien. I'm impressed." He was absolutely sincere.

"Thanks."

"You always were a stubborn bastard."

We both laughed, and I remembered how much I'd missed him after he'd left. Funny how someone could be a major player in your life for years — and then be little more than a stranger. Was that how it would be between me and Jake one day?

To fill that suddenly empty place inside me, I spoke quickly, bringing him up to speed on the last three years — the general release, not the director's cut. By the end of it he was very nearly goggling.

"I can't believe I never heard any of this."

I could believe it. Mel's family hadn't been thrilled at our relationship. Polite but cool was about the most I'd got from them. When it had ended between us, they'd been only too delighted to close the doors — and change the locks.

"So you're like a…an amateur sleuth?"

"God no. I'm more like the hapless guys in those film-noir flicks we used to watch. I keep getting tangled up in bizarro events."

"Oh yes?" His eyes lit with enthusiasm. I was speaking his language now. "Guy Pearce in *L.A. Confidential* or William Hurt in *Body Heat*?"

"I was thinking more like Woody Allen in *Play It Again, Sam*."

"No. You'd be one of the classic lads. Farley Granger or Monty Clift." The fond appraisal in his eyes took me aback. Maybe he was viewing me through the rose-colored glasses of the past. "The funny thing is, you always were as curious as a cat. And you *loved* a puzzle. You used to read about murders in the paper and theorize who the killer was."

"I *did*?" Now that was something I did not remember.

"I don't remember you ever being right," he admitted.

I laughed. Tried not to wince at the inevitable yank of stitches and wires.

"So," he said slowly, "is it you and this ex-cop or you and this nutty professor?"

"Apparently I'm attracted to nutty professors."

"That hurts." He was chuckling, though.

I'd skimmed over a lot of the parts that had to do with Jake — old habits. I guess Mel knew me pretty well. Even after all these years. Maybe not so surprising, given that we'd been together five years, by far the longest I'd been with anyone. And we'd have still been together if he hadn't dumped me.

"It's nobody at the moment. I'm just…"

"Sure," he said with immediate understanding. "You've been through the wars." I could feel his hesitation before he asked, "And the doctors are sure that you're going to make a complete recovery? Your heart's okay?"

Once, this had been an area of discussion fraught with peril. Maybe after all this time it was only a tender spot for me. I said shortly, "They were able to repair the valve instead of having to replace it, which was the best-case scenario. So, yeah, everybody seems to think I'm going to be feeling better and stronger than I have in years."

He automatically rechecked the empty breadbasket — expecting further miracles? — and said, "Adrien…"

I didn't say anything. I knew what was coming.

"This is way overdue. I want to apologize for how things ended between us."

Mel met my eyes, looked away again. "I'd like to plead age and ignorance, but that's really not an excuse. I was…afraid."

I shrugged. "We both made mistakes. We were young." Not that it hadn't hurt like hell — and still did sometimes — but I'd had a lot of time to come to terms with it.

"I know. I know you couldn't care less at this point. It still needs to be said." His eyes met mine, veered away. "It wasn't… You were so sure you wouldn't…" His lips tightened. "You took it for granted that you were probably going to die before you were fifty, and I was young enough and dumb enough to think you were probably right. And I…cared for you. You know that. And I couldn't handle the thought…"

"It's okay, Mel," I said when he seemed at a loss for words. "Fifty seems like a lifetime away when you're twenty. I wasn't very realistic about my health or the future either."

I didn't bother reminding him that part of his decision had also been based on his family's belief that he couldn't really be gay, and even if he was, he was way too young to settle down — let alone commit to someone who was liable to end up as a complete liability.

"It was good what we had. It was special."

It seemed to be my week for apologies from ex-lovers. I wondered if I'd be hearing from Guy soon. Probably not. Guy was comfortably certain that he was generally, if not always, in the right. The idea of that made me grin inwardly. "It was. It was also a long time ago."

Mel drew a quick breath and sighed. "Yes. It was." His brows knitted. "You look tired. I wasn't thinking. Do you want to go?"

I nodded. "Sorry, but yeah. To be honest, I'm beat." It was normal. They'd warned me in the hospital that I was going to find that I tired fast at first, that I'd need to plan for naps and plenty of rest. It was still aggravating. When was the feeling-better part supposed to start?

To my relief, Mel kept the conversation low-key and casual on the drive back to the bookstore. He parked in front and turned off the engine.

"This was… I wish we'd done this a long time ago."

I smiled, although I was thinking what a bad idea that would have been at any point during the last three years. "It was great seeing you again." I reached for the door handle. "Thanks for lunch. Let me know how your dad's surgery goes."

"Adrien?" Mel said quickly, "There's a film-noir festival at LACMA this week. Thursday's double feature is *The Blue Dahlia* and *The Big Sleep*. Assuming everything goes well with Dad's surgery, would you want to see it together? You always loved Chandler."

I wasn't sure what to say. I wasn't sure what he wanted. Sure, we had stayed friendly. That wasn't the same as being friends. We had not stayed friends. I didn't know if — even now — I could be friends with Mel.

"I hate to admit this, but I don't know if I'm really up to —"

"We'd leave the minute you wanted to go. Totally up to you how long we stay. I — It's driving me nuts sitting around that house. It would be good to get out for a few hours, wouldn't it?"

Maybe. The fact was, I preferred staying home on my own and sleeping. Sleep was currently my favorite thing.

"We used to have a lot of fun at those things," he added persuasively.

Sometimes that life seemed to belong to someone else.

"Can I let you know?" I hedged.

If he was disappointed, he hid it well. "Of course. I'll call you tomorrow. How about that?"

I nodded reluctantly. I think part of my unease was that my instinctive response had been a jolt of excitement at the idea maybe Mel was... Well, I truly didn't want to start thinking that way. Merely ego, wasn't it? "Okay, then. Call me tomorrow, and I'll see how I'm feeling."

"Great." He hesitated and offered that warm smile that showed the dimple in his left cheek. "Talk to you Wednesday."

Nodding, I got out of the car, lifted my hand in farewell. Mel raised his hand in acknowledgment, pulled away from the curb.

I crossed the sidewalk, absently noting the art-deco black tile on the building's façade. The old guy — Henry Harrison — was right. It was a beautiful building.

As I drew near the building, I heard two things: absolute silence from the construction crew — and Natalie screaming.

CHAPTER THREE

I burst through the doors of Cloak and Dagger, and Natalie, who must have seen my approach through the windows, threw herself into my arms, sobbing.

"What is it, Nat? What's wrong?"

She wept something into my shoulder, and I said bewilderedly, "What the hell happened? Did someone…?" I looked around. Obviously it was something more than a declined credit card or a missing shipment. My imagination boggled.

There were a few alarmed customers grouped nearby. Half the plastic wall was down, and the entire construction crew stood in the opening it made. I saw shocked, even pale, faces. Fernando called to me, "I think you better see this, Mr. English."

"Okay." I tried to detach Natalie. She clung harder. "Nat. Natty. I have to see this. Whatever it is."

"No." She raised a tearstained face. "You shouldn't go up those stairs."

Upstairs? I had quick, crazy visions of mysterious locked rooms and madwomen in the attic, which was ridiculous, since I'd been through the entire building and there were no boarded-up rooms or anything more sinister than mold beneath the window casings — which, come to think of it, *was* pretty sinister.

I tried pulling her arms from around my neck, and she latched back on like an amorous octopus. "Nat, there's no reason I can't walk upstairs. It's not Everest." I peeled her arms from around me.

She cried, "*No.* Don't go up there. They found the body."

I froze. "What body?"

"The body that old man told us about this morning. The trumpet player's body."

Clarinet player, though he was probably past caring. I turned to Fernando, and he said apologetically, "It's true. We found a body in the floor upstairs."

"A body in the *floor*?"

He nodded.

"There's a *body* in the floor upstairs?"

Another nod. "A skeleton. He's been there a long time."

In the stricken silence the cat stuck a cautious nose around the nearest bookshelf, whiskers twitching. He sensibly retreated.

"A skeleton?" Not that I really thought he could be mistaken about this.

A final nod.

"It's *horrible*, Adrien," Natalie told me. "Don't go up there."

"Which floor?"

Not that it really mattered.

"Third," Fernando supplied.

Maybe it did matter. The third floor had been blocked off for the last decade or so. That was probably significant.

"Has anyone called the police yet?"

"We found him a couple of minutes ago," Fernando explained. "We showed the lady..." He let that trail, probably realizing after the fact that "showing the lady" had not been the smartest move of the afternoon.

"All right. Now show me." I thought quickly. "Natalie, you'd better lock up for the day."

Bodies under floorboards would not be good for business. Not even at a mystery bookstore.

She assented, pulling herself together, and shepherding the remaining — and surprisingly reluctant — customers out. They went, offering helpful advice such as telling us to call the paramedics. Personally, I thought it sounded late for that.

The workmen shuffled in silence to the side as I followed Fernando through the part of the building still under construction.

We headed up the long staircase, the crew following at an uneasy distance while Fernando explained how they had been ripping up floorboards near the window in preparation for treating the mold.

"And there he was," he finished glumly over the crunch of our shoes' soles on bits of plaster, dust and paint.

This side of the building was three stories tall, as opposed to the two stories on the Cloak and Dagger side. We climbed slowly, Fernando clearly reluctant to return to the chamber of horrors, and me pacing myself. It was my building, and if there was a skeleton hidden in here, I was sure as hell going to see it.

Could the mystery of Jay Stevens's disappearance really be solved after all these years? Maybe *solved* wasn't the right word. Obviously if his body had been shoved under the floor in the old hotel, he hadn't died a natural death. This discovery might open more questions than it answered.

We climbed past the second floor, and I absently noted that the crew had finished replastering the walls and sanding the floors. Nice to see that progress was being made, although this latest discovery was guaranteed to set things even further back than the revelation of a bunch of dead rats in the attic had.

Up on the third story, the renovation was much less further along. In addition to battling fungus and wood rot, the crew was still stripping wallpaper and ripping out the old wiring.

Fernando led me down the long hallway to the back. The floorboards squeaked ominously beneath our feet. We came at last to one of the small corner rooms. Water-browned wallpaper curled in sheets from the still-intact walls. The light fixture was hanging from the ceiling like a gouged-out eye. There were two double-hung windows, one with a view of the alley below and the other of the busy street to the south, where life went on as usual.

Fernando closed the door on the crowd in the hall, and I saw the pulled-up, battered planks stacked to the side of the window. Something lay inside the gaping hole in the floor. I walked over and looked down at the raggedly clothed skeleton.

Introducing Jay Stevens?

He'd been wedged between the deep wooden joists. Then the planks had been nailed down again. Pretty simple, really. Assuming you had a crowbar, a hammer, and a chunk of uninterrupted time. If it hadn't been for the mold staining the walls and creeping into the baseboards, the construction crew would have simply sanded the floors, refinished them, and moved on to the next room. He might have rested there for another fifty years.

"Is there anything unusual about the room?"

Fernando looked at me like I was insane.

"Besides the dead guy in the floor."

"No." He reminded me, "This level was sealed off. Nobody used it for years."

I nodded, unable to tear my gaze away from skeleton in the cavity at our feet: the empty, staring eye sockets, wispy, tarnished remnants of hair on the not-quite-clean skull, the yellowed and protruding teeth that gave the impression it — he — had been screaming when he died. Not an attractive sight. Natalie had been right about that.

It would have been pleasant to take an academic view, to think of this like the twelve-thousand-year-old skeleton of a Natufian shaman I'd been reading about at my cardiologist's office yesterday.

"There's a suitcase in there too." Fernando squatted down. He reached beneath and hauled out a long, flat suitcase before I could stop him. A fat spider scuttled toward my shoe, and I absently stepped on it.

The shaman had been discovered with burial offerings that included fifty complete tortoise shells, the pelvis of a leopard, and a human foot. This skeleton had been walled up with a vintage Samsonite that bore faded labels for Delta-C&S Airlines and a couple of eastern hotels.

Maybe it wasn't archeology, let alone forensics, but it sort of indicated to me that the dead man — man, based on the filthy remnants of the polka-dot shirt — was circa the 1950s.

It looked more and more likely that this *was* Jay Stevens.

Judging by his luggage, he had been a man who liked to travel.

"What do you think happened to him?" Fernando asked in a hushed voice.

"Nothing good."

It looked to me like there were dark stains on the upper shoulders of the ratty shirt, and I knelt to get a better look, although, frankly, I didn't want to get too close. He wasn't the sweetest-smelling artifact to come out of this old building. Still, he didn't smell as horrifying as something newly, freshly dead. All the same, I wondered how no one had…well…noticed him all these years? Even if the Huntsman's Lodge had been pretty run-down by that time, surely the odor of a decomposing body would have made its presence known?

"He must have been here a long time."

"Fifty years," I said, "if he's who I think he is."

"All this time he's been waiting here for us to find him."

Happy thought. I opened my mouth to reply, but when Fernando had leaned over the broken floor to lift out the suitcase, he must have brushed against the bag of bones, because as we were studying it, the skeleton's jaw dropped as though he were about to speak. Fernando swore and stepped back. I sucked in a sharp breath.

I turned to Fernando, who was staring at me with horrified eyes.

"Time to call the police," I said.

∫ ∫ ∫

I'd had the unique pleasure of making LAPD Homicide Detective Alonzo's acquaintance a few weeks earlier when I'd been seduced — almost literally — into getting involved in the murder investigation of a Hollywood producer by the name of Porter Jones. Alonzo had found it hard to believe that an innocent citizen could be involved in four murder cases and not be guilty, at the very least, of considerable bad judgment. I tended to agree with him.

More so after getting shot.

So I can't say that my heart exactly leaped for joy when he walked into Cloak and Dagger Books wearing that familiar cheap suit, mirrored shades, and bad attitude.

"Mr. English. We meet again." Alonzo was showing lots of teeth, though I don't think it was meant to be a smile. He wasn't a bad-looking guy. Hispanic, mid-thirties, medium height, and compactly built. He scanned the empty bookstore, his gaze lingering too long on Natalie, while the crime-scene team pushed through with their usual brusque officiousness.

"It's a small world," I said.

"About the size of a jail cell."

"I like your optimistic spirit, but even you're going to have trouble pinning a fifty-year-old murder on me. If this case were any colder, they'd have called an anthropologist."

He raised his eyebrows. "Oh, you think you know how old this murder is? You get your online degree in forensics or something?"

"Fair enough. I think this might be Jay Stevens. He lived at the Huntsman's Lodge back in the fifties. He disappeared in fifty nine, and the rumor was that he was murdered. I'm guessing the rumor was right."

"How about you leave the guesswork to the police?"

I opened my mouth; that was really too easy a shot. And if I were honest, I didn't feel up to tangling with Alonzo again.

He must have read the thought that crossed my face. He said with grim good humor, "First thing is, we're going to have to close your shop till further notice. This is a crime scene now."

"Further notice?" I repeated. I tried to keep my voice calm, so as not to antagonize him further. "I understand closing the bookstore for today. And I realize that construction has to stop while you investigate, but this part of the building isn't a crime scene. There's no reason we can't be allowed to open for business tomorrow."

"You don't think so? And here you're supposed to be a famous master detective."

"I don't consider myself any kind of a detective, and I've zero desire to get involved in another murder investigation, okay?"

"But here you are, right in the middle of another one, aren't you?"

"The crime scene is over there on the other side of the wall."

"And what wall would that be?"

We both looked at where the plastic divider hung, torn and drooping.

Alonzo smiled. "That's about as much protection as a condom with a hole in it. No offense."

Was inadequate self-protection supposed to be a specialty of mine?

Actually, maybe he had a point. I said, "Look, Detective. I know you don't like me, and I know you resent the way —"

"You don't know shit," he interrupted. "This isn't personal. This is strictly police business."

"Then you have to know that I didn't — couldn't possibly — have anything to do with this. I wasn't even born when Jay Stevens disappeared. And this part of the building has —"

"Sorry, English," he said with that same cheery aggression. "Rules is rules."

He strode off but stopped as he reached the open space between the bookstore and the construction site. "Hey, give my regards to your boyfriend, *ex*-Lieutenant Riordan."

I didn't have an answer, which clearly pleased him. He strolled away with a big smile on his face.

"What an *ass*," Natalie muttered, joining me.

Answering was beyond me. I felt numb as a wave of fatigue seemed to roll in out of nowhere, sucking the sand out from my under my feet, nearly knocking me over. I needed to lie down. Now.

I said, "I'll be upstairs."

"Are you okay?"

I nodded. I didn't feel okay, though. I felt nauseated, with a combination of reaction and exhaustion. I just wanted peace and quiet while I lay perfectly flat and perfectly still in an imitation of the corpse I felt like.

"Do you need any help?"

I shook my head impatiently and went upstairs. The cat appeared out of nowhere, springing along beside me — and again, nearly underfoot — equally happy to escape to the privacy of our quarters.

Closing the door behind me, I staggered into the bedroom. I kicked my shoes off and flopped down on the bed.

The next thing I knew, Natalie was bending over me saying, "*Adrien?*"

I blinked up at her worried face. "What?"

"I've been calling and calling you. Are you all right?"

"Yeah." The lamp was on; the corners of the room were in shadow. I wiped the corners of my eyes with the heels of my hands and sat up. "What time is it?"

"Seven." She was frowning. "Have you been sleeping this whole time? Are you sure you're all right?"

"Of course I'm sure."

"The police *finally* finished downstairs."

I pushed myself to my feet. "Is Alonzo waiting to talk to me?"

"No. They've left."

"*Left?* Without talking to me? What did they say?"

"Nothing. Do you want me to go pick up something for dinner?"

Dinner? The cops had shut us down, and she was worried about *dinner?*

I sank down on the edge of the bed again, trying to understand. "They didn't say anything about what they found?"

"They — that asshole in charge — said we can't open the store tomorrow."

"The hell we can't."

She was shaking her head. "I don't think you should push him, Adrien. I have a feeling he's dying for a reason to hassle you. He tried to insist that you had to vacate the premises."

"Oh *really?*" I said dangerously, rising again.

"It's okay," she said quickly. "You don't have to do anything. Everything's been taken care of for you."

"What?"

"I called Daddy, and *he* called the chief of police, and the final decision was Detective Asshole can't make you leave, but he does get to make the call about when the shop can open again." She smiled reassuringly. "As you can imagine, Daddy had a thing or two to say ab —"

"Goddamn it. I don't need your *daddy* running interference for me." I heard the echo of that in the harsh silence that followed my interruption.

"I" — her expression was stricken — "I was trying to help."

What was I doing? None of this was her fault. I was lucky to have her. Lucky to have Bill Dauten willing to go to the mat for me. And he would. He'd do anything for Lisa and, by extension, me.

"I know you were. I don't even know why I said that." I didn't know how to explain the raw compound of frustration and resentment that surfaced lately when I least expected it. "I'm sorry. It's not that I'm not grateful. I am. Truly."

Natalie was still hurt, still waiting for me to say whatever it was that would make her understand why I was being such a prick when she and everyone else were doing their best to take care of me. I offered lamely, "I thought I'd be feeling better by now."

About a lot of things.

She softened. "I know. The doctors said you'd be up and down. Like an emotional roller coaster. They told us what to watch for."

I resisted the temptation to undo my apology by throttling her. "Uh, yeah."

Bucking for sainthood, she volunteered, "Would you like me to make you something to eat?"

Natalie's cooking skills were even worse than my own, so it was a truly noble gesture. Or revenge. I shook my head. "I'll figure something out."

"Like what?"

"I don't know. Soup," I said irritably. "Tuna. I'll find something. What did the cops say?"

"Why don't you come home tonight?" she coaxed. "Lisa said she'll make chicken potpie just for you."

"I *am* home."

"I know." It was the tone of one humoring a crabby child. "But wouldn't you feel better in a house with other people than in this creepy old building where someone was murdered?"

I sighed. "He was murdered fifty years ago, Nat. I don't think I'm in any danger."

"You don't know who that skeleton belonged to. You *think* it was the trumpet player the old guy was talking about. Maybe it was someone else. Maybe that murder was a lot more recent than you think."

I ignored the suggestion of wholesale slaughter in my home and hearth. "Did the locksmith show up?"

"Yes. The new keys are on the table in the hall."

"What happened to that old guy, anyway? What was his name? Henry Harrison?"

She nodded. "I think so. I don't remember. I think he wandered out again after your — Mel — arrived."

I didn't like the delicate inflection on *my* Mel. The legendary Mel, no less. God only knew what information Lisa had shared about my past. Not that it was much of a past, but it was my own, and I'd have preferred to keep it that way.

"He didn't leave a card or anything?"

She shook her head as she stooped to pick up Tomkins, who had wandered in. "Hello, bootiful boy. He looks *so* much healthier now, doesn't he, Mr. Tomkins?"

I wasn't sure if she meant me or the cat. Probably the cat. I wisely remained silent.

Mr. Tomkins put up with being cuddled with better grace than I did, although his eyes did slant my way in a silent appeal for aid when she started kissing his nose.

"So what's the problem with the temporary help?" I asked.

Natalie hesitated before admitting, "Well, as you may have noticed, there *was* no temporary help today. This is the third day she's called in sick."

"Tell the agency we need someone new."

"I did."

"And?"

"The thing is, you've got sort of a reputation."

"I have?"

"The bookstore has."

Oh. I considered this glumly. Yes, I could see where Cloak and Dagger Books might not win any Employer of Choice awards.

"Let's try a new agency."

"I did. Several of them. I finally found one who said they'd send someone out tomorrow. Or at least they were going to try. Now I'll have to get them to postpone until we're open again."

I nodded, preoccupied. If I really wasn't going to be able to work — and admittedly, I'd felt ready to die with weariness by the time I'd dragged myself upstairs to rest that afternoon — we were going to need more help.

Natalie let Tomkins down, and he sprang onto the bed and shook his head as though he'd been on the roller-coaster ride with me.

"Are you sure you won't come back to the house tonight?" she coaxed. "You'd make Lisa so happy, and you'd save Lauren a drive tomorrow, and Emma misses you *so* much."

"At the risk of seeming more ungrateful than I already do, I want to spend the night in my own bed."

She didn't like it, though she had to accept it in the end.

Following Natalie's departure — after reciting the usual list of warnings people seemed to feel obliged to deliver to me — I felt relief — for all of an hour. Long enough to feed the cat, make myself a small dinner salad, and relax in front of the TV.

Usually the Partners and Crime writing group would be meeting downstairs, but I didn't have the energy for it that night. Instead I watched TV and caught the tail end of the 1944 noir classic *Laura*, directed by Otto Preminger. Naturally that reminded me of Mel and his invite to the LACMA noir festival on Thursday. Thinking of Mel made me restless. I couldn't seem to decide if I wanted to go out with him or not. I was flattered that he'd asked, that he seemed to want to resume a…friendship, at the least. There was a time I'd have given anything to believe he regretted walking out. Now I felt little. But then, I felt little, period. It had to be some lingering emotional miasma following the trauma of getting shot and nearly dying. I couldn't seem to make myself care about much of anything. I just wanted to be alone, but when I was alone, I felt edgy, almost nervous. Had I lost the knack of living by myself?

In the midst of these gloomy thoughts, the phone rang, and my heart jumped. I went to the phone, made myself take a deep breath, and answered.

"So you *are* there," Guy said in that slightly affected accent, and I felt a flicker of disappointment. Not that I wasn't happy to hear from Guy. I missed Guy, truth be told. I guess I'd been hoping…

"I'm here."

"I was sure you'd be at Riordan's."

"No."

I could feel a dozen questions in that brief pause. He said easily enough, "Good. I'm glad of that. How are you feeling?"

I was really quite tired of that question.

"I'm fine."

"Lisa sounded…"

"Lisa is ticked off because I left the nest AMA."

"Against medical advice?"

"Against Mother's advice."

Guy chuckled. "That sounds about right. I heard you had a spot of excitement at the bookstore today?"

I filled him in on the discovery of the skeleton in the floor, and he said, "I don't think there can be much mystery about it. They're all but announcing on the telly that it's this Stevens bloke."

"It's on the *TV*?"

"Of course."

Of course. I'd slept through the afternoon and missed a lot of the excitement. Naturally the media would have turned out for a story like this. And naturally Natalie would have neglected to mention anything she figured might upset me.

Guy was saying, "What the hell is it about you that attracts murder and mayhem?"

"Something in my body language?"

He groaned. "That was bad — even for you."

"What are they saying?"

"Oh, you know. It's a slow week for news. They're making it sound like the Black Dahlia murderer has been revealed at last."

"Is there any real information on Stevens? I remember when I first bought this place, I tried to find out what I could, and there didn't seem to be anything on him."

"How hard did you look? After all, the press is going to have resources you didn't. Not to mention the fact that you weren't the supersleuth then that you are now."

"Don't even joke about it. Do you know who's in charge of this investigation? Detective Alonzo."

"Christ." That was heartfelt. "But it's a-a what do they call it? A cold case, isn't it? Don't they have special departments for that?"

"I have no idea." And as for my LAPD contact — I remembered Alonzo's *"hey, give my regards to your boyfriend, ex-Lieutenant Riordan."* I felt another surge of anger on Jake's behalf. Jake had been ten times the cop that incompetent, homophobic asshole would ever be.

I realized that Guy was still talking, and I hadn't heard a word he'd said.

"…dinner one evening."

I replied automatically, "That sounds great." And it did. I realized again how much I missed Guy. It had been good between us, hadn't it? Why hadn't it been enough?

We chatted a bit more, and Guy rang off. Three minutes later the phone rang again, and my heart did another of those fish-on-a-hook leaps. This time the caller was Lisa. Right on schedule.

"Darling, you *have* to come home," she started in as soon as I answered. "You cannot *possibly* want to stay in that...that *tomb* with bodies falling out of the wall!"

"Floor," I corrected. "Anyway, I don't know why not. It's everything a ghoul could ask for."

"There's nothing humorous about this, Adrien. Your heart still isn't strong enough to withstand any kind of strain."

My amusement faded. "Please don't start."

"You're going to undo everything the doctors worked so hard for."

"Lisa."

"You *have* to be realistic now. You *know* what the doctors said."

"Lisa."

"Why do you so resent the idea that your family loves you and wants to take care of you? Sometimes I think you'd rather d —" She caught herself, though not really in time.

There was a shocked silence between us.

I clamped down on my anger and said as gently as I could, "I wouldn't. I don't. I appreciate everything everyone is doing for me. Or trying to do for me. But...sooner or later you're going to have to come to terms with the fact that I'm...okay."

She objected, "Three weeks ago —"

"Three weeks ago I was *shot*."

"Thanks to that *swine*, Jake Riordan."

I'd known that was coming. She'd been uncharacteristically forbearing on the subject of Jake ever since I'd regained consciousness in the hospital. It couldn't last.

"Lisa," I warned, still striving for patience, "Jake saved my life. Twice."

"Your life would never have been at risk if it hadn't been for him."

"Let it go." That time I didn't bother to gentle my tone.

"I don't understand you," she protested.

That made two of us. I didn't say that, though. Instead I did my best to soothe her, reassure her that I was feeling fine, following doctor's orders, and keeping the doors locked and the security system on. When she'd finally worn us both down, she bade me good night and rang off to go terrorize her own household.

I replaced the phone on the hook, collapsed on the sofa, and turned on the TV. I got the usual depressing dose of murder and mayhem on the mean streets of LA; and then, as I started to nod off again, the front of the bookstore flashed onto the screen. An earnest-looking young reporter described the shocking circumstances of the skeleton discovered by a construction crew in the flooring of a historic old building.

The reporter did a brief interview with a discomfited Fernando, who looked ready to sink into the sidewalk, no doubt remembering the green-card statuses of most of his crew.

The news anchor speculated as to the identity of the cold-case victim. A photo appeared of a tall young man in a dinner jacket blowing a clarinet. Given the closed eyes, chipmunk cheeks, and double chin, that image could have been anyone from Richard Mühlfeld to Benny Goodman.

I concluded the local news didn't really have any more information than I did. Not about the gruesome discovery itself or Jay Stevens.

Clicking off the television, I was dismayed to realize that, despite having slept all afternoon, I was now ready for bed again. Could this excessive need for sleep really be normal?

I selected a book at random from the living-room shelf — Chandler's *The Long Goodbye* — and retired to read in bed.

No need to set the alarm clock. Even if we'd been allowed to open for business on Wednesday, I'd have been banned from participating. Was that the reason for the apathy that held me in its sway now? Did I really have nothing going on in my life beyond running Cloak and Dagger Books? Was that the sole purpose of my existence? Or was this emotional fugue a combination of meds and the toil of healing?

Tomkins joined me and set about grooming himself at the foot of the bed. I eyed him critically. Natalie was right. He was filling out nicely, and a bath had done wonders for him. With those big, almond-shaped eyes and that silky fawn coat, he wasn't nearly as ugly as I'd originally thought.

"You're looking pretty fit these days. Ready to go back on the street?"

He offered a jeering sort of *meow*, curled up, and went to sleep.

I went back to my book.

When I woke the next time, the lamp was still shining, the book was a weight on my still-tender chest, and the alarm was going off downstairs.

CHAPTER FOUR

Surely it was a sign of the strangeness of my life that on being jolted out of a sound sleep by the hysterical clamor of a security alarm, my first reaction was, *not again.*

Not a-*fucking*-gain, if we wanted to be precise.

So much for new locks on the doors. I threw aside the sheet and reached for the phone. The bells were still clamoring downstairs, but we'd had so many false alarms, I wasn't sure the police would show up. This time the 911 operator came on immediately, and I reported the break-in.

I verified that I was safe — I assumed the new dead bolt on my flat door would hold — and agreed to wait on the line while a patrol car was dispatched.

The minutes ticked by. Tomkins played with the lamp cord until I scooped him up and tossed him on the bed.

After what seemed like a very long time though, according to the clock, was a mere seven minutes, I heard the downstairs buzzer. I thanked the operator and hung up.

I turned off the alarm, unbolted the door, and went down to let the cops in.

It was the same two uniformed officers from the night before. A young Hispanic man who didn't look old enough to be out past curfew, and a matronly-looking black woman who identified herself as Sergeant Frame.

"Somebody sure wants in here pretty bad," Frame remarked. "Come have a look at this."

I followed them into the warm, smoggy night and over to the construction side. Around the corner of the building, they showed me where the bay window had been partially cut away.

"He must have been counting on you not expecting another break-in."

"Not kids," I said. I couldn't believe kids would be using a glass cutter. Tools seemed to indicate a professional mind-set.

"Not kids," agreed Frame. "Definitely not kids. There's crime-scene tape across the door, and the perp went for it anyway."

The rookie, Martinez, said, "I guess he wasn't expecting the alarm. He must have fled when it went off."

I opened my mouth, and Frame said, "Don't worry, Mr. English. We'll make sure. We'll check the premises from top to bottom."

They did too. I went back into the bookstore, sat on the steps, and waited while they investigated the building, floor by floor. A floorboard squeaked, and I tensed. Nothing moved in the gloom. Behind the sales desk, the shiny eye of the Maltese Falcon replica caught the gleam of the emergency lights.

Occasionally Frame's and Martinez's voices drifted down to me — and the crackle of their radios.

"Nothing to indicate he made it inside," Martinez called to me when they came back downstairs.

Frame signified that they were going to check the alley behind the bookstore, and I nodded. A short time later I heard the *clang* and banging of trash bins.

When all had been checked out to their satisfaction, they returned to the bookstore.

"I don't think he'll be back," Frame assured me while Martinez went out to radio all clear. "Not tonight."

"Thanks." I thought she was probably right. Then again, I hadn't thought there was a chance in hell my intruder would show up two nights in a row, so what did I know? Whoever this guy was, he was determined.

As though reading my mind, she commented, "This is a busy address these days."

I nodded glumly.

"Any idea what he'd be looking for?"

I shrugged. "Books? Construction equipment? Termites?"

She smiled politely. "There are a lot of stories about this old place."

"I've heard one or two."

"I guess you know it used to be a hotel. The Huntsman's Lodge. It was a swanky place at one time, but a lot of lowlifes used to hang out here in the fifties and sixties."

"I heard that too."

"The place belonged to the Swierzy brothers. They owned a lot of properties through this part of town. Most of them were sold and demolished after Teddy Swierzy died. This old beauty managed to survive the cut."

"There was a move to have it placed on the historical register." I eyed her with new interest. "It didn't succeed, but it delayed the building being torn down. In the end, it was subdivided and sold off."

"Funny in all these years, all these renovations, nobody ever found what was buried in the floor of that back bedroom."

Hilarious.

"The top level was blocked off for years as unsafe. I know the remodel I did on this half when I purchased it a decade ago was the first real renovation the building had. Most of the businesses renting on that side were fly-by-nights. I don't think the second story was used much for anything except storage."

She shook her head, whether over the waste of floor space or the shabby treatment of what should have been a historical landmark was unclear.

It occurred to me that Sergeant Frame had something on her mind. She didn't strike me as the type to stand around in the middle of the night reminiscing about the good old days — although I'm sure it made a pleasant change from domestic-dispute calls.

"When I first bought this side of the building, I tried to find out what I could about Jay Stevens. There wasn't much."

"Guys like Jay Stevens were a dime a dozen," Frame said easily. "Part-time musicians and full-time hustlers."

"You couldn't have known him." She had to have been a baby in 1959. A baby with an intimidating gaze.

"No. I knew the officer who investigated Stevens's disappearance, and I remember his stories about this town back then. Stevens played at a club on the beach. It was called The Tides. It's long gone now."

I made a mental note of it. "Was there much of an investigation after Stevens disappeared?"

"Some. According to Argyle, he was the disappearing kind, if you know what I mean."

I thought I did. "This Argyle was the investigating officer?"

She nodded, glanced out the window to where her partner was waiting by the squad car. She looked back at me. Slowly, quietly, she said, "Jake Riordan was my lieutenant."

Funny how the unexpected mention of Jake's name rippled through my nervous system like an electric shock. I sat up straight, bracing for…whatever was coming.

"He was a hard ass all the way."

Before I could respond, Frame added evenly, "But I never met anyone more fair. Riordan backed his people. He never tried to pass the buck. Never asked you to do anything he wasn't willing to do himself. That means a lot in a job like this. Sometimes it means everything."

I didn't know what to say; I was wondering why she thought this was anything like my business — what the official word was about me and Jake.

Into my silence, she said, "Riordan's still got friends on the force."

"Thanks. I'm glad."

She nodded politely. "You have a good rest of your night, Mr. English."

ʃ ʃ ʃ ʃ

Despite the adventures of the night, I was up at the crack of dawn, prowling restlessly around my flat and finally going downstairs to the empty bookstore. The silence was almost eerie, especially on the side of the building under construction. I went to the wall of plastic — refastened with crime-scene tape — and stared through at the empty rooms. I could see the broken window from where I stood.

There had been occasional break-ins on that side of the premises through the years; there had even been the occasional attempt at burglary on this side. But *this* was plain weird, wasn't it? Either I had been targeted by the dumbest burglar on the planet, or someone was desperate to get into this place. Why? We did a decent business, though Cloak and Dagger Books hardly made the irresistible target a 7-Eleven did. Construction equipment couldn't be that hard to steal. And if it had something to do with Jay Stevens, well, surely the burglar was aware Mr. Stevens had left the building?

Sipping my coffee — a gourmet flavor known as "decaf swill" — I noted that there was no sign of Detective Alonzo or any kind of police investigation this bright and sunny a.m.

I turned away as the bookshop phone began to ring. Natalie had recorded a message informing customers that we were temporarily closed. I listened to her unreasonably cheerful recorded voice followed by the incensed voice of one of our regular customers asking how she was supposed to pick up a book we were holding for her.

Terrific.

The next three phone calls were local media outlets requesting tours of the building.

Uh-huh.

I wondered how long Alonzo's vindictive streak was going to last. Even a week of this was liable to put a serious dent in my finances. If Lisa hadn't chosen to shell out an ungodly amount of money, my hospital bills would have already left me in serious fiscal jeopardy.

I trailed up and down the aisles of books, facing a title out here, reshelving a book there...

The building creaked emptily as I took another turn around the floor. Outside, the street was busy with traffic; people strolled along the sidewalk. It was sort of like being walled up inside the building, and I thought of Jay Stevens — if that's whom the skeleton belonged to — waiting to be found all these years.

That started me thinking. I went into my office and, shrugging off the illogical feeling of guilt, turned on my laptop. I wasn't going to *work*, merely glance at my e-mail and maybe check our web-site orders. No harm in that.

However, as I watched an alarming amount of e-mail loading into my in-box — sure enough Mel's e-mail address flashed by — a better thought occurred to me, and I clicked onto the Internet and Googled "Jay Stevens."

I was quickly reminded of why I hadn't pursued the puzzle of Stevens's disappearance when I'd first taken possession of Cloak and Dagger Books. Not only had I had my hands full trying to get a new business up and running, but "Jay Stevens" was a popular name. A lot more popular than, for example, "Adrien English." Not that I wasn't happy about *that*.

Never mind all the Facebook, MySpace, and LinkedIn Jay Stevenses. There was the hair-salon Jay Stevens, the big-and-tall Jay Stevens, and the assorted writer, historian, photographer, and other business-owner Jay Stevenses.

Mama, don't let your babies grow up to be Jay Stevenses.

Four pages in, there was still nothing on a missing 1950s clarinet-player Jay Stevens. I remembered what the elderly shutterbug had said about a jazz band called the Moonglows, so I plugged that into Google.

To my surprise, I scored. My search brought up a small and now-defunct record label by the name of Vibe. *Vibe* as in *vibraphone*, not *good vibrations*. Vibe had been based in Los Angeles and had only managed to stay afloat three years, but in its stable of talent was a jazz ensemble called Jay Stevens and the Moonglows, featuring Jay Stevens on clarinet, Jinx Stevens on vocals, Orrie New Orleans on trombone, Paulie St. Cyr on piano and guitar, and Todd Thomas on drums.

The Moonglows had made one recording, titled *Kaleidoscope*. There was a miniature black-and-white photo of the record cover, which I was totally unable to make out.

I jotted down the names of the other members of the Moonglows. Next I tried a search for "The Moonglows" and "Kaleidoscope" and got a couple of hits. One was a passing reference on a jazz discussion board to Paulie St. Cyr's "locked hands" style of playing, but the other was for an eBay sale long passed. I was able to zoom in on the record cover, which featured an enraptured-looking lady in a slinky cocktail dress, lying on what appeared to be a red carpet. She was spying through a kaleidoscope. The back of the record cover offered a small black-and-white photo of the uncomfortable-looking Moonglows (probably thinking about that kaleidoscope) grouped around a piano. I was able to pick out who was whom based on the instruments they held. The man holding the clarinet was tall and thin and fair. His suit looked too big for him. He had an engaging grin. The chick singer, Jinx Stevens, leaned with easy familiarity against his shoulder. She wore a ponytail and a cocktail dress. She looked too much like Jay to be anything other than his sister.

Surprise. I'd automatically assumed wife.

I tried another search for the Moonglows and their sole album. All that came up were references made in passing to other members. Paulie St. Cyr had gone on to become quite well-known before his early death in 1967. Todd Thomas had given up music for selling ski boats. He'd apparently retired in the eighties and moved to Canada. His wife kept a family web site which offered "news" updates and lots of photos of spectacularly plain children. Orrie New Orleans had a long, if unspectacular, career as a backup player. He had passed away last year. I couldn't find any information on Jinx Stevens. The only time her name popped up was in reference to the Moonglows and *Kaleidoscope*.

She seemed to have vanished as effectively as her brother, though it seemed there was no mystery about it.

But then, there wasn't a lot made of Jay Stevens's disappearance either. Maybe it had only been news in Los Angeles. The Moonglows were strictly famous (and that was relative) for having been Paulie St. Cyr's first band. For that reason, and that reason alone, a copy of *Kaleidoscope* was worth a small fortune.

I plugged it into my eBay searches. I was curious. Plus, listening to music was on my doctor-approved list of activities.

I spent the next hour scanning through jazz discussion boards and coming up with not so much in the way of information. The next time I surfaced, I realized that it was nearly ten o'clock, and Lauren would be showing up to drag me to cardiac rehab.

I signed out, turned off the laptop, and went upstairs to change into sweats and a T-shirt.

♪ ♪ ♪ ♪

"Depression is perfectly normal after a cardiac event, Adrien." Dr. Shearing studied me over the top of her spectacles.

Dr. Shearing was my therapist, yet another member of my rehabilitation team, which included my cardiologist, physical therapist, exercise therapist, dietitian, and…shrink. I didn't care for her. I didn't care for any part of cardiac rehab. Not that I didn't know how lucky I was to be in such a program, but I'd never been much for team sports, and that was increasingly what my recovery felt like. All this fucking attention on *everything* I did. It was close to unbearable. And most unbearable was Dr. Shearing's poking and probing into my emotional state.

"I'm not depressed." I gave her a smile perfected through years of dealing with my mother's nosy cronies at interminable high-society shindigs.

Dr. Shearing smiled politely in return. She was, as they say in legend, small but terrible. Barely five feet tall and built like a pixie. She had one of those pixie haircuts too. The kind of thing that looks best on elderly women or kindergarteners. The walls of her office were plastered in a disturbing mix of angel pictures and diplomas.

"What about stress? Are you using your stress-management techniques when things seem to be getting on top of you?"

"Nothing is getting on top of me." As I said it, a totally inappropriate picture popped into my mind.

"What are you feeling?" Jake's breath warm against my face, my bruised lips tingling from his kisses. *"Tell me what it feels like with me inside you."*

I felt my face warm. I think Dr. Shearing mistook it for guilt. She said rather impatiently, "You're an intelligent, educated man, Adrien. You must realize we can't treat the heart without treating the entire mind and body. Did you know that depressed cardiac patients have at least *twice* the risk of repeat events in the two years following their first heart attack?"

"Yep," I said shortly. "Depressed patients are less likely to take their meds, stick to their diets and exercise regimes, and continue cardiac-rehab sessions. I'm not depressed, and I'm doing everything I'm supposed to do." Including this waste of time thrice weekly for twelve weeks. That was how long my rehab was scheduled for. Twelve weeks of closely supervised... everything.

I added, "So can I please go do my workout?"

She shook her head as though she didn't get it — or more likely, that I didn't. "We talked about you bringing a support partner to rehab today."

"No, we didn't. *You* did." And now I was losing my temper. "Even if I wanted to put someone else through this, there isn't anyone."

"I know that's not true. Your mother —"

"Jesus. You don't give up, do you? I'm thirty-five years old. I don't want to go through cardiac rehab with my mom, although I sincerely appreciate the fact that she's paying for all this. I can get through it on my own. I *prefer* to do it on my own."

Mother, please, Mother, I'd rather do it myself!

Dr. Shearing gave me a long, unsmiling look. "There's not a lot I can do with that attitude."

Fortunately.

♫ ♫ ♫ ♫

"How'd it go?" Lauren asked when I climbed into her BMW about thirty minutes later.

"It's going fine." I relaxed against the headrest.

She glanced at me. "That was a heavy sigh."

Lauren was the eldest of my stepsisters. Like Natalie, she was a tall, leggy blonde; classic California girl. She possessed a much more serious temperament, though. Her days were spent working for a nonprofit organization, and her evenings went to charity work. She was in the middle of an ugly divorce and had moved back home, which right there meant she already had her own problems and didn't need mine.

I smiled wearily. "Everything's fine. It's only that I'm tired of being tired."

"I know," she commiserated, starting the car.

She didn't know, of course. That didn't change the fact that she wanted to help — genuinely wanted to help, wasn't simply offering lip service. That was one of the strangest parts of having acquired an extended family this late in life. Having all these people who genuinely cared, were genuinely interested, were not only willing but eager to help. It took getting used to. Even after two years, it caught me off guard.

Even more surprising to me was that, despite what everyone seemed to think, I sort of reciprocated. I was mildly fond of gruff Bill Dauten, and I was, well, very fond of the girls. In fact, when Natalie had hurled herself sobbing into my arms yesterday, I'd experienced the completely unfamiliar urge to break someone's face in her defense. I couldn't remember a time when anyone had relied on me, really relied on me, let alone turned to me for protection and comfort.

It had felt…good.

We drove out of the crowded lot — another sore spot: I wasn't allowed to drive yet and probably had to put up with another two or more weeks of being a passenger in my own life.

"Why don't we go by the house?" Lauren said out of the blue. "I mean, the bookstore is closed today anyway. Emma is dying to show you pictures of ponies. And it would do wonders for Lisa's nerves."

I studied her profile. "I guess she's still upset about the… er…"

"The skeleton in the floor? You could say that." She spared me a quick, wry smile. "It was all over the local news last night. She tried to send Daddy out to bring you home."

I raised my head and stared. At last I managed, "I guess I owe Bill one."

Lauren nodded. Her lips quivered, and I could see she was working not to laugh. "Don't tell Lisa. I thought your skeleton sounded kind of interesting."

"It is, kind of," I admitted. I considered telling her that someone had tried to break in to the bookstore for two nights running, but no way would she be able to refrain from passing that intel on to Lisa. It's like these women had signed a blood oath to put loyalty to their sub rosa sisterhood above all else.

"She's afraid you're going to get involved in another murder investigation."

"No."

Lauren didn't reply.

"Even if I did look into it…most of the principals would be long gone. It's a cold case. I mean, I'm *not* considering getting involved, but…"

Lauren shrugged. "Fifty years ago. If someone was in their twenties back then, they could still be around."

"Even Lisa can't think I'm at risk from the seventy-and-up demographic."

She bit her lip, still clearly amused at my woes. "Shall we drop by the house and reassure her that you're still alive?"

"Home, Jane," I ordered languidly.

§ § § §

"I like *him* best," Emma confided, handing me a photo of a five-year-old black gelding. "Adagio."

We were sitting on the wide sofa in the Dautens' family room, which opened into the large kitchen, where Natalie stood quietly arguing on the phone with her boyfriend and Lisa pretended not to listen as she dished out lunch.

"He's a beauty," I agreed, studying the graceful tail, arched neck, wide eyes, and classic dish face of an Arabian horse.

"We've been through this, Emma. A pony is much more suitable." Lisa set a plate of eggplant cannelloni on the coffee table in front of me.

Emma's face took on a mutinous expression. She was the youngest of my stepsisters, and if I were going to be honest, she was my favorite. I'd never been remotely interested in children, but Emma — somehow she was different. She even sort of looked like me. Well, she had dark hair and blue eyes. At fourteen, she still had to grow into her lanky height, and she seemed to be all knees and elbows.

I said, "A pony isn't necessarily the best choice for a child." Emma opened her mouth, and I amended, "*Or* a teenybopper."

Torn between indignation and gratification, she volunteered, "Adagio is fourteen and a half hands."

I picked up the plate, saying, "That's relatively small. Cutoff for a pony is fourteen point two."

"Tall enough for someone to break her little neck falling off."

"I won't," Emma protested.

"She could break her little neck falling off a Shetland pony," I said. "Or tripping over her little feet." I added to Emma, "Try to avoid that."

She smothered a giggle. I actually liked her giggle. Sue me. I sampled the cannelloni. It was good: olives, shallots, goat cheese. But it was hard to make myself eat now. I surreptitiously set the plate aside.

Lisa wore the expression I recognized only too well from many thwarted attempts to coerce her into letting me have something besides tropical fish during my formative years. "I think it would be better to start with a pony. I'm not wild about *that* idea, let alone buying a horse."

"Ponies can be stubborn and spoiled. A lot of it's going to depend on the previous owner. Arabians are smart, alert, gentle. So much so that they're about the only breed of which the United States Equestrian Federation will permit kids younger than eighteen to show stallions."

My grandmother had raised Arabians. In fact, my childhood ambition had been to raise Arabians. I'd probably have outgrown that even if I hadn't gotten sick in my teens. I still enjoyed riding — and hopefully would be well enough to start again soon.

"She's not going to have a *stallion*," Lisa exclaimed.

"Adagio's not a stallion," Emma said. "He's a gelding."

At that unconsciously possessive tone, Lisa gave me a long look. I intervened before she could.

"Don't set your heart on Adagio, kiddo. You're going by a photo. We haven't seen him in the flesh, let alone ridden him. And you'd want to ride him a couple of times, not make a decision based on seeing him once."

"But I *know*. If I ride him once and I think he's the right one, why can't I have him?"

"Arabians aren't much good as jumpers," I reminded her. "They jump flat. You still want to show jump, right? Show me the other ponies."

It was clear that I had let her down big-time. She fought to keep her mouth from quivering as she handed me the next photos. I tried not to notice, though it was hard to ignore, when she was shaking with the effort not to cry. It reminded me of something I hadn't thought of in a very long time: a cardboard box with an old pillow and a cheap dog collar for an unknown dog to be named Scout that I had confidently believed would one day be mine. I had held on to that box for two years, believing that I could wear my mother down.

In the end, the cardboard box, pillow, and collar had gone in the trash, along with my dreams of dog ownership. And I'd gotten over it just fine. So would she. I picked up my plate, ate a bite of cannelloni.

"This chestnut is nice-looking."

Nothing from Emma.

"The Welsh pony?"

She nodded. Pressed her lips still more firmly when they would have betrayed her.

"Or what about the Welara?" For Lisa's benefit, I said, "That's an Arabian and Welsh pony mix. They're supposed to be very gentle."

Emma nodded bravely, her fingers clutching the photo of Adagio so tightly, it was starting to crinkle.

Appetite gone, I set my plate on the table. "I'm not saying Adagio's *not* the right horse."

She gave another of those tight nods, wiped her nose with her hand, sniffed fiercely.

"Emma, you're being a goose," Lisa said sharply. "You're lucky that your father and I are willing to consider a pony."

Emma jumped up and ran from the room, ignoring Lisa's exasperated "Emma!"

In the wake of a distant bedroom door slamming, Lisa turned to me. "I do *not* understand that child. You were never like this. Girls are so…so *unreasonable*."

"It's not going to hurt if I go take a look at this horse, right?"

She paled. "Adrien, you are *not* well enough to ride. You *know* that."

"Yes, I know that." I clamped down on my own impatience. "I'll have a look at Adagio and see if it's worth taking her out there for a test drive."

"She's had her heart set on that bloody nag from the minute she saw his picture. It's ridiculous."

"Yes. Probably. What's the harm in letting me vet him? Osseo Farms is a reputable breeder, and I like Arabians. If I were in the market for a horse, I'd be looking at Arabians."

"Are you sure you're *not* in the market?" my mother asked drily.

I grinned at her, and after a moment she smiled reluctantly.

Despite the flare-up with Emma, it was a pleasant visit. We sat in the large, shady backyard and drank lemonade and talked. Or they talked. Mostly I listened. And admittedly, I dozed off a couple of times as Lauren and Natalie discussed their romantic woes.

Fortunately no one asked my opinion, because I believed Lauren couldn't unload her cheating, corporate-clone spouse fast enough, and Natalie's on-and-off boyfriend, Warren was a waste of space. Not that my track record was enviable, though with the exception of Mel, I didn't think I had ever kidded myself that my relationships were going to last forever.

"Guy called here last night," Lisa said, jolting me out of a somnolent contemplation of bees buzzing the purple clematis climbing up the redwood pergola. "Did he get hold of you?"

"Yes."

Three pairs of eyes watched and waited.

"What?"

Natalie said to the others, "I told you."

I asked shortly, "What did you tell them?"

"That it's over with Guy."

I closed my eyes, raised my face to the sun. "You worry about your own love life," I said finally.

Not exactly a crushing rejoinder. Surprisingly, they left it alone.

After a time, Emma came out to join us on the patio, and everyone carefully ignored the fact that her eyes and nose were pink. Bill arrived home, and cocktails were served — though none for me. I was looking forward to the following week, when I'd finally be allowed a glass of wine again. Not that I needed to be drunk to be around my family, but it didn't hurt to take the edge off.

The only awkward time was when Lisa popped out with, "Darling, the house in Porter Ranch is still sitting empty."

"I thought you were putting it on the market?" I said.

"This is a dreadful time to try and sell a house."

"Okay."

My bemusement must have been clear. She pushed a fraction harder. "Have you given any more thought to what we discussed?"

"What did we discuss?" I asked cautiously.

"You moving into the Porter Ranch house."

I peered more closely at her. "That was like…two years ago."

She said brightly, "Then you've had plenty of time to think about it. The house is perfect for you. It's quiet and private, and it has the swimming pool, which would be so good for you now. The doc—"

"It's sort of big for one, don't you think?"

"It won't *always* be one." She was giving me that maternal look that always raised the hair on the back of my neck.

"That's true. I do have a cat now."

She laughed her silvery laugh, and I knew I'd better not encourage her.

"I appreciate the thought. I can't afford a new house *and* a bookstore renovation."

To my horror, Bill looked up out of his paper and said, "You can have the house, Adrien. Your mother and I already discussed it. It would put Lisa's mind at ease."

I made a sound that generally precedes having a doctor inspect your tonsils and managed feebly, "It's too far from the bookstore."

"Darling, you don't need to live over the bookstore."

"No, but I *like* living over the bookstore."

"But living over the bookstore is hardly conducive to developing a healthier lifestyle and more-sensible work habits, which is what the doctors warned you *has* to happen, or you're going to be right back where you were."

I said to the others, "Is this better than reality TV or what?"

Emma made a squeaky sound that was probably a laugh swallowed in the nick of time.

"Adrien, you need to take this seriously."

"Serious as a heart attack," I assured her.

Her face tightened. "That's hardly amusing, under the circumstances."

"If it has a pool, why can't *we* move there?" Emma inquired.

"*There*," I said, pointing at her. "Excellent idea."

"Oh, Adrien." Lisa abandoned the discussion.

Another round of cocktails was served, and plans for dinner got under way. I felt that peculiar, inevitable restlessness again.

To Lisa's displeasure — and my surprise — Lauren asked if I wanted to go home. I hardened my heart against Lisa's and Emma's obvious disappointment and admitted I did. It wasn't merely the fatigue, although it continued to worry me how tired

I was all the time. I had a strange sense of missing something, of being in the wrong place — no matter where I was.

I said my good-byes, and Lauren drove me back to Pasadena. "Thanks for the intervention," I said when we were on our way.

She brushed it off. "I know how it is when you need quiet to think things out."

I remembered her impending divorce. She probably did know. For all that Lauren seemed to agree with the other womenfolk that she was doing the right thing, I got the feeling she was in a lot of pain.

We reached the bookstore. I thanked Lauren again, lifted a hand in farewell, and let myself into the big, empty building.

It was warm and very still inside. The heady scent of old books floated with the dust motes in the fading light. Old and used books have a particular scent — very different from new books. That evening it was a mix of old leather, worn cloth, crumbling paper, and wood polish. It smelled like home. I couldn't imagine willingly leaving Cloak and Dagger ever. Maybe they could stick *me* under the floorboards when I was done.

I walked over to the plastic wall dividing the bookstore from the other half of the building. There was no sign that the cops had been there during the day. No sign anyone had. Perhaps that was good news.

I went upstairs and unlocked my flat. It was too warm and stuffy upstairs, a bit too redolent of cat. I opened the windows to catch whatever evening breeze there was.

What had been the rush to get here again? Everything was exactly as I'd left it. As it would always be.

I sat down on the sofa, and Tomkins leaped onto the cushion beside me, rubbing his face against my arm.

"Miss me?"

Apparently so. Well, there was no accounting for taste; I'd be the first to admit that.

I dealt with the litter box, fed the cat, decided I'd opt for a snack later, considered having a drink, reconsidered, and returned to the sofa, where I stared at the ceiling for a time.

What the hell was my problem?

If I'd wanted company, why hadn't I stayed at Lisa's?

I listened to the distant street sounds as this part of town began to roll up the sidewalks for the evening. I listened to the building settling in for the long evening, stretching out wooden joints, cracking its knuckles.

"Oh, what the hell," I said.

Tomkins briefly abandoned his pursuit of an ailing fly to throw me a curious look as I rose and went to the phone.

"He's probably not even home," I told him.

Tomkins offered no opinion. He sat down to watch, as though my dialing a phone was one of the most fascinating things he'd ever witnessed in his brief life.

The phone rang on the other end.

Once.

Twice.

I closed my eyes, trying to decide if I was going to leave a message.

"Riordan."

I opened my eyes. Funny how the sound of his voice could still make my heart speed up. You'd have thought I'd be over it by now. You'd have thought wrong.

"Hi."

"Hey." One syllable, but his voice warmed perceptibly. "How are you doing?"

"Okay." I wondered how long it would be before that statement was true.

"Yeah?"

I didn't think there was any telltale note in my voice, yet his single questioning word held instant and complete discernment. Sometimes I thought Jake, ironically, knew me better than about anyone on the planet.

"Not really," I admitted. "Did you hear about yesterday?"

"The skeleton in the floor? I heard."

You could take the boy out of the police force, but you couldn't take the police force out of the boy.

"We had another break-in too. That's why I'm calling."

His voice didn't cool exactly, though it lost warmth. "Yes?"

"How's the PI biz?"

He said colorlessly, "I got my first case yesterday. A woman wants me to follow her ex."

"He's already her ex?"

"Yeah."

No wonder his voice sounded flat. "Are you going to take it?"

"Yes." And clearly it was not up for discussion.

"Do you think you'd have time for another case?"

He sounded almost wary as he asked, "What case? Who's the client?"

"Me," I said. "I want to hire you."

CHAPTER FIVE

Since Jake's key no longer worked following rekeying the building, I had to go downstairs to the side entrance to let him in. I opened the door.

He was wearing jeans and a black T-shirt. The dying rays of the sun gilded his close-cropped blond hair. His hazel eyes seemed lighter than usual in his tanned face. There was something else different about him; I told myself it was the Thai food. He held up a brown paper sack of takeout from Saladong Song.

I quoted, "To know things in the same way a duck does."

"That's what I always say."

"It's a Thai proverb. I've never understood what it means."

"Maybe it'll become clear after dinner."

I turned and led the way upstairs, conscious of Jake behind me on the staircase, the quiet, measured tread of his feet. He'd been here the night before last, so I wasn't sure why it felt like a lifetime.

We went inside the flat. He still remembered where everything was in the kitchen. I considered that while he got out plates and silverware. Was it a commentary on him or me? I wasn't sure.

"What made you think I hadn't eaten dinner?" I inquired, folding my arms and leaning back against the counter.

"Nothing. I was going by the fact I hadn't eaten yet." His eyes met mine, and I could feel my mouth twitching into a smile. He never ate tom yum goong soup.

All at once, for the first time in weeks, I was starving. I got him a beer out of the fridge and a bottle of mineral water for myself.

We carried our plates into the living room and settled side by side on the couch.

"When did you get the cat?" Jake asked, observing Tomkins, who was eyeing him distrustfully from beneath the chair by the window.

"It's kind of a long story," I said vaguely. "He got mauled by a dog. I'm not keeping him, though. He's only staying here until he's healed. After that he goes back to the alley."

"Uh-huh. Did you name him?"

"Tomkins. John Tomkins." I felt it necessary to explain. "I had to name him for the vet. He was a pirate."

"Only you would have a pirate for a vet."

I laughed, tried not to wince at the pull of sutures and wires. "Hey, he's great with the tropical fish. Anyway, if I *wanted* a pet — which I don't — it would be a dog."

Jake said seriously, "You can't have a dog without a yard. Unless you want one of those earmuffs with feet."

"No. I'd want a real dog."

That reminded me of Emma and Adagio. I filled Jake in on the domestic drama chez Dauten, and he said, "If you want me to drive you out to the breeder one afternoon, let me know. My current caseload allows for flexibility."

He sounded sardonic. I wondered how he was doing financially. I'd yet to hear the details of his resignation from the force. And then there was his impending divorce — assuming that was still on. Would he have to sell his house?

I opened my mouth to ask a lot of questions that were probably none of my business, but the phone rang. I put down my bowl and went to answer it.

"Holy moly. It is the same phone number," Mel remarked. "You have no idea the memories…"

He sounded mildly shaken — which matched my feeling on hearing his voice so unexpectedly. Not that it should have been entirely unexpected; he'd said he would call. Unusual that I'd forgotten.

"Hi." I was acutely conscious of Jake listening on the sofa a few feet away. "How's your dad doing?"

"Excellent. He came through surgery with flying colors." He filled in the details — as though I hadn't had enough heart surgery lately — and I listened politely, watching out of the corner of my eye as Jake calmly ate his supper.

"Which is probably more than you wanted to know." Mel concluded at last. "How are *you* feeling?"

"Fine. Better every day."

"Are you up for tomorrow night?"

I felt a flicker of amusement, which I firmly squelched. In my peripheral vision Jake lifted the beer bottle to his mouth, and I watched his throat move as he swallowed. It would probably do me a world of good to go out with someone else, now that I thought about it.

"Okay. It sounds like fun, actually. Thanks for thinking of me."

"I think of you more than you might realize."

I had no answer to that. I wasn't even sure I wanted to hear it. I was pretty sure Mel was suffering some kind of *Back to the Future* emotional retrograde on this visit home.

"What time?" I asked neutrally.

We worked out the details, and I hung up, returning to the sofa and my now-cool soup. The silence seemed newly awkward.

Jake said, "So what exactly is it you want me to do for you?"

I opened my mouth, but the vision that suddenly flooded my mind seemed to short-circuit my speech center.

Jake whispering against my face, *"I missed you."* His kisses — for a guy who sometimes had all the subtlety of a blunt instrument, Jake's kisses — the intimate exploration of tongue, the tease of teeth, the melting, unexpected softness of his lips...

I cleared my throat. "Well, for starters, I want you to see if you can find a guy named Henry Harrison."

"Okay. Why?"

"Because yesterday he showed up asking questions about the hotel and talking about the murder of Jay Stevens. I find it too much of a coincidence. Seriously. The very day after an attempted break-in?"

Jake considered it. Nodded. "I agree. Do you have any kind of a lead on him?"

"No. Harrison might not even be his real name. He claimed to be visiting from Milwaukee, but he didn't sound like he was from Milwaukee. In fact, nothing about him jibed. Well, I take that back. He did seem to know something about architecture."

Jake asked a few pertinent questions about Harrison, and I answered to the best of my ability. Mel's showing up when he had the day before had completely distracted me. I didn't want to admit that to Jake.

"Here's the intriguing part," I said. "Harrison looked to me to be in his late sixties or so. Which means he could have been a contemporary of Jay Stevens."

I liked the way Jake's eyes lit with interest. "That *is* intriguing." He thought it over. "Okay. Locate a.k.a. Henry Harrison. What else?"

"Secondly, and finding Harrison might answer this, I want to know what it is someone thinks is hidden in this building. It can't be Jay Stevens's body, because that's been found, and the discovery was all over the news last night, so I don't see how anyone could have missed it."

"Your intruder may not watch the news." He pointed out, "You don't."

"True, but if he's interested enough to break in to the building twice, he's got to be keeping an eye on the bookstore, and this place was a zoo yesterday." I added, "The ape in charge was our good friend Detective Alonzo."

Jake said impassively, "So I heard."

"What else did you hear?"

"What do you mean?"

"You still have contacts, right? Is there confirmation that the skeleton is Jay Stevens?"

"It's going to take a while to verify that one way or the other. It's a good bet that it's Stevens. The skeleton is male and probably belonged to someone in his early- to mid twenties. His is the only mysterious death associated with the hotel that I'm aware of."

"I've been checking on Stevens." I told Jake about the Moonglows and *Kaleidoscope*.

"If the sister is still alive, she might be a lead."

"I couldn't find any trace of her, though Sergeant Frame mentioned the name of the investigating officer. Somebody Argyle."

Jake shook his head. "Doesn't ring a bell."

Argyle was probably long gone. Frame had about ten years on Jake, so she would remember people who had moved on or retired by the time Jake joined the force.

"Frame also mentioned that Jay Stevens and the Moonglows used to play at a club near the beach called The Tides. She didn't say whether it was up the coast or down." I smothered a yawn. Eight thirty and I was ready for bed. For sleep. As party animals went, I appeared to be going into hibernation.

"Okay. Those are both good leads." Jake rose, picked up our empty dishes, and vanished into the kitchen. I heard the taps running, and I stared out the window at the first pale stars in the pink and yellow sky. One thing about smog: it made for beautiful sunsets.

Jake returned to the living room. "I'm taking off. I'll let you know how it goes."

I turned around to study him. I hadn't expected this. On the one hand, I was relieved he was giving up without a fight. On the other...

I rose too. "We rekeyed. I have to lock the door after you."

"Right."

He paused at the table and picked up the DVD lying there. "*The Maltese Falcon*?" He said with a faint smile, "I'd have expected *Captain Blood*."

"I'm kind of off pirates just now."

"Ah." His smile faded. "Yeah."

Into the sudden silence between us, I said, "I heard Paul Kane is suing you too?"

"Hmm?" It seemed to take him a second to follow what I was saying. "Yeah."

Not a big deal for him, it seemed. I opened my mouth to say...I have no idea what. Jake cut me off with a brisk "It doesn't matter. Kane's going away for a long time, and the lawsuits are strictly nuisance bullshit." The expression in his eyes was one of curiosity. "You're not worried about that?"

"No." I really wasn't. He looked unconvinced.

"There's more than enough evidence to convict Kane a couple of times over."

"I know."

He waited for me to spit out whatever was on my mind. When I didn't, he turned away again and opened the door. I followed him downstairs.

At the side entrance, he said with a long, straight look, "Night, Adrien."

"Jake?"

He nodded.

"Maybe this isn't my business. All the time we were seeing each other —"

"Ten months."

Ten months. Not that long, really. Making it all the more difficult to explain why it sometimes seemed like one of the most important relationships of my life.

"Were you still seeing Kane all that time?"

Had he been expecting the question? Jake answered without hesitation. "At first, yes. I quit seeing him after we spent those days at the ranch." His gaze met mine steadily, seriously. There seemed to be a message there. I wasn't sure what it was.

I said, and I was astonished to hear the pain in my voice, "I'd thought — I don't know why — that I was sort of your first." I added quickly, "I mean, I know I wasn't your first, because you said —"

He said, "You were the first in every way that counted. You were the first guy I ever kissed." He smiled faintly, unreadably. "Come to think of it, you were the first guy I had sex with in a bed."

I had no idea what to say to that. The images that it conjured were enough to shut anyone up, I guessed.

"You're comparing apples and oranges. Paul and I didn't date. We weren't friends. We didn't have a relationship outside of the club we both belonged to. He had a voracious appetite for pain, and I had a powerful desire to inflict it."

I wished that I hadn't asked. It was more than I wanted to know.

"However, when I went back to the club after my marriage, my relationship with Paul did change. We became friends. Or if not friends, at least I allowed the relationship to extend outside of the confines of the club. I was fond of him."

"I know."

"I'm sorry you were hurt. I'm sorry Paul hurt you. I'm sorry I hurt you." Straightforward, sincere, take it or leave it.

I nodded.

"Good night," he said.

"Good night."

I locked the door after him and went upstairs.

ʃ ʃ ʃ ʃ

The bookstore remained closed on Thursday. I was a model prisoner.

By now I was getting the morning routine down to a science: I weighed myself, took my temperature, checked my blood pressure and heart rate, inspected the ugly incision on my chest. Everything indicated I was recovering right on schedule. And I did feel more cheerful, despite the daunting array of medications I was still on.

I did my tai chi, had breakfast — forcing myself to eat a bowl of oatmeal — opened my e-mail, promptly closed it again, and decided to go for a stroll.

As I walked, I couldn't help noticing how loud and busy and smoggy the city was. It had never bothered me before. Now I felt…vulnerable, and the noise and crowds unsettled me in a way they never had before.

Reluctantly, I thought of the house in Porter Ranch — and the pool in the backyard. It would be nice to swim again. Nice to lie in the sun and enjoy the peace and quiet of the surrounding hills. And it *would* be good for me. Lisa was right about that.

But the house was far too large for one. Too large for two, really — although if it were two people used to needing their own space…?

I walked for about twenty minutes, stopping only to buy a couple of CDs — *The Essential Glenn Miller* and *The Very Best of Cole Porter* — came home, put Cole Porter on, and fell asleep listening to Carmen McRae's version of "Every Time We Say Goodbye." I woke reenergized, went downstairs, and opened my e-mail for real — this time dealing with about half of it.

On impulse, I sent off an e-mail to the Thomas family web site asking Todd to get in touch with me.

That did wonders for my morale, and I spent the rest of the afternoon upstairs working on the third Jason Leland mystery, *A Deed of Dreadful Note*.

This was my third novel about a gay Shakespearean actor and amateur sleuth. When I'd left college, I had fond dreams of writing for a living. The plan was even parent approved. Perhaps that was the problem. Or perhaps it was simply that I didn't have much to write about at that stage in my life. I'd liked the idea of writing more than the actual writing. Now I enjoyed writing, but I didn't kid myself that it was ever going to be anything other than an enjoyable diversion. I took pride in selling books. In fostering literacy. I loved talking books and writing to people. I appreciated the absence of deadlines in my life and the fact that I was my own boss. I was successful, but not so successful that it was an obsession. There was still room in my life for other things. Like…murder.

There was no question Leland was a much-better amateur sleuth than I. Granted, he was lucky in the amount of clues that conveniently fell into his lap.

The first book in the series, *Murder Will Out*, had even been optioned briefly for film, though that had fallen through. And how.

I worked on the novel, pushing words around, and then I took another brief walk around the block, came back, and made myself a salad for dinner. Food was kind of a problem for me. The second day of cardiac rehab, I'd met with a nutritionist and received a brochure to go with the lecture on what I should and shouldn't eat. Which was fine. I wanted to eat the right things, but I wasn't particularly hungry, and I'd never been much of a cook.

I showered and dressed for my — I didn't really want to call it a date — with Mel. Appointment sounded a tad medicinal, though, and rendezvous seemed to require passports. In the end I settled on a clean pair of Levi's — I didn't want to overdress in case it looked like I was taking this outing too seriously — and a blue jacquard short-sleeved shirt. I experimented, turning this way and that to see if the scar below my collarbone showed, and it did at certain angles. If Mel and I achieved those angles, clearly the shirt would be coming off anyway. And I really couldn't picture that.

I filled in the time waiting for Mel to pick me up by surfing the Net, looking to see what I could find on a club called The

Tides. Unexpectedly, there was a quite a bit of information. In fact, for a brief time in the 1950s, The Tides had been *the* place to go for a romantic evening.

I studied the black-and-white photos of smiling Hollywood starlets and Korean War vets, of couples dressed in cocktail dresses and dinner jackets dancing in front of giant picture windows that offered panoramic views of the Southern California coast from Santa Monica to Palos Verdes.

I peered at photographs of different bands. Tommy Reynolds, Si Zentner, Annie Laurie, the Johnny Long Orchestra — most of these names were unknown to me, but there were other names that I did recognize. Benny Goodman, Ella Fitzgerald, Peggy Lee. The Tides owner, Dan Hale, had brought in the best and the brightest.

There were a number of passing references to a "house band," Jay Stevens and the Moonglows.

On a site describing now-defunct jazz clubs, I read a description of The Tides.

Set back a few yards from the pier was the cobalt blue door of The Tides. A short, narrow flight of steps led to a long, wide room with picture windows facing the ocean. The room featured tiled mosaics of the sea, zigzagging wood inlays, and undulating wrought-iron handrails. Playful, ocean-themed shapes popped up everywhere in sconces, moldings, and upholstery. The large, polished dance floor could easily accommodate one hundred couples, while latticework sculptures of sea life caught in nets of dark wood stretched across the ceiling.

Mel rang to say he was waiting outside. I turned off the laptop and went to meet him.

He was standing beside a silver rental car. I remembered that he had owned a classic BMC Mini when we had been together. I wondered what he drove those days. Knowing Mel, he probably still drove a Mini. "I can't leave you alone for a minute, can I?"

"History would seem to dispute that."

"No, but I've only just heard about the skeleton in your attic."

"Third-floor bedroom, but…right. An upgrade the Realtor forgot to mention."

"I can't believe you haven't put this place on the market yet. It's the first thing I'd have done."

"Are you kidding? I'm the envy of every mystery-bookstore owner in the country." I was turning, still smiling at the sound of a car engine down the alley. My smile faded at the sight of Jake's black Honda S2000.

I was surprised I recognized it, given how rarely I'd been invited to ride shotgun in its comfortable bucket seats.

"Who's this?" Mel inquired. Something in my expression must have told him what he needed to know. He said in a different tone, "Oh."

The Honda rolled up beside us. Jake rolled down the car window. His expression was impassive as his hazel gaze flicked from Mel to me. "Sorry. I should have called first."

He should have, of course. I was surprised he hadn't. "No problem," I said automatically.

There was a beat — or more of a dropped beat — and I said reluctantly, "Jake, this is Mel Davis. Mel, Jake Riordan."

Mel was on the other side of his car, and Jake hadn't got out, so nothing more was called for than a nodding of heads and minimal greetings — and that was exactly the extent of it.

"Nice to meet you," Mel said.

"Davis," Jake returned. Since I couldn't believe that Jake remembered the name of my ex, the terseness had to be merely his natural charm shining through. His gaze met mine, and by some quirk of the fading light, his eyes looked green. "I found Nick Argyle."

"You did?"

His mouth quirked. "Don't sound so surprised."

"No, only I figured even odds he'd be sitting at that big sergeant's desk in the sky by now."

"Nope. I hope I sound that sharp at seventy-plus. I've got a meet with him tomorrow. I thought you might want to tag along."

"Seriously?"

He nodded.

I didn't have to think about it. Today's taste had been all the solitary confinement I could swallow. I'd be going stir-crazy before long. "I'd like to, yeah."

"Eleven o'clock in the morning. Will that work for you?"

"Works for me. Thanks for inviting me."

"Don't mention it." By now it had dawned on all three of us that Jake hadn't had to drive over to the bookstore to deliver this news.

Mel said, "We've got to go, Adrien, or we'll be late."

Jake's expression was totally blank.

Too much drama in my life, as Natalie would say. I was irritated to hear the note of apology in my voice. "Mel and I are going to catch a film-noir double feature at LACMA. You know the film series the County Museum of Arts puts on?"

"You'll enjoy that." He inclined his head politely to Mel. "Have a great evening." The window of his car slowly rolled up.

He nodded to me through the glass and put the car into reverse, making the neat, tight half circle in the alley with the ease of long practice.

Mel and I got into his car.

"So that was the cop?"

"That's Jake, yes."

"He's…a presence, that's for sure." Mel was smiling, curious. "Not what I would have pictured for you."

"What did you picture for me? Clearly not yourself."

"Yeeouch." Mel was still keeping it light. "I can see why you're having doubts. He seems like a roughneck."

"A roughneck?" To hide my illogical irritation — illogical, because who was I kidding? Of course I was having doubts — I returned lightly, "Well, you know what they say about opposites attracting."

"I've never believed that."

Neither did I, actually. I said, "I may have done something unfair. Jake's working as a PI now, and I hired him to look into the weird stuff that's been happening at the bookstore." I filled him in on the second break-in. Before I'd finished, he was reaching for his antacids. I'd forgotten what a worrier Mel was.

"Anyway, I thought it would help both of us. Jake needs the work, and I need the security breaches to stop."

"And he's misinterpreting your gesture?" When I didn't answer, Mel asked, only half joking, "Or you are?"

§ § § §

The evening went better than I expected. It helped that Mel and I had always seen eye to eye on films — and these classics were two of my favorites. *The Big Sleep* with Humphrey Bogart was pretty much the film everyone thought of when they thought of Chandler, and *The Blue Dahlia* was the only script Chandler wrote for the screen. Everything else was mostly adapted from his stories.

It was a pleasure to see the films again and under such primo conditions — and these *were* primo conditions. The county museum's Leo S. Bing Theater was equipped with an amazing sound system — three amazing sound systems, if you wanted to get technical — and it looked as good as it sounded, though that was really Mel's realm of expertise rather than mine. I was all about story. Mel was more into technique. Even if I wasn't an expert, I appreciated seeing the movies on the big screen again.

"It's going to be a shame if they lose this," Mel said during the intermission.

I agreed.

The forty-year-old LACMA weekend film series was still relatively unknown, which was a shame, considering the role Hollywood and the film industry played in shaping Southern California. In recent months, dwindling audiences and lack of funds had put the program in jeopardy, but the city — and the film community — stepped up to the plate. For now, the weekend film series was saved.

I admit I was very close to dozing off at the last bit of *The Big Sleep*, and in fact, Mel did razz me about life imitating art.

"Would you like to stop somewhere for coffee or a drink?"

I shook my head. "As much as I'd like to, I'm bushed."

"Another time?"

"Sure."

"How about dinner tomorrow night?"

"*Tomorrow* night?"

Mel said. "I don't want to play games. I enjoyed tonight more than I've enjoyed any night in a long, long time. I want to see you again. I hope you feel the same way."

"I enjoyed tonight, no question," I said. "I just…"

Mel filled in the blank. "Don't want to see me again?"

I stared at him.

"No, definitely not that."

He leaned forward, and we kissed. His mouth was warm and pliable and disconcertingly familiar. Uncomplicated. Nice. Safe.

Our lips parted. I said, "Definitely not that."

CHAPTER SIX

Early Friday morning, Natalie arrived at Cloak and Dagger to receive book shipments and complain about the music I was playing.

"What *is* that?" Her expression was as pained as though an air-raid siren were going off.

"That's Glenn Miller. 'The Nearness of You.'"

"I don't mean the song. I mean…what kind of music is that? Classical is bad enough. This is…old-people music."

"You say that about the Beatles. You say that about the Pretenders."

"Yes, okay, this is…ancient-civilization music."

I made a dismissive sound. "I like it."

"Warren says…"

I turned the volume down on her and glanced over the bills of lading — which I'd practically had to arm wrestle her for.

Shortly after ten thirty the front door on the other side of the building opened, and Natalie and I watched two plainclothes detectives — presumably one of them was the detective I'd spoken to on the phone first thing that morning — enter. We were acknowledged with a flash of badges. The detectives went upstairs.

"What now?" Natalie asked.

I shook my head. I was waiting for Detective Alonzo to make an appearance; to my relief, there was no sign of him. It seemed to be only the two detectives. "Maybe it's the post investigation walk-through."

"The what?"

"Exit procedures for the detectives in charge of a crime scene. At the conclusion of the case, the investigator does a walk-through to ensure the scene investigation is complete."

"You mean the case is closed?"

"I don't know. I don't see how it could be this soon. Hopefully it means they'll let us open for business."

Jake arrived shortly after, and I went to the side door to let him in.

"Argyle lives in Ojai, so make sure you've got whatever you need for the next few hours."

"*Ojai?*"

His gaze was curious. "Is that a problem?"

"I don't know." I said reluctantly, "That's — what? An hour and a half, two hours, each way?"

"Yeah?"

"I'm not sure I'm up to it." It was painful to admit, painful to acknowledge how uncertain I was of myself. Even more than convalescence, I felt tethered by my fear of what might happen. It was frightening and frustrating. Was I ever going to be up for anything again? It didn't feel like it.

I could feel Jake assessing me, though I didn't meet his eyes.

"I'll make sure you don't get into any trouble."

"Thanks." I had to work at a smile. "I should probably play it safe."

"I think it'd do you good to get out of here for a while."

I nodded. I agreed with him, but it wasn't that simple. What if something happened? Did he really want to try and deal with that? I didn't.

"Why don't you phone your doctor?"

I looked up, startled.

Jake clarified, "Why don't you ask him if you're well enough to spend about three or four hours in a car?"

Uh, Hello Kitty, as Em would say. So simple it was disconcerting that it hadn't occurred to me.

I left Jake to Natalie's mercy while I went into my office and called Dr. Cardigan. I was reassured that, provided I wasn't doing the driving, I was permitted to travel, although there were a few restrictions.

I dutifully reported back to Jake. "I'm supposed to get out and stretch my legs for five to ten minutes every hour or so."

"That's easy enough. Anything else?"

Dr. Cardigan had suggested that if the trip was more than two hours one way, I should spend the night at a motel or hotel. I wasn't about to suggest that to Jake.

"No. That ought to do it."

I grabbed my meds and a tea towel to place between the seat belt and my chest to minimize irritation to the incision. "I'll be glad when this bullshit is over," I commented as Jake pulled out onto East Colorado Boulevard.

"What's that?"

"I'm fed up with being scared all the time."

He threw me a quick glance. It was weird the stuff I told Jake. Stuff that I wouldn't tell anyone else for love or money. Weird, because no one would ever think of Jake as someone patient with weakness — his own or anyone else's.

He didn't reply to that. "How was the movie?"

"Movie? Oh. Two movies. *The Big Sleep* — which I nearly did, because I have the stamina of a goddamned infant — and *The Blue Dahlia*. They're both quintessential Chandler. He was nominated for an Oscar for the screenplay on *The Blue Dahlia*, and *The Big Sleep* has Bogart and Bacall, so —"

"A good time was had by all?"

"You could say that."

Instead, he said hesitantly, "I didn't realize Davis was back in the picture. Doesn't he teach at UC Berkeley?"

He had remembered. Well, one thing about Jake: he paid attention to details.

I said, "Yes. He's down visiting. His dad recently had heart surgery."

The silence between us was filled by Marc Cohn's "Walking in Memphis."

"He's not in the picture," I said. "It's hard to explain. The way it ended between us — things were unresolved. That's all."

He asked drily, "Isn't that pretty much the way it is when most relationships end? Is anything ever really completely resolved?"

"I think so, yeah."

Jake nodded thoughtfully and, to my relief, did not ask the question I dreaded. He changed the subject. "I'm hitting a wall with Henry Harrison. Not unexpected, because we've got almost nothing to go on. I tried contacting hotels in the area. There's not a lot more I can do unless he resurfaces."

"If he resurfaces."

"If you're right and he's somehow connected with this case, he'll resurface."

"This Argyle remembered Jay Stevens?"

"It took some prodding. It was a long time ago, and it never really was officially a murder case, but he did finally remember a few details, and he was willing to talk, so we'll see what comes of it."

"How'd you find him so fast?"

"I've still got a contact or two downtown." The satisfaction in his voice made me smile inwardly.

"Whatever is going on at the bookstore, it's got to tie into Jay Stevens's murder."

"It is homicide," he agreed. "The preliminary indicates Stevens was killed by blunt-force trauma to the head. There's a big crack down the side of his skull. He must have been struck by something pretty damn heavy. He probably died almost instantly."

Nice to still have friends on the force. The papers had been remarkably silent on the topic of Jay Stevens once the excitement of the discovery of the skeleton in the floor had been milked.

Jake said, "It's been handed over to the CCHU. The cold case homicide unit. But you have to remember, despite the media attention on the discovery of Stevens's remains, this isn't a high-profile case."

"What does that mean?"

"It means that it all went down half a century ago. Our resources are limited. CCHU has six detectives trying to choose among eight thousand unsolved homicides dating all the way back to 1960."

I groused, "You'd think they could move the cutoff to permit one case from 1959. Couldn't they temporarily add an extra detective or two?" Granted, if the extra detective was going to be Alonzo, I'd be just as happy if they let it go.

"The focus has to remain on clearing up current caseloads that not only stand a better chance of being solved but have citizens pushing for resolution. No grieving family member is begging us to find Stevens's killer. No one is begging us to give them closure."

Our. Us.

Once a cop, always a cop, I guessed.

"I'm begging," I said.

He looked at me and grinned. "You never begged in your life."

"I suppose you have?"

An odd expression flickered in his eyes, a sudden recognition of something in the distance — or the past. "I begged for something once."

To be straight? That would be about right. Or did he mean it in sexual context I didn't want to know anything about?

I said drily, "And did you get what you begged for?"

"Yeah." His voice sounded funny. "I did."

I glanced at him. There was nothing to read on his face. Same handsome, unforgiving profile.

I changed the subject. "Have they confirmed that the skeleton belongs to Jay Stevens?"

"It's not a rock-solid ID. We don't have any family members to match the remaining DNA to, but Stevens's fingerprints were all over the suitcase the skeleton was boarded up with. The suitcase and the clarinet inside."

"Stevens's fingerprints are on file?"

"Oh yeah. Once for possession of marijuana and once for theft." I could tell by the satisfaction in Jake's voice that there was more.

"He doesn't exactly sound like a master criminal."

"I'll let Argyle fill you in."

Yep, he sounded way too pleased with himself.

I said, "What I don't get is, why now? Why, after all these years, is someone looking for whatever it is they're looking for in that building?"

"You tell me."

I thought about it. "Because whatever it is will either be found during the renovation or be lost forever."

"That's my guess."

We made good time on the 101 and got off on Highway 33. At Lake Casitas, we stopped so I could stretch my legs. We strolled down to the small store and bought bottles of water and ice-cream bars. We ate the ice cream, watching the boats on the lake.

Maybe it was the perfect combination of fresh air, sunshine, and ice cream that gave me that rare sense of well-being. Or maybe it was Jake's standing beside me eating an Eskimo Pie with complete sangfroid that brought a grin to my face.

He raised his brows. "Something funny?"

I balled my wrapper and tossed it into the nearby trash. "Nope."

He considered this, but what he said was, "Your hair is the longest I've ever seen it." His fingers brushed the strands curling behind my ear — a feathery touch that I felt to the roots.

"Is it? I guess it is." I rubbed my jaw. "But I shaved for you."

"True. You looked pretty disreputable the other night." He added, "Sexy, though."

Yeah, right. Shaggy and half-naked and skeletal. He obviously thought I needed cheering up. I said ruefully, "You just liked the leather jacket."

There was a glint in Jake's eye as he replied, "I did like the leather jacket. Yeah."

♪ ♪ ♪ ♪

Nick Argyle lived on a small horse ranch in the golden hills of Ojai horse country.

We followed a dirt road a few miles until we came to the front drive. The main house was set well back in shady oak trees. A dog was barking from somewhere behind the house as we parked and walked down to the barn. The pungent smell of horse reached us before we spotted Argyle in the entrance of the twelve-stall breezeway barn. When we reached him, he was talking to a ranch hand about adding warm water to the feed for senior horses.

Argyle was tall, lean, weathered. He wore Western boots and a straw Stetson, wore them like his own skin. This was no weekend cowboy. His eyes were that shade of blue that was often mistaken for gray. He'd have been a very handsome man and still had great bone structure. He moved well, seemed vigorous, although I figured him for mid seventies. Jake was right; I hoped I'd be half as spry at that age. Funny to think that I actually had a shot at it now.

Argyle shook hands with Jake, eyed him with that keen, steady gaze, and seemed to like what he saw. He kind of reminded me of Jake, in fact. Jake introduced us, and I received that same keen, steady appraisal.

Argyle's face didn't quite fall. He directed an old-fashioned look Jake's way. He was cordial enough, though.

"So I hear the bad penny finally turned up. You want to know about Jay Stevens?"

We walked out to the corrals, which smelled of horse and hay, where a young woman in jeans and a cowboy hat stood in a round arena, taking an Appaloosa mare through its paces on a lunge line. Argyle observed for a few seconds and called out, "She's starting to rely on the fence, Francine."

The woman nodded and cracked the lunge whip.

Argyle turned back to us. "Jay Stevens. My God. That was a hell of a long time ago."

"Fifty years," Jake agreed as Argyle shook his head in disbelief. "You were the investigating officer?"

Argyle raised an eyebrow at Jake. "Investigating officer? You could say that, I guess. I tried to nail that bastard for nearly two years."

I asked, "Nail him for what?"

"Theft. Burglary. Stevens was a high-class cat burglar." He gave a bark of a laugh at my expression. "From the time he and the kid sister arrived here from…New Haven, I think it was? Someplace in Connecticut. Over an eighteen-month period, Stevens pulled off a series of upscale burglaries in Bel Air, Brentwood, and Beverly Hills. Oh, I knew he was our boy. Proving it was something else. I tried. Jesus, I tried to catch the bastard red-handed."

"So the musician gig was only part-time?"

"Isn't it always? They — he and his band — played a couple times a week at Dan Hale's place."

"Dan Hale?" Jake repeated alertly.

Argyle gave another of those bitten-off laughs. "Name rings a bell, does it? I bet. You're right. Hale had a few ties to the old

LA mob. He wasn't a bad guy, really. Very personable. It just happened that he'd do anything to hang on to that club." He added, "He's still around, you know. Hale, I mean. Lives in Santa Barbara, last I heard."

"Hale owned The Tides club where Stevens and the Moonglows used to play?"

"That's right. The club was in financial difficulty by fifty-nine. It was all Elvis Presley and Buddy Holly. Rock and roll. Nobody wanted to hear the kind of music they played at Hale's place."

I remembered the discussions and articles I'd skimmed. "Swing?"

"Yeah. Jazz, but not that stuff with no melody. The Moonglows, well, all the bands at The Tides, played the old stuff — Benny Goodman, Glenn Miller — but that music was falling out of fashion by the late fifties." He broke off to yell more instructions to the girl using the lunge line.

"Francine, do not change your aim to suit the horse. The horse has gotta change her ways to suit *your* aim."

Francine, looking harassed, straightened her hat and nodded.

"How'd you come to focus on Stevens?" Jake asked.

"You'll know what I mean when I say LA wasn't quite so big a town in the fifties. Not like it is now. I was working robbery-homicide in those days, and I noticed a pattern to a series of cat burglaries occurring in the west side. That pattern matched a series of expertly executed burglaries in places Jay Stevens and the Moonglows had spent time."

"What first drew your attention to Stevens?"

"A hunch mostly." Argyle's smile was more of a grimace. "I hate to admit that, though it's the truth. The burglaries always occurred on the nights Stevens didn't play, and a large percentage of the victims were patrons of The Tides."

I wasn't sure if that answered Jake's question or not — something must have first caught Argyle's attention in order for him to notice the pattern.

I was starting to feel the heat by then. I wiped my forehead. There were a couple of scrub oaks near a water trough and a skinny bar of shade cast by the fence. Otherwise there was no shelter from the blazing sun overhead. Slowly but surely I became more and more aware of the harsh light shimmering off the dirt and bouncing off the whitewashed sheds and buildings.

All at once, the ground seemed to slide out from under me, and I reached for the fence. At the same instant, Jake slipped an unobtrusive, steadying hand beneath my elbow.

The world stabilized.

"You mind if we talk in the shade?" Jake asked. "Adrien's still recuperating from surgery."

I didn't know what Argyle made of that. He gave me a narrow look. "You do look a little peaked, son."

I wiped my face on my shoulder. "I wouldn't mind sitting down."

"Sure, why don't we go inside," he agreed. "It's cooler there." He called out a final word to Francine and led the way back to the house.

"Okay?" Jake asked in an undervoice as we followed. His hand was a warm weight at the base of my spine. Prepared to scoop me off the path if necessary, I suppose. There was a time when he'd have viewed touching me in public in the same light as exposing himself.

I nodded. "I felt…off for a second. It's the heat."

"It's hot as hell," Argyle agreed without glancing back.

We trooped up the road into the comfortable ranch house. It had that trademark sixties architecture. A sunken living area opened onto a spacious main room with an impressive view of the mountains. At one end of the room was a massive raw-stone fireplace. At the other were an equally impressive gun case and a wall studded with hunting trophies, including a buffalo's head.

There were no pictures and surprisingly few photos. A couple of old-fashioned framed portraits of a married couple circa

1920, a couple of photos of Argyle receiving commendations or promotions, and that was about it.

"Have a seat," Argyle invited, and I was only too grateful to accept.

I leaned back on the long leather- and brass-studded couch and closed my eyes. The cool was a relief. So was sitting down.

"He okay?" Argyle asked.

"Maybe a glass of water," Jake suggested.

I heard footsteps retreating.

Please let me be okay. Please don't let this be anything. Why can't I be all right? It made me angry to even ask. It had been years — childhood — since I'd hoped. Or feared.

Jake asked quietly, "Do you need to take something?"

I moved my head in slight negation.

He picked up my wrist, and I jerked my hand away, opening my eyes and glaring at him. "I'm all right."

He nodded curtly.

I closed my eyes again. I wasn't angry with Jake. It was simply...

In fact, I was conscious of the familiar, comfortable scent of him. Deodorant soap and Le Male aftershave. Abruptly I remembered those minutes on the *Pirate's Gambit* when he'd put his arm around me. I almost wished he'd put his arm around me now.

Argyle returned, and I opened my eyes, sat up, and took the glass of water. I drank while they both observed, as though waiting for Dr. Hyde to make an appearance.

I really did feel mostly all right again. Too hot and too tired, and it was way past my naptime. No wonder I was cranky. I glanced at Jake. He was sitting close to me. Probably too close. I saw Argyle take that in, and I remembered a line from *The Long Goodbye*. "Patient and careful eyes, cool disdainful eyes, cops' eyes." Jake had those eyes too, though he wasn't looking at me that way now.

I couldn't deal with the feeling in his eyes.

To Argyle, I said, "Do you think Stevens was killed because of his criminal activities?"

"It occurred to me." He shrugged. "It seems the most likely explanation."

Jake asked, "Who did you think was responsible for Stevens's disappearance?"

"Well, to be entirely honest, I was never sure Stevens didn't skip town. He was pretty much a rolling stone, and I admit I'd made things pretty hot for him in the City of Angels. I'd told him I'd see him behind bars sooner or later. I guess I thought he took me at my word and split." His smile was rueful.

"Knowing what you know now?"

Argyle looked reflective. "Fifty years is a long time. My best guess would be he had a falling-out with a partner. Or his fence — whoever that was. I never did know."

"Did he have a partner?"

"The girl. His sister. Jinx, her name was. I'm pretty sure she was his accomplice. But there's no way she was involved in his murder. She idolized him."

Argyle's determination to see Stevens behind bars didn't seem to have extended to the kid sister. That seemed revealing. Maybe he'd had a soft spot for her, or maybe she was too small a fish to bother with. Stevens had apparently been the driving force.

"Did you ever hear of a guy named Henry Harrison?"

His brow wrinkled as he thought. Reluctantly, he shook his head. "It's not an uncommon name. Is he connected with Stevens's disappearance?"

"We don't know. It's probably not even his real name."

There was a *click* of nails on the hardwood floor, and a nervous black and tan German shepherd bitch, teats hanging low, came over to check us out. She gave Jake and then me a quick, thorough sniffing over.

"All right, Gerda. All right."

Gerda thrust her head beneath my hand, and I stroked her head. "Hello, Gerda."

"She's a beauty," Jake said, and Gerda flicked her ears in acknowledgment, although I seemed to have won her affections. Maybe she preferred my aftershave. Maybe she sensed I might soon be doggy food.

"You happen to be in the market for a German shepherd?" Argyle inquired. "Gerda has a litter of eight looking for good homes. Five boys and three girls."

"Me? No. I don't have any kind of a yard." I looked at Jake, remembering that he'd lost Rufus, his own shepherd, a year ago.

"I may be moving."

My stomach flopped. "What? Where?"

He gave me an unfathomable look. "I've got a couple of options."

I turned back to Gerda, who was panting affectionately into my face. So he was going to have to sell the house. I'd been afraid of that. He'd had that house in Glendale a long time. Would he have to take an apartment somewhere? Or would he rent another, smaller house? What were his finances like?

Probably not my business. Certainly not my problem. I couldn't help worrying.

Argyle glanced at the clock on the mantel. "Boys, as much as I enjoy talking over old times, I've got the vet due any minute. Any other questions for me?"

I asked at random, "Did you like Stevens?"

Argyle appeared surprised. He narrowed his eyes, reviewing those long-ago memories. "In a funny way, I did. We were adversaries, you understand. He didn't seem to mind that. *I*, on the other hand, took it all pretty seriously." His smile was tinged with acid. "I think it sort of amused him. The thing about cat burglars is, they're thrill seekers. They enter the residence while the victim is home — sometimes while the victim is wide awake and moving about. Cat burglars are risk takers. That makes them dangerous in my book. But Stevens was…engaging. Charming. And a very good musician. He had a way of playing that clarinet." He shook his head. "There was a song they used to do, him and the girl. 'Every Time We Say Goodbye.' You know that song?"

"I know that song. Cole Porter."

His smile was twisted. "It's a shame it ended up the way it did. I wish he *had* skipped town."

That was it. He rose, asking if we wanted to see the puppies. I thought that was a very bad idea. Jake did the socially correct thing and said yes. We walked out behind the house, and there were several German shepherd puppies in a pen in the shade, rolling over and playing with each other.

"How old are they?"

"Seven weeks. Old enough. I've started giving them away."

"They're pretty cute," I admitted.

"I don't have the papers on them, but they're purebred. The sire is a black sable from down the road. Ex-bomb-detection dog. Son of a bitch got hold of Gerda one night."

A fat, sleek puppy with a black and reddish coat finished beating up his sisters and waddled over to look up at me with shiny button eyes, pink tongue lolling like he was laughing.

"Yeah, you're a little reprobate."

He jumped up and put his paws — big paws — on the chicken-wire fence.

"He likes you," Argyle remarked.

"You say that to all the suckers."

"Sure," he agreed genially, adding, "You can pick him up."

"That would be a very bad idea."

Argyle laughed.

I said to Jake, catching a peculiar expression on his face, "We ought to get going."

He nodded. We thanked Argyle again. As we walked away, the puppy barked a high-pitched, stuffed-toy bark after us.

"That was informative," Jake commented with satisfaction as the ranch grew small in the distance of the rearview mirror.

"Yes."

"I meant to ask if he had an address on Hale. I'll follow up with him this evening."

I stared out at the sea swell of gold weeds rippling in the summer wind. It looked like wheat. What was it called? Tare? Darnel? Proverbs, was it? Some lesson about learning to tell the real thing from the false, separating the chaff.

"Tired?" he asked at last.

"I didn't realize you were thinking of moving."

He said neutrally, "Nothing's decided, but I either have to buy out Kate's share of the house or sell, and at this point, selling is the more realistic option."

"If you do sell…?"

He didn't answer right away, and I knew I was not going to like what he had to say. "I've got a job offer back East."

"Back East where? What kind of job?"

"Vermont. Sheriff." He added deprecatingly, "It's a very small town."

When I could speak, I said, "What happened to Sam Spade? I thought you were going into the PI business?"

"Business isn't exactly booming. It's a tough time to try to start a new business. I don't have the financial resources to float for long."

"You only got your license. It's only been a couple of weeks."

"I realize that."

"You could…you could join someone else's agency."

"Yes. That is one option."

"But you're not considering it." Why was I so angry? What was I giving Jake at this point? What support had I offered him at what was probably the toughest time of his life? If he had a better offer, why the hell wouldn't he take it?

"I'm considering all the options."

I went back to staring out the window. "So…"

He said with that rare gentleness, "Just ask, Adrien. Whatever it is on your mind, just go ahead and ask."

What about us? That's what I wanted to ask. But what kind of a question was that when I couldn't seem to make up my mind whether I wanted there to *be* an *us* or not? How fair was that? But how fair was it to spring this on me? I resented like hell the feeling that I was being rushed into making a decision.

"My observation is, when a guy comes out, the next few months — years — even, are spent at the all-you-can-eat sexual smorgasbord."

"Speaking from your own experience?" Jake inquired gravely.

"Excluding myself and Mel."

I don't know exactly why I dragged Mel's name into it, because Mel had pretty much feasted at the table after we broke up, and I'd known plenty of other guys who *hadn't* gone hog wild, except I'd never known anyone as closeted as Jake who hadn't glutted himself on sexual freedom once he finally threw open the closet door.

Then again, I'd never known *anyone* as closeted as Jake.

"Good old Mel," Jake drawled. "The guy who walked out for fear he might get saddled with a cardiac cripple."

"Oh fuck you, Riordan. You've got a hell of a lot of nerve talking about someone walking away."

Like that, I was furious. I used to be such an even-tempered guy, too.

Jake pulled over to the side of the road, tires bumping as he left the highway for the dirt turnoff to a small, deserted picnic site. Dust flew in a golden cloud over the Honda's pristine hood. The car jerked to a halt, and he turned off the engine. "Let's get out here. You should stretch your legs, and I'm not going to try to argue while I'm driving."

He got out of the car and slammed the door, and after a fuming instant, I did too. He was already striding down over to a picnic table, and I followed, heart slamming, preparing for anything from a shouting match to maybe a knock-down, drag-out brawl — stranger things had happened between us.

Halfway down the path he stopped to wait for me, and as I reached him, he moved into step beside me, his hand brushing my elbow in a half-courtly gesture. Against my will, I was disarmed, because I was braced for his full rage — something equal to the rage I'd been holding in for…way too long.

As we walked, shoulders and arms occasionally brushing on the narrow path, I found my anger was dwindling. More than anything, I felt saddened. I suspected he had already made his choice — as had I, whether I wanted to admit it or not.

We walked down the trail till it gave way to hills and rocks and scrub oaks, and then we walked back and stopped at the picnic tables beneath a rough wood covering. I propped a hip on a tabletop, and Jake leaned against the brick barbecue, facing me.

"So assuming there was a question in there somewhere, what are you asking? Can I be faithful to you?"

"That's part of it."

He seemed to weigh his words. "Here's the part you seem to forget. I haven't had many what you'd call *relationships* with guys. But I've had a lot of sex. I've had sex with women and men, all the sex anyone could ask for. And since you seem to want to know this, the sex with men was the kind of thing you would consider kinky. The sex with women was, for the most part, as… wholesome as June and Ward Cleaver."

"I don't want to know." I couldn't help adding, "Didn't the Cleavers have twin beds?"

"The point is, I don't need to reserve a seat at In-N-Out or wherever you imagine sexual smorgasbord is served. I've had it. I've been there and done everyone. Okay?"

The words burst out of me; I didn't even feel them coming. "I can't *take* it," I cried. "I can't go through it again."

An owl, nesting in the corner of the patio roof, startled and took wing. We both ducked as it swooped down under the edge of the roof and flew away. I was reminded of the owl Jake had hit when we were driving back to Pine Shadow Ranch three springtimes ago. Bad omens, owls.

Jake said quietly, "Now we're getting down to it."

"I'm not blaming you for anything," I said, and there was no holding it back now. "Nothing. Not the...not wanting to acknowledge we were friends or that you even *knew* me, not walking out on me when you decided you wanted to marry, not...any of it. Not really. But..." I hardened my voice. "I can't go through it again. You changing your mind. Because I think you will, Jake. You've spent your entire life wanting to be Ward Cleaver, and I can't see you giving that up this easily."

"*Easily?*"

There was disbelief and anger both in that. I forced myself on, forced myself to say the simple truth. "You know what I mean. Maybe it is gutless. I don't want to be hurt again. I don't think I could survive it this time." My voice cracked, and I turned away and leaned on the table, glaring out at the tall pine trees.

Into that naked and humiliating pause, he said mildly, "I think you're tougher than you give yourself credit for."

"You're not helping your case."

A pause. "I can't promise that I'll never hurt you again. I never deliberately hurt you. I wouldn't deliberately hurt you. But..."

"Yes," I clipped out, "I know. Hurt happens."

I heard that long, weary exhalation. "It does. That's life. It's the good and the bad, the ugly and the beautiful, the wins and the losses. I never thought you'd be too afraid to try. I thought you were stronger than that."

I hoped to hell they'd never used him in trying to talk potential suicides down from ledges. I turned back to face him. "I'm strong enough to face facts. I'm not afraid to say good-bye to a dream that I wanted too much for too long. I'm tough enough to say no. Even to you. Even to this, whatever the hell it was going to be, and as much as I love you. And I do. Love you. More than…" I shook my head.

He was motionless for what seemed like a long time. He said, "I see."

That was it. *I see.*

I see, said the blind man. Who was the real blind man here? Obviously not worth fighting for, was it? Not worth —

"Can we go back to the car?" I grated.

He seemed to come to, like someone in a dream. He nodded. I walked ahead of him on the path, and as tired as I was, I kept a brisk pace all the way back to the car. We climbed inside. He turned on the engine.

The CD player filled the blank silence between us.

Marc Cohn. "Strangers in a Car."

I put my seat back, staring out the window at the blue cloudless sky rushing by, an empty blue highway.

What was that line from *The Long Goodbye*? Chandler had it right. "There is no trap so deadly as the trap you set for yourself."

CHAPTER SEVEN

Baby? A delicate brush of lips worked itself into my dreams. *Adrien?*

"Adrien?" a voice asked outside the dream.

I started. Opened my eyes. I was reclining in a car in broad daylight on the busy street in front of Cloak and Dagger Books. Pedestrians strolled by, talking and laughing. Jake sat back behind the steering wheel, watching me.

"See? Home again, safe and sound."

I uncricked my neck, arched my back. "Mmmhmm, thanks." I levered the seat up and scrubbed my face, trying to wake up. I'd been really zonked. The dream had been a nice one. Too bad about reality.

"Good news. You're open for business again."

I looked over and saw that he was right. Customers were walking in and out of the bookstore, those exiting carrying the familiar green and white bags that always made my spirits lift. The construction side still looked closed, but I'd take what I could get.

I risked another look at Jake's unrevealing features. "Thanks for letting me come along today."

"Sure."

Earlier in the afternoon I'd thought we might stop and get something to eat on the way back — or get takeout once we got home. But the day trip was over. A lot of things were over.

I said, "Well —"

He said at the same time, "Do you —"

We both stopped, and I said, "You first."

"Do you want me to keep looking for Henry Harrison? Or do you know all you need to?"

Was there a double meaning to that? I said, "Yes, I want you to keep looking. We still don't know what my burglar is looking for, and we don't know what happened to Jay Stevens."

"You didn't hire me to find out what happened to Stevens."

"It's all part of the same puzzle."

"Not necessarily."

"So the case is more complex than you expected. You need the money, right?"

His eyes met mine. He said evenly, "Yeah, I need the money."

"Then what do you care? I'd like to know what happened. The whole story."

"You're the boss."

I didn't care for the cool edge to his tone, but I was fairly pissed myself — about a number of things.

"Great. Thank you."

He nodded in cursory and clear farewell.

I climbed out of the car and walked across the sidewalk. As I opened the door to the bookstore, I saw the reflection of the Honda pulling away from the curb and merging into the flow of end-of-workday traffic. One more fish in the sea.

I nearly collided with two customers pushing through the glass door. The woman nearest said, "Yes, very nice selection, but they need to hire enough staff. That wait was *ridiculous*."

"I'm thinking of writing a letter!"

Fabulous. Fan mail.

"Well, it's about time." Natalie exclaimed as I appeared in front of the tall wooden desk that had once served as the hotel's check-in counter. "Do you realize it's nearly five o'clock? I was afraid something had happened to you."

"Nothing worse than a stiff neck." I rubbed the back of the neck in question. "I told you we were driving up to Ojai." I noticed Warren ensconced in his usual place in one of the leather club chairs near the counter. Ideally situated to distract Natalie and inconvenience customers. "Warren," I said politely.

He stood up: tall, thin, sandy hair, and scraggy goatee. "Mr. English."

Warren usually didn't bother addressing me at all, let alone wasting breath on courtesy titles. And his rising to his feet was cause for concern. I spared a closer look than usual. He was not wearing a suit; however, the khaki Dockers and tweed jacket — in July — were probably the closest things he had to it.

Hell.

"The police have given us permission to open the bookstore again," Natalie announced, in case I'd missed those customers wandering zombielike through the aisles and hovering like vultures over the bargain-book table.

"Excellent." She opened her mouth again. I could see what was coming. "I have to make a couple of quick calls, and then you can fill me in."

I beat a hasty retreat. In vain. She followed me into the office. "Adrien."

Phone in hand, I sighed. "You'd better close the door."

She pushed it shut and came over to the desk.

"Warren's band split up."

I put the receiver down. "Good news for music lovers."

She let that go. "And Warren is looking for a job again."

"No."

She looked wounded. "You haven't even heard what I'm going to say."

"You're going to ask me to hire Warren, and the answer is no."

"*Why?*"

"Nat, we've been through this."

"You don't like him."

I said cravenly, "I don't think he's a good match for the bookstore."

"You mean you don't like him."

That was exactly what I meant, but as I stared into her angry, glittery eyes, my nerve nearly failed again. I drew a deep breath. "No, I don't like Warren. And I especially don't like him for you."

"Why *especially* not for me?"

I hadn't noticed how deep the water was. I did a few backstrokes. "Because…because you're my sister."

"Oh." She relented. It was only for an instant. "But you're not being very fair to me. We needed help when it was both of us. Now I'm here all by myself. It's too much."

There was no answer to that, because she was absolutely right. "Look, I'll call the agency. I promise I'll get someone here. And until then, I'll take care of the —"

"I knew it. I *knew* this was going to happen when I drove you home Monday evening."

"Huh? What did you know?"

"That you would try to go back to work. But you pleaded—"

"I didn't *plead.*"

"And you promised that you would rest and follow every single one of the doctor's orders."

"I *am* resting. I *am* following orders. I'm talking about handling some of the phone calls and paperwork, that's all."

To my astonishment, she said quite sternly, "No, Adrien. There's no gray area here. Your doctor said it would be six weeks before you could return to work. He didn't say three —"

"Hey, technically I'm in the middle of the f—"

"He didn't say four weeks or that it would be okay if you worked part-time or if you worked in your office or if you simply did paperwork. You're supposed to be resting and recovering."

"Jesus, I *am* resting and recovering. How much resting and recovering can one person do in a day? It's wearing me out. I have to have something to keep my mind occupied." I felt close to panic at the suggestion that I wouldn't be allowed to work. At all? For six *weeks*? That was crazy. What the hell was I supposed to do with myself?

"Read a book, Adrien. We've got a store full of them. I bet I could find you a title you'd enjoy."

"Very funny. It's not like I work in a shoe store. I own this place. I can't ignore it for months."

I could hear the agitation in my voice, and so could Natalie, because she said soothingly, "That's what family's for."

Oh, *that's* what family was for. I thought they were just there to monopolize my holidays and critique my love life.

She continued, unmoved. "You're going to have to be patient and have trust, because under *no* circumstances are you coming back to work. If you won't hire Warren, I'll have to manage on my own till one of the agencies finds us someone, but you are *not* working until your doctor gives you permission."

I opened my mouth, and she threatened, "I swear I'll call Lisa."

"You wouldn't dare."

"Make. My. Day." She went out and closed the door. Pointedly.

I shook off my incredulity and dialed Jake's cell phone. He picked up on the second ring.

"Listen," I said. "I apologize for the crack about needing money."

"Hey, it's true. I do need the money." There was nothing to read in his tone. Business as usual.

"If you…if you're short of cash, I'd be happy to —"

"Thanks. It's not necessary."

I stumbled over the words. Got them out anyway. "In fact, maybe I can help you buy out Kate's share of the house. Advance you whatever you need."

The silence that followed lasted so long, I thought maybe he was out of range. In every sense.

"Why?" he asked tersely, at last.

"Because…because you shouldn't have to lose the house. Because we're friends. Because you'd do it for me."

"That's all true, and I appreciate the offer, especially because I know you're overextended yourself, but no."

"Why not?"

He said painstakingly, as though explaining the ABC's of the law to a rookie, "Because the best thing for me now will be to get out of this town and start over someplace new."

I had no answer to that. He was right. Even I could see that. Jake needed a fresh start, a new beginning somewhere, without all the history and emotional baggage. But the idea of his leaving filled me with sadness. Totally selfish. I knew that. Totally illogical.

I said mechanically, "If you change your mind…"

"Sure," he said. And then, "I'll be in touch."

He clicked off.

Having slept surprisingly well in the car, I felt more alert and energetic than I typically did in the early evening. Maybe I *was* getting better. I wanted to believe that, even if it seemed like too much to hope for.

I did a tentative search of the Internet and discovered that Dan Hale was a very popular name — nearly as popular as Jay Stevens. However, a combined search for Hale and The Tides yielded better results in the way of a number of vintage photos of a lean, dangerous-looking young man with a wolfish smile, an ever-present cigarette, and a black calla lily in the buttonhole of his white dinner jacket.

There wasn't much information on Hale. He'd been born in Los Angeles, had served in the merchant marine during the Korean War, had opened The Tides after his stint, and had run it successfully for five years. He was reputed to have mob ties.

There was nothing about his personal life or background. No contact information. He had been linked romantically to a number of starlets and Los Angeles socialites. There were plenty of photographs where he appeared as one of the glamorous subjects, although he was rarely the primary focus.

I read more about The Tides. In those days the stretch between Point Dume and Malibu had been a wilderness, yet a lot of people had fond memories of driving out to the coast for dining and dancing at Hale's place. I read those accounts carefully, but there wasn't much to glean other than historical perspective. A few folks mentioned Hale and his supposed mob connections. It didn't sound like anyone had actually witnessed evidence of mob influence, though apparently the possibility had added a little spice to the entertainment. Occasionally there were references to the house band, though no one specified Jay Stevens or the Moonglows by name. Mostly it sounded like Hale had run a tight ship.

Argyle had said Hale was still alive and his last-known address was in Santa Barbara. I decided to give information a call. I learned that there were two Daniel Hales in Santa Barbara.

The first Dan Hale was not at home. I was pretty sure I had the wrong one.

"Yo! Danny's answering machine is broken. This is his refrigerator. Please speak very slowly, and I'll stick your message to myself with the pineapple magnets."

I was tempted to ask to speak to the stove. I restrained myself.

The second Dan Hale didn't answer. At all. Who didn't have an answering machine in this day and age?

Natalie poked her head into the office to say good night. She eyed me suspiciously.

I said, "This is recreational computer use. Please don't tell my mom."

Unwillingly, she started to laugh. "You're a nut, you know that."

"That's what all the guys in the white dinner jackets tell me."

The bookstore was very quiet after she left. I read up more on the swing-music scene and ordered a couple of CDs online.

The phone rang next to me, and I jumped. I picked up before the answering machine could, and Guy said, "*Why* am I not surprised?"

"Because you're wise in the way of the world? How many guesses do I get?"

"Aren't you supposed to be resting and relaxing?"

"I am."

"Downstairs in your office?"

"Did you merely call to berate me, or did you have a higher purpose?"

"Could there be a higher purpose? In fact, I was thinking of dropping by tonight if you're not too busy pretending to rest and relax?"

Frankly, I was delighted at the idea and said so.

"How does barbecue chicken sound?"

"Probably very quiet. I'm just guessing."

"You're in rare form."

I admitted, "I'm bored and lonely."

"I'm on my way."

§ § § §

Guy rang me from the outside the building. "Permission to come aboard, captain?"

"Aye, aye. Hang about."

I signed out of the laptop, locked my office, and went over to open the side door.

Guy was medium height, lean, with long, loose silvery hair, an imperious face, and knowing, bright green eyes. Tonight he smelled irresistibly of barbecue chicken.

"You didn't waste any time changing the locks."

"What's that?" I realized what he meant and said, as I leaned forward to kiss him, "That wasn't on your behalf. Don't be a dope."

He asked about the break-in as we marched upstairs, and I filled him in on the developments as well as my trip to Ojai with Jake.

Guy heard me out. "Riordan seems to be playing a starring role in your latest adventures."

"Yeah, well he's the only cop I know."

"Ex-cop." There was a certain pithy satisfaction in Guy's voice.

"Yes."

He couldn't resist observing. "You know Paul Chan."

"True. But no way would Chan —"

"Humor you?"

I shrugged.

"And has it occurred to you to wonder why Riordan continues to humor you?"

"Yes. Except this time I dragged him into it, and I'm paying him to humor me."

"Yes," Guy said drily. "I find that fascinating."

We dished out the food in the kitchen and sat down at the table. Tomkins stole into the room, and Guy nearly choked on his potato wedge.

"Where did the cat come from?" he questioned hoarsely.

I'd completely forgotten Guy's allergies.

I got up, cornered Tomkins, and threw him — to his astonishment — into the bedroom, closing the door after.

"Sorry," I said, coming back to the table. "He just sort of happened."

"Yes." Guy sighed. "Well, I'd say that doesn't bode well for the rest of the evening."

Our gazes caught, and I smiled sheepishly.

I was relieved that I'd put off dinner with Mel one more night. It was comfortable and relaxed with Guy in a way it wasn't with Mel, let alone Jake. We talked about the summer courses he was teaching. He asked me how the work was going on *A Deed of Dreadful Note*, and I detailed Jason's latest adventures.

Interestingly, Guy had always found my writing as unrealistic as Jake, although his reasons were totally different. Guy deplored my *pulp sensibilities*. Jake deplored my lack of realistic police procedure.

Guy told me he was thinking of writing another book himself, this time based on his part in the Blade Sable murder case.

"Speaking of Blade Sable," I said, "How *is* Harry Potter?"

"Peter is…adjusting. He's back in school, and he's doing quite well. I wish you could find it in your heart to forgive him."

"I've got this funny resentful streak about people who try to kill me."

Guy sighed, long-suffering. "He didn't. You know he didn't."

"I don't know that. If it makes you feel better, I don't wish him any harm. I hope he is rehabilitated. I hope he does…whatever it is you hope he's going to do for you." I lifted my lashes, grinned lazily.

Guy was gazing at me with such an intent expression, I stopped smiling, puzzled. "Something wrong?"

His smile was twisted. "I think it's finally sank in on me that it really is over between us, isn't it?"

"I... Yeah. I suppose it is." I managed to bite back the one about always being friends. Not because it wasn't true — it was — but I knew he didn't want to hear it. Didn't need to hear it.

He nodded, looked away. His shoulders sagged. He glanced back at me. "Tell me it's not that asshole Riordan."

"It isn't anything to do with Jake."

"He won't ever change, Adrien. It doesn't matter the promises he makes; it doesn't matter even that he might *want* to change."

The correct response was to repeat the truth: that it had nothing to do with Jake. I heard myself argue, "He already *has* changed, Guy."

He was shaking his head stubbornly. "He was forced into coming out. Circumstances forced it. If your life hadn't been on the line, he'd still be safely in the closet and married."

I didn't have a response, because I feared that *was* the truth. Not that I wasn't grateful that Jake had chosen to sacrifice the lie of heterosexuality in order to spare my life, but there really had never been a question of that. Okay, maybe for a few seconds there had been a question in my mind. Looking back...realistically, there shouldn't have been. He was simply too good a cop — too good a man — to have let me be murdered.

He did care for me. I did believe that.

"Would you like another beer?"

Guy nodded.

I got up and went to the fridge. "Harp okay?"

"It doesn't matter."

He sounded dispirited. I tried to think of something that would ease his pain. I didn't believe Guy loved me, though I knew he was pretty fond of me, and I knew he thought I was headed for disaster with Jake.

I took the beer to the sink, picked up the bottle opener, and stared out the window. My gaze fell on the lamp-lit streets and the alley below — sharpened as I caught a shadow moving along the deep shade of the tall cinder-block wall that separated the alley from the apartments across the way.

As I watched I saw it again: a figure creeping through the long shadows and squares of window light.

I stepped back and said urgently, "Guy, there's someone in the alley."

"So?"

"He's lurking."

His expression reminded me of the looks Dr. Shearing threw my way when I resisted her helpful efforts on my behalf.

"He's *skulking*," I clarified impatiently. "He's...furtive. Come here. See for yourself. He's up to something."

Guy shoved his chair back at once and started to the window. I said quickly, "Don't let him see you."

He muttered something. I caught the words *right nutter*. The rest of it escaped me.

"*There*," I whispered. "You see?"

"I can't see a bloody thing. Are you sure —" He stopped short.

"See?"

He nodded.

"I think it's my burglar."

Guy's profile grew forbidding.

"Can you follow him?"

He whipped around to face me. "Can I *what*?"

"Can you see where he goes? Can you follow him?"

"You're joking."

"No." The plan, to use the term loosely, took form instantly in my mind. "You follow him. If he manages to break in to the building, we'll see what it is he's after. And if he doesn't break in, follow him. See where he goes. Maybe we'll get an address on him. Meantime, I'll grab my camera and see if I can get a photo of him. But in case I can't get down there fast enough —"

"Are you out of your bloody mind?" He was looking at me with something like horror. "Sometimes I wonder if your mother isn't right. Sometimes I wonder if you *haven't* got a self-destructive streak."

"Later, Guy. Right now just do this for me." I added belatedly, "Please."

I could see the internal struggle. Unfortunately we didn't have time for it. I spared a harried glance back at the alley. I couldn't see the prowler any longer. We were liable to lose this chance. I started for the doorway, and Guy grabbed my shoulder.

"Oh no, you don't." He gave me an exasperated shake. "Right. I'll do this. However, *you* don't leave this flat. Understand? Stay put. I'll see what the bastard is doing in your alley."

"That almost sounds salac —" He was moving for the door, and I went after him warning, "Be *careful*, for God's sake. And remember he can't see you, Guy. Don't confront him. If it were simply a matter of talking to him, I'd —"

He was out the door. I heard him taking the stairs quickly. I went to the window, standing well to the side as I stared down.

There.

The prowler was trying for one of the back windows, perhaps thinking — rightly — that I would delay arming the alarm system till my visitor left.

"You stubborn son of a bitch," I murmured, watching the shadow prying at the frame. I looked for Guy but saw no sign of him. It wouldn't take him more than thirty seconds to get down the stairs and out the back door. Hopefully he was already getting into position. Maybe now we'd find out what this guy was after.

I left the window, heading for the bedroom. Tomkins, contently putting claw marks on the bottom drawer of an antique dresser *meowed*, and I *meowed* back louder, which shut him up. I'd received a very nice camera for my last birthday — with a terrific zoom lens. I'd never really learned to work it. Still, I thought I could fumble my way through this photo op.

The camera wasn't in my bedroom, though. I'd relegated it to the room I was supposed to use as my upstairs office. I found it at last, only to hear the alarming crash and bang of trash cans.

I ran back to the window and saw Guy struggling with a slim figure in black. "*Shit.*"

Belatedly, it occurred to me that Guy might be seriously injured. Because the prowler had fled the previous times, didn't mean he wouldn't turn violent if he thought he was in real jeopardy.

"Hey!" I yelled from the window. "You'd *better* run, you bastard."

Guy went sprawling back into a mound of black trash bags. The intruder sprinted away, although he seemed to be limping.

"Guy, are you all right?" I shouted.

I couldn't make out his answer, although it was encouragingly vigorous.

I got down the stairs and out to the alley as Guy was getting to his feet. He brushed off the pieces of colored packing peanuts — and less-innocuous materials — clinging to his clothes.

"Are you all right?" I gasped again as I reached him.

"Yes, I'm fucking brilliant. No thanks to you."

"What the hell happened? How did he see you?"

He wiped his face on his forearm. "He saw me when I took his picture with my cell phone."

"You did what?" I was torn between alarm and delight. "Why did you do that? Jesus. I *told* you not to let him see you. I *told* you to be careful. He could have been armed, for all we knew."

Guy's head snapped up. "*You* of all people have one hell of a nerve telling me off for not being careful."

"Well, Guy." I really didn't have an answer to that one. Shutting up seemed my best bet.

He reached into his pocket and pulled out his cell phone, thrusting it into my hands. "Download whatever is on there so I can get the hell out of here."

I started to speak, but his face, a jaundiced yellow in the waxen light from overhead, was not encouraging. I turned away, pausing at the sight of something flat and furry in the alley. For one repelled instant I thought it was a dead animal. I realized it was a toupee.

"Look at this."

I bent to pick it up, and Guy said with savage satisfaction, "I thought so."

I dangled the toupee. "I think you're supposed to count coup or something."

"Ugh."

"*This* is what I call a clue."

Guy followed me inside the bookstore. I found a bag for the toupee. We went into my office, and I downloaded a couple of blurry photographs.

"Aha," I exclaimed as the jet-black hair, pencil-thin mustache, and seamed face materialized on my laptop screen. "I knew it was too much of a coincidence."

"Do you know who this is?"

"Henry Harrison."

"Who?"

"Actually, that might not be his real name."

"I'm lost." And he sounded lost — uncharacteristically so.

"He came to the bookstore the morning after the first break-in. He claimed to be a tourist from Milwaukee by the name of

Henry Harrison. I'd bet money that's not his real name. And I know someone who might recognize him."

"Let me guess. Jake Riordan."

"No. Although…"

Guy put his hand up. "I don't care. I don't want to know."

I saved the photos and turned to face him. "Thanks for doing this, Guy. I really didn't intend for you to put yourself in harm's way. Why don't we go finish dinner?"

He sighed. "Thank you, but no, thank you. I need a shower and a drink and a fuck — in that order."

"I can do the drink and the shower." I wasn't up to the other, although in a way it would have been comforting to be together one last time. Not fair to Guy, however.

"I wouldn't be satisfied with the drink and the shower." He bent to kiss me. "I'll call you."

I had a wistful feeling it wouldn't be anytime soon.

After Guy left I turned on the alarm and debated calling the police. Since the prowler was gone, was there any point in taking up the rest of my evening with making a police report? Yes, I had a photo of sorts and a toupee soaked with DNA, and I'd turn those over if Jake thought that was the way to go. I believed I had a better idea.

I sat down to e-mail Jake and realized I didn't have his e-mail address. E-mail had been strictly verboten. As I had heard many times, e-mail lasted longer than Styrofoam and was ten times more deadly.

I called him.

"Riordan."

"Sorry, I know it's late. I've got a photo of Henry Harrison. I want to send it to you if you've got e-mail."

"How the hell did you manage that?"

"Guy managed it. Harrison tried to break in again tonight, and Guy ran downstairs and took a couple of photos on his cell phone. Neither is great, but the image on one of them is distinct enough that I was thinking maybe Nick Argyle might be able to ID Harrison."

One of the — many — things I liked best about Jake was it didn't take him long to process information. "You're sure now Harrison is an alias?"

"The more I think about it, the more I have trouble believing he'd walk into my bookstore and volunteer his real name."

Whatever Jake thought of that, and I was sure it was plenty, he restrained himself to giving me the e-mail address.

"Okay. I'm attaching the files to the e-mail now."

And then neither of us said anything.

Into that lull where all that was unspoken seemed to lap against the silence, he spoke. "I'll let you know what I find out."

And again neither of us seemed able to say good-bye and hang up.

I said, "Oh, I found a couple of Dan Hales in Santa Barbara. One we can scratch off our list. The other —"

"Right," he said crisply, and it was a very different tone of voice. "I know you're bored and restless, and I've got no problem with you coming along with me on any interviews that might develop, but you are *not* — let's get this straight now — to go forging off on your own. Not three weeks after heart surgery."

"Four."

"Not on my watch. You got that?"

"Yes, I've got that," I responded testily. "If you'll notice, I'm not forging off on my own. I let Guy take the photos, and I'm telling you exactly what I found, which is not a hell of a lot."

"Uh-huh." And there was a wealth of sardonic derision in those two syllables.

"I'm not sure what that's supposed to mean." I was annoyed to hear that huffy note in my voice — giving away that I knew exactly what he meant.

"It means I know you, Adrien with an *e*, and I know you get reckless when you're impatient. You're paying for this investigation, and I'll keep you apprised every step of the way, but if you even think about going rogue on this one, I'm turning in my fedora and you can hire some other dick."

I don't want any other dick. I closed my mouth on that one — metaphorically speaking — and said, "I don't know why the hell everyone seems to think I'm so reckless —"

"One of life's little mysteries."

"Guy is the one who took the risk in getting that photo of Harrison."

"Good for Gandalf. I'm sure he only did it to keep you from doing it yourself."

"Good night," I said shortly.

"Talk to you tomorrow."

I hung up and pressed Send on the computer.

CHAPTER EIGHT

"You do remember that I'm not exactly an equestrian." Mel glanced away from the Saturday-morning traffic. We were on our way to Osseo Farms in Chino to have a look at Adagio.

"Oh I remember."

He must have seen I was struggling to keep a straight face — both of us remembering a particular weekend when we were still in college when we'd rented horses for an afternoon from a local stable. Mel's horse had quickly figured out he didn't know his stirrup from his snaffle bit. The horse had refused to budge on a tricky bit of trail. We'd dismounted, traded horses, and I'd got Mel's horse down the trail — only to discover that my own horse had balked and was impersonating a mule. Needless to say, it was the last time we went riding.

"I can't believe I'm letting myself in for this."

I said, "Relax. I want to see how this horse behaves with an inexperienced rider."

"You'll certainly get that."

It was a long drive, though it flew by as we talked — not about anything very important — and caught up on the last few years.

"You remember when you called about three years ago?" Mel asked. "You were staying at your grandmother's ranch in Basking? You wanted information about a former colleague of mine."

"I remember."

"I almost called you back and asked if you wanted company for the weekend."

I was still, remembering that trip. My relationship with Jake had altered substantially after the week we spent at Pine Shadow Ranch — had become what I believed was a genuine relationship. Or as much of a relationship as we could manage, given Jake's insistence on remaining in the closet. Nor could I be alone in thinking there had been a genuine bond, if Jake had broken off with Paul Kane afterward.

Things *had* changed between us, though not enough. That had been okay — partly because I had always warned myself not to expect much of my relationship with Jake. From the very beginning I had told myself it wasn't — couldn't — lead to anything lasting.

But I'd still hoped. I had still wanted it. It had still hurt too much when it ended.

"I wish I had," Mel added.

I returned to the present. "You wish you had what?"

"Phoned you. Joined you for the weekend. It might have changed a lot of things."

Sliding doors? I knew I was only kidding myself. I would never have chosen Mel over Jake at that time in my life. For one thing I'd still been too bitter over Mel's defection. For another... I swallowed hard, remembering the taste of Jake's mouth, the feel of his arms around me, the feel of his cock pressing into my body.

Heat suffused me from head to foot. I was sitting next to Mel thinking about Jake fucking me. There was something wrong with me, all right, and it wasn't my heart. It was my brain.

"Jake was staying with me at the time."

"Oh." Mel's voice matched his disconcerted expression. "I didn't realize. I keep thinking that you didn't see each other very long."

"Ten months."

He said softly, "We were together five years."

True. Of course, we'd been in college part of that time. It wasn't like we had tried to live together. And when we had — but what was the point of rehashing all this?

"Obviously I haven't seen enough of Riordan to form an opinion —" He must have caught my derisive smile, because he said with a trace of defensiveness, "Okay, yes, I've formed an opinion. He's obviously got sexual magnetism, but I'm having a hard time picturing anyone more wrong for you."

If everyone around you saw what was apparently obvious, but you couldn't see it...the skewed vision was probably your own, right? Mel was saying what all my friends and family believed, so getting defensive was a waste of time.

I asked coolly, "How so?"

"Well, don't you want someone who shares your interests? Or at least your values?"

I opened my mouth. Changed my mind. Even if I knew how to explain it, I wasn't going to get into how Jake made me think and made me laugh and challenged me in a way no one else did. That his differences intrigued me; I enjoyed exploring them. That I couldn't ever imagine running out of things to talk about with Jake.

The bastard.

"And..."

I knew that tone. I said, "And?"

He said diffidently, "Even if the valves on your heart are repaired, you're still not...invincible. There will be times you'll need someone who's going to...be willing to take care of you, be there for you."

"Like you were there for me?"

His hands tightened on the wheel. He didn't say anything for so long, I thought he wasn't going to, but at last he replied, "No, I wasn't there for you. But...*he's* sure as hell not going to be there for you. He's not going to be there for anyone except himself. From the bit you've told me —"

I laughed.

"Is that funny?"

"Sort of. Everyone is so intent on convincing me what a disaster Jake would be in my life."

"I'm glad you think it's funny."

"Sorry. Look, the funny part is, I agree with you. At least, I agree that I don't think Jake is a good bet for a relationship."

I felt a funny sense of guilt as I delivered that pronouncement. I could have as easily said, *The guy walked into a bullet for me, Mel.* That was certainly true, but frankly I thought Jake might have done that for anyone. I could have said, *He manages to look out for me, take care of me, without unmanning me, which is more than anyone else has ever managed.* I could have said, *I don't have to pull my punches with him.* Mel wouldn't have had a clue what I meant. But it was all true. It didn't mean that Jake and I could make a real day-in, day-out relationship work. And maybe as much because of me as because of Jake.

But there was a time I'd have at least had the guts to try.

"You don't?" Mel queried.

"No, I don't. In fact, Jake and I have sort of agreed…to let it be."

"Oh." He clearly hadn't considered this possibility. I watched him think it over. He confided at last, "Believe it or not, I've always thought you were kind of a lone wolf, Adrien. That whether you knew it or not, you were happier on your own."

I said sweetly, "Yeah? That must have simplified a few things for you."

He nervously cleared his throat. A few seconds later he changed the subject.

At the horse farm, we recovered our earlier harmony. One thing I'd learned the hard way: people loved you in the way they knew how to — and often it was not the way you knew. Or needed. Mel had done his best. Was still doing his best, I guessed. Besides, he was doing me a big favor driving me out to Osseo Farms.

I'd forgotten how really bad a rider he was — as in the sack-of-potatoes class — but he was such a good sport about it, so willing to laugh at himself, that it was sort of endearing.

And Adagio turned out to be a beauty — and a horse with a sense of humor. I longed to ride him myself, however, proof that I really was a lot more sensible than people seemed to give me credit for, I contented myself watching Mel put him through his paces. Or vice versa. It was reassuring to see that Adagio didn't take too much advantage of his rider's lack of experience.

When the owner, Karin Schultie, couldn't bear the circus performance any longer, she whistled Mel over, ordered him down, mounted up herself, and took Adagio around the small arena. He was beautiful to behold. Quick, responsive, intuitive the way only a smart and well-trained horse can be.

Karin brought him back to the fence, and I stroked Adagio's glossy neck while he accepted his due.

"I like him," I told her. "If I were buying him for myself, I'd make you an offer right now, but he's for my kid sister. She's going to have to ride him herself."

Karin was agreeable. "So you know, I've got another buyer interested. I'll hold off having him out for one week. I want our baby to go to the best possible home."

We shook hands on it, and then Mel and I headed back to Los Angeles. On the way, we stopped for a late lunch at a Basque restaurant.

"I fly out tomorrow." He uncapped the bottle of Zantac to prepare for eating his lamb stew.

"I figured. It's been good spending time together again."

"Yeah." He hesitated. "You know, Berkeley isn't the end of the earth. I could fly down…well, next weekend." He hesitated. "I mean, if you'd…like that."

I'd have been lying if I tried to deny that it didn't go a long way to healing that old hurt to see the warmth in his eyes, that hopeful smile. And he was saying all the right things. This was the sensible direction, the logical direction to go.

Assuming I wanted to go any direction at all.

I said slowly, "I'd like that, but there's a lot of truth to what you said in the car. I'm happy on my own. I don't see changing that."

"Fair enough. I'm fresh out of one relationship. The last thing I need is a hot-and-heavy romance, but I can't tell you what a pleasure it's been spending time with an adult again. We always were compatible."

"We were," I agreed. And companionship was about sharing the same interests, the same values. It couldn't all be about solving crimes together. Or sex.

Well, it couldn't all be about solving crimes together.

What *was* it that made people love each other? Was it as simple as answering twenty questions on a compatibility quiz?

The drive back to the bookstore passed quickly — for me anyway, since I dozed much of the way. I woke up as we reached Pasadena, and I was wide awake by the time we pulled up in front of Cloak and Dagger in time to see Detective Alonzo climbing out of a blue sedan bristling with antennae.

"Oh hell."

"What?"

"The fuzz."

"Do you want me to come with you?" Mel asked, frowning at the vision of Alonzo squaring his shoulders as he viewed himself in the plate-glass windows of the store. Readying for battle?

"No, I've got it," I said.

"Are you sure?"

I nodded.

"I'll call you." Mel leaned forward. Our mouths brushed quickly. We had an audience; something I didn't enjoy.

As I climbed out of the car to face Alonzo, I couldn't help thinking that Jake wouldn't have asked whether I wanted him to come with me. He wouldn't have asked, because he'd have been right there with me, if not in front of me running defense. Maybe this was the more normal reaction. Maybe this was how the civilized world handled this kind of thing.

"Detective Alonzo," I greeted him. "Working on a Saturday?"

He flashed his teeth like a guard dog who enjoyed his work. "Missed you yesterday, Mr. English."

"But your aim is getting better?"

"Ha-ha." Another baring of teeth. "I thought maybe we could have a chat?"

"About?"

"Do you really have to ask? About the skeletons in your closet."

I could see he'd been storing that one up. "I thought the CCHU was handling this case?"

Alonzo didn't like that.

"Is there a reason you don't want to talk to me, Mr. English?"

"Is that a rhetorical question?"

His face darkened. "There's the attitude. I wonder about that. I gotta wonder why you have to be such a smart-ass all the time. What are you hiding?"

"What a nice guy I really am?"

"Yeah, right." He was sincere about that. He really did think I was some kind of creep. He really did believe there were skeletons in my closet — as well as beneath my floorboards.

We went inside the bookstore. Natalie, efficiently dealing with a short line in front of the register, looked up smiling. Her smile straight lined at the sight of Alonzo, and it was so noticeable, he colored.

"Adrien, do you want me to —"

"Everything's cool," I assured her, leading Alonzo into my office.

I closed the door as Alonzo announced, "I heard Paul Kane is suing you and your boyfriend, Jake Riordan."

"Is he?" I leaned back against the edge of my desk, folded my arms. "I leave that kind of bullshit for my lawyer to deal with."

I knew that pretense at a blasé attitude would piss him off, and sure enough… "So here's my first question for you, English. This is what I can't stop thinking about. How is it that that skeleton was never discovered till now?"

I studied his face, wondering what he really suspected me of. He was neither stupid nor insane, so he had to know that I couldn't possibly have had anything to do with the death of Jay Stevens. It seemed most likely this was simply…harassment. I don't know why it came as a surprise, but it did.

"I only bought that side of the building last spring, so I can't tell you. What I do know is they never renovated beyond the first floor over there. The second floor was used for storage. At some point the third floor was blocked off as unsafe. My contractor found termites, wood rot, mold, and a bunch of dead rats in the attic. The place is in bad shape. The property owner wasn't into improvements. He didn't have to be, because this part of town is prime real estate. He never had trouble finding businesses to lease, although no one ever lasted more than a year — usually not more than a few months."

"I don't see what that has to do with anything."

"I told you. This is the first time that side of the building has been renovated."

"Why would that be? If it was such a valuable property, why wouldn't the owners take care of it?"

I hung onto my patience. "I don't know. I didn't own the building then. You'd have to ask the previous owner. Or his heirs."

"If that building was in such bad shape, why did you buy it?"

"Because I wanted to expand my store, and the guy on the other side isn't about to sell. Besides, it makes sense, since this all used to be one building."

"If it's in such bad shape, why not knock it down and build from scratch?"

I opened my mouth to answer, though it was clear to me that I was speaking a foreign language. "I like old buildings," I said lamely. "They don't make them like this anymore."

He laughed. "You can say that again."

I resisted saying that again.

Alonzo said, "It seems to me that there's more of a story here than you're willing to talk about."

"What exactly is it you suspect me of? I wasn't even born in 1959."

"What makes you think I'm interested in 1959?"

"Aren't you?"

He smiled.

"Doesn't the skeleton belong to Jay Stevens?"

"It hasn't been proven one way or the other."

"The fingerprints on the instrument case and clarinet belong to Jay Stevens, don't they?"

His smile disappeared, his eyes narrowed. "How would you know that?"

I wasn't sure if that was information Jake was supposed to have access to or not. "It was on the news, wasn't it?"

He continued to eye me suspiciously, and I surmised that he wasn't absolutely sure on that point. Which indicated to me that this wasn't his case. That he probably had no business poking his nose in at all.

"*Is* the CCHU going to investigate this?"

"*I'm* investigating the case in these five seconds. That's all you need to worry about. Tell me about these break-ins you reported."

He surely had access to the police reports; even so, I dutifully went through the whole story again, including the disturbance the night before. I told him about Guy going downstairs to confront the prowler. I neglected to let him know about the photos Guy had taken on his phone, but I offered him the bag with the toupee in it.

He took it, looked inside it distastefully. "What the hell is this supposed to be?"

"It's got the burglar's DNA all over it, right?"

"So? Why didn't you report this alleged attempted break-in last night? Why didn't you hand this evidence over?"

"I'm handing it over now. As for why I didn't report it last night, once again the guy was long gone. I guess I thought three attempted break-ins in a row might be getting monotonous, even for LAPD."

"This is crap." He thrust the bag back at me. "That whole story is crap. You know what? I'm having a lot of trouble believing in these alleged break-ins."

"Why would I make something like that up?"

He shrugged. "Attention for your bookstore? I could see that. Or maybe it's an insurance scam."

I stared at him in fascination.

"I'll tell you what I think, English. I think you're up to something. And I plan on keeping a very close eye on you."

"Great. Police protection. I won't have to worry about any more burglars, will I?"

"No," he said darkly. "You'll have other things to worry about."

It was a good parting line, and he made use of it. I followed him out onto the book floor. He left with a long look at Natalie, who raised her chin and delivered the snub direct.

"What was that about?" she asked after the jangle of bells signaled Alonzo was well and truly departed.

"The usual."

I filled her in, and she said dazedly, "He thinks you're making this all up for a publicity stunt?"

"That's the way it sounded, though I can't believe he's that stupid."

"He's not stupid," she said. "He hates you — or maybe it's Jake — so much he's willing to convince himself of anything."

"Yeah, well, do me a favor and don't call Bill or Lisa. Please. I can handle that asshole."

"I don't understand why you're so hostile to the idea of your family's wanting to help."

"I'm not hostile. I appreciate the help. I do. But I don't need help with this."

"We *like* to help."

"Sure. But I need to start feeling normal again. I need to start feeling like myself. And part of that is being allowed to solve my own problems."

She considered this. "You're never going to convince Lisa of that."

"But if I can at least keep the rest of you from ganging up on me, it'll be a start."

She rolled her eyes, looking disconcertingly like Emma for an instant.

"And I promise I'll let you all help as soon as I get in over my head. Which will probably be any minute."

She reminded me that we were supposed to go to the house for dinner. I went up and changed, and we drove out to Chatsworth. As we got out of the car, the scent of barbecue reached us on the summer breeze.

Natalie sniffed the air. "Uh-oh. Hide the salami. Daddy's got the Weber out."

Bill was a devotee of outdoor grilling, but he tended to get carried away. I'd often thought it was a good thing the Dautens didn't own any pets.

We found the family out on the patio having cocktails. Bill was enthusiastically barbecuing enough steaks to feed the troops for the next week — the troops overseas — and discussing the merits of mesquite wood chips over hickory with Lauren, who had the glazed look of a woman rethinking her plans for divorce.

I celebrated the next phase of my recovery with a glass of red wine — after Alonzo, I felt I'd earned it even if it was a few days early — and told Lisa about the trip to Chino to look over Adagio, concluding with, "I think he's worth every penny. I think we should make plans to drive down there with Em on Tuesday."

Lisa moaned. "I saw this on Lifetime only last night. A young girl's parents bought her a horse for show jumping, and she was paralyzed in a fall. It was a dreadful."

"Lisa —"

"And Anna Kelly's daughter broke her jaw falling from her horse. She lost all her front teeth. Anna broke her own wrist in a spill."

Bill interrupted the wood-chip lecture to say calmly, "Em's not going to break her jaw or her neck, my dear. She's a very good rider."

Lisa threw him a reproachful look that managed to convey that, despite his *many* fine qualities, he was either heartless or obtuse. "I don't think you should bring it up, Adrien. Emma hasn't mentioned that bloody horse since you were here last. I think she's forgotten all about it."

"I don't think she's forgotten."

She stared at me with those wide blue-violet eyes. If she read something in my face, it certainly wasn't anything I intended her to see. Her expression altered. She bit her lip. "Oh bother. If it's so *awfully* important to you." Her gaze sharpened. "Are you seeing Mel again?"

"We're just friends."

She continued to watch me with that alert look.

"Really."

"Perhaps he's grown up."

Hadn't we all?

Cryptically, she added, "But there's no question Jake Riordan is mad about you."

I blinked. "There...isn't?"

"Although I suppose it's beside the point."

"It is?"

"Of course."

Was I drunk on one glass of wine? "Anyway, Mel and I are *just* friends."

She raised her elegant brows and sipped her drink.

Emma was providing inadequate supervision to a naked Barbie and Ken when I sat down across from her on the floor in the den. At fourteen, she didn't exactly *play* with Barbie so much as act out elaborate and occasionally disconcerting screenplays. My kid sister, the budding performance artist.

"Kiddo."

She smiled and jammed Ken into the pink Corvette beside Barbie. Ken looked pretty uncomfortable to me. Barbie seemed smug. Granted, she had the car keys.

"I drove out with a friend today to have a look at Adagio."

Like that Emma was bolt upright, a look of painful intensity in her gaze. She swallowed.

I smiled. "I like him. I think maybe you should come with me to check him out on Tuesday."

She threw herself into my arms, hugging me tightly. I looked down at her silky, dark hair, touched it lightly. Baby hair. Skinny arms wrapped around me. Fourteen was so *young*. She was making snuffling noises into my shirt.

Oh. Man.

"Hey, at least you could stop laughing for a minute."

She raised her wet face with a watery giggle. Her face fell. "But Lisa won't…"

"Yes, she will," I said firmly. "Lisa knows all about this. In fact, she's going to drive us out to the farm on Tuesday."

She wiped her wet face on my shirt, nodded doubtfully.

"Em?"

She raised those big blue eyes that looked so uncannily like Lisa's.

"I know it hasn't been very long for you, but Lisa — she really does love you. Pretty much from the minute she saw you. She's trying to keep you safe, you know?"

She nodded, clearly unconvinced she didn't have Maleficent for a stepmom.

"She worries about…stuff because of my dad dying. And then I got sick when I was only a little older than you are now."

Emma considered this. "My mom died. I'm not afraid."

"It's different for Lisa. She thinks it's her job to keep us all safe."

She lifted a bony shoulder in dismissal.

I left Barbie and Ken to Emma's matchmaking skills and went to join the others on the patio. I had to pass through the kitchen, and as I crossed the threshold, I heard Natalie say coldly, "But it's not your business, is it?"

Lisa answered, "For heaven's sake, Natalie. What kind of man takes money from his girlfriend? How often has he done this?"

"It's none of your business." Natalie's voice rose. "You turned Daddy against Warren."

"Your father didn't need me to point out that Warren is *at best* a slacker."

I was already retreating, but both turned my way like lionesses on the Serengeti scenting an unlucky zebra.

"Don't go, Adrien. This concerns you too." Natalie's tone was chillier than dry ice.

"I'm pretty sure it doesn't."

"You're part of this conspiracy."

I stopped. "Say what?"

The look in her eyes should have pinned me to the paneling. "You don't like Warren. You wouldn't help him when he needed help — not even for me. You all think you can break us up by making things hard for us."

I opened my mouth, but Lisa got in first.

"Leave. Adrien. Out of it." The warning in my mother's tone even sent a prickle down *my* spine. Maybe the Maleficent analogy wasn't so far off. It shut Natalie down for an instant, and unwisely, I pressed on.

"Natalie, it isn't anything personal. I don't think hiring family is a good idea. It worked out with you, but I'm not bringing Warren on board."

She said defiantly, "You're not going to keep Warren out of my life. You'll both be interested to know that Warren and I are moving in together."

"Does Warren know?"

I had no idea why that came out of my mouth, but the effect was instant and awful. Natalie's face crumpled.

"*I hate you, Adrien!*" She turned and fled down the hallway. A door slammed in a nether region of the house.

"He stole money from her purse," Lisa said bleakly. "And it's not the first time."

I looked at her but managed to keep my mouth shut this time.

Lisa shook off her preoccupation. "Darling, don't look like that. She'll have a good cry and be over it by supper."

Natalie did not join us for supper, however. In fact, her car was not in the drive when Lauren drove me home later in the evening.

Rarely had I been more relieved to return to the peace and quiet of my bachelor sanctuary.

And yet the first thing I did — after verifying that there had been no further attempt at a break-in — was check to see if there was a message from Jake.

There wasn't.

Sunday was quiet. Too quiet. Natalie worked downstairs. I worked upstairs.

Midmorning, I used my morning walk to buy doughnuts as a peace offering, but Natalie informed me that she was on a Zone diet and was not currently entertaining pastries. Or the men who offered them.

I left the pink box on the sales desk in a hope of luring her later in the day, and I retired to my lair to work on *A Deed of Dreadful Note*. It was a relief to focus on the made-up problems of someone else's life. I appreciated my wisdom in making Jason an orphan.

As I wrote, I listened to one of the CDs from the Women in Jazz collection.

"You and I and moonlight in Vermont," crooned Ella Fitzgerald, rudely interrupting my train of thought.

"But there's no question Jake Riordan is mad about you."

Was Jake really going to leave? Or more to the point, was I really going to let Jake leave? I thought of those long two years when he had been out of my life.

I thought of the ten months we'd been together. Okay, "together" was probably not the word for it. Still…

I thought about how it had felt after he'd told me he was going to marry Kate.

I didn't blame him for the choices he'd made. He'd done the best he could. I believed him when he said he'd never intended to hurt me. That he would never deliberately hurt me. I understood intellectually that there was no insurance policy on affairs of the heart.

But something had happened to me between waking up in the hospital and those moments on the *Pirate's Gambit* when I had believed — for a few terrible seconds — that he was willing to sacrifice me to protect himself, his web of lies. I never wanted to feel that again. That...broken, that betrayed. Because for those fleeting seconds, I really hadn't cared if I died. I knew in some shadowy corner of my brain, I'd hoped that I *would* die. That I would never have to face the day after.

I didn't want Jake to go to Vermont. Couldn't bear the thought of it. I couldn't make myself stop him either. It was like getting thrown from a horse and waiting too long to remount. I'd lost my nerve.

I worked all afternoon in between napping and listening to music. Very productive from the viewpoint of the rest-and-relaxation crowd.

Natalie did not relent. She locked up and left without looking in to say good-bye. I hated to admit how much it bothered me.

In the evening I made fruit salad with cocktail olives and maraschino cherries and read more of *The Long Goodbye*. It was not my favorite Chandler novel — that would have been *The Lady in the Lake* — though Chandler at his weakest was still better than almost anybody else at full strength. Not that this Edgar-winning novel was Chandler's weakest effort. It was an interesting work both for the social commentary and the way Chandler cannibalized his own life for material. As always, when reading Chandler I resolved to keep my day job.

When the phone rang a bit after eight, it occurred to me that I had been waiting all day for it. The number that flashed up was like the winning fruit combo on a slot machine.

Jake was brisk. "I've got progress to report. First thing. I found Dan Hale."

"That's great."

"He's living at one of those retirement-home things in Santa Barbara. Sea View Manor."

"Is he all there? Mentally, I mean." I thought it was safe to assume that, at what must be an advanced age, Hale was probably missing a few of the original parts. "Is he well enough to talk to us?"

"I didn't get the impression he's in great health. He seems alert, and he's willing to talk to us, yes. Would you like to take a drive out to Santa Barbara tomorrow?"

I opened my mouth to say yes — only to remember my cardiac-rehab session. I'd cut Friday's session to go to Ojai. I could imagine the hue and cry if I dared to miss two appointments in a row.

"I can't tomorrow."

"Hot date?"

"Yeah, with my cardiac-rehab team. I don't get out of there until lunchtime."

"So we'll go after lunch."

I felt a surge of gratitude that he didn't simply do the easy thing and say, in that case, he'd head up the coast on his own.

"If you're okay with it?"

"Hey, I'm at your disposal."

And dispose of him I had, right? I pressed my lips closed on that as he continued. "The second break we caught is, Argyle recognized your photos, although how the hell he did is beyond me. Guy is clearly no relation to Ansel Adams. He says your Henry Harrison is a retired PI by the name of Harry Newman."

"Oh wow."

I heard the faint smile in his voice. "I figured you'd like that. You'll like this even better. The reason Argyle remembers Newman is because Newman was hired to find Jay Stevens after he disappeared."

"Hired by whom?"

"Hired by Stevens's girlfriend."

CHAPTER NINE

Jake was waiting for me when I got out of cardiac rehab the next day.

I thought seeing him leaning against the side of the Honda, long legs encased in faded denim, arms folded across the broad chest beneath the navy polo shirt, sunglasses reflecting my slightly disheveled approach, did my heart more good than all the previous hour of team effort.

"You're smiling. Good session?" he asked as I reached him.

It was unsettling how easy it would have been to walk into his arms. It was as though we were operating on the same brain wave; he shifted, as though prepared to draw me close, and I almost forgot and reached for him. I wasn't sure why it was so hard to remember that all that was over now. I settled for giving his arm a friendly punch.

"It was, yeah. They're going to let me start swimming."

Jake smiled one of those rare, warm smiles. "That's great."

"Yep. I love swimming."

"You do?"

I could see why he might be surprised, as I'd never gone swimming or done much of anything in the way of athletics during the ten months we'd gone out. "There's a pool at Lisa's old house. I'm going to swim there."

I saw caution flash across his face, and I knew exactly what he was thinking, but he didn't say it, which I appreciated. "I'll have to bribe someone to go out there with me at first, of course."

"I'll go with you." He added offhandedly, "If you can't get anyone else."

"Thanks," I said quickly, awkwardly. I hadn't got that far along in my plans. I figured I could persuade Lauren to go with me a couple of times a week, or maybe Natalie in the evenings. Assuming she ever spoke to me again.

Mel on the weekends? Somehow thinking about Mel with Jake standing right in front of me felt wrong.

He let me off the hook, saying, "You must be making pretty good progress if they're letting you swim this early."

"It's been five weeks." Well, that was pushing it a little. I'd be starting week five tomorrow. Still. "Apparently I've turned the corner." Funny how I hadn't felt the proof of that until this very moment, with him smiling at me in the bright July sunshine. It brought a smile to my face.

"Congratulations."

"Thanks." I was grinning like a goof as we got into the car, and I didn't think I stopped chattering for the next half hour. As happy and energized as I was, I gradually felt that familiar sleepiness steal over me. I thought I would close my eyes for a bit, and the next thing I knew there was a hand on my shoulder, a light, warm weight that worked itself into my dream.

I opened my eyes, blinked up at Jake. "Hi."

His mouth twitched. "Hi."

I lifted my head. We were in a mostly deserted parking lot. Beyond wind-tattered eucalyptus trees, I could see the hazy blue of the ocean. Overhead, gulls mewed. "Where are we? We can't be in Santa Barbara already."

"No. We're near Point Dume. I thought we might as well stop for lunch. I figured you'd want to stretch your legs."

"Oh right." He must have left the 101 at Las Virgenes Canyon. Not exactly on the way. In fact, about an hour out of the way. Not that I didn't prefer the coast road to inland freeway. I opened the car door and unfolded. The breeze off the sea was cool and salty. The scent of burgers mingled with the ocean and eucalyptus.

I walked to the edge of the parking lot and looked down. Sandy stairs led to a stretch of pale beach. A silvered pier sat crumbling in the green-blue water. A few yards away from the tumbling surf was a battered-looking restaurant. POINT DUME CAFÉ read a pitted sign. Something about the outline of the building caught my attention.

"*Hey.*"

Jake's grin was crooked. "I thought you might enjoy a look at the original Tides."

"Is it still open?"

"Looks like it."

"This is the actual building?"

He nodded.

"Wow."

We walked down the rickety steps to the pale sand. The gulls soared and dived against the blue sky. Far out on the water, sailboats skimmed along like seabirds.

"You want to walk on the pier?"

Jake shrugged, although he didn't look thrilled.

We walked out to the end of the pier. It was solid enough underfoot, but the railings looked pretty wobbly. I stood at the end, staring down at the green water, the seaweed floating atop like a golden net, sun spots flashing off the surface.

Something glimmered beneath the water. Something else, long and pale, glided silently past. A shark?

I leaned over, careful not to rest my weight on the railing.

Jake's hand fastened around my upper arm, and I looked back in surprise. His expression was unexpectedly stern.

"We ought to eat and get going."

"Okay. Sure."

He let go of me as I turned away from the railing. I smiled quizzically. But then it occurred to me that whatever this was, maybe it wasn't something to kid him about.

We walked back to the shore, our feet pounding the wood planks. The sand was cushiony and slippery beneath our shoes.

When we reached the café there was a sign in the window.

TO ALL OUR LOYAL CUSTOMERS:

THANK YOU FOR TEN YEARS OF YOUR BUSINESS AND FRIENDSHIP. IT IS WITH GREAT REGRET THAT WE WILL BE CLOSING OUR DOORS ON JULY 19TH. WE WISH YOU EVERY SUCCESS AND HAPPINESS.

EARL AND PETA

"Sad," I said. "Ten years."

"Things change."

I threw him a quick look; his face was impassive behind the sunglasses. His cop face.

The door to the café was white now, but beneath the milky white was a blue shadow. We went inside, went up the short flight of steps to a big room remarkable for the enormous windows looking out over the ocean. There were a number of plastic chairs and tables though only one other couple was eating lunch — and complaining about the food, if I read their expressions correctly.

I recognized the old decor — what was left of it — from the photos I'd seen on the web. The zigzagging wood inlays and wavy wrought-iron handrails were long gone, but the blue-and-gray-tiled mosaics of the sea still adorned the long walls, and the ceiling was covered in the remnants of grimy, dust-coated latticework meant to counterfeit fishing nets.

A skinny, leathered woman in shorts, halter top, and flip-flops took our order. I ordered grilled cheese and asked to substitute the fries for a piece of fruit. Her expression was priceless. Jake ordered the fishwich.

I stared out the big picture windows at the boats dotting the blue water.

"Thanks," I said to Jake.

He smiled back, that wry grimace. I thought of Guy's comment about Jake's humoring me. I thought Guy probably had a point. But in certain ways Jake had been humoring me for as long as I'd known him. Maybe not when he'd suspected me of murder; certainly from our time at Pine Shadow Ranch. For such a hard ass, he had always been strangely indulgent with me.

Lunch arrived on paper plates. We dug in.

"How's the fishwich?" I inquired.

"Old. How's the grilled cheese?"

"It's hard to go wrong with grilled cheese."

He nodded.

"But somehow they've managed."

He laughed.

The play of sun on the water was almost hypnotic. It glowed softly against the old dance floor. I really had to get over my desire to sleep all the time. I glanced at Jake and caught him studying me.

I thought of something I'd been wanting to ask him. "You never said how your family reacted to your coming out."

He leaned back in the plastic chair, which gave a protesting squeak. "You know those stories you hear about someone finally coming out to their family, only to hear that their folks knew it all the time?"

"Yes."

"That's not how it was."

"Oh." I looked at the greasy remnants of my grilled cheese. "Lisa claims now she always knew, but I remember how it was. She was flabbergasted."

"This was when you were in college?"

I nodded. "She did come to terms with it pretty fast. Within the course of a weekend, as I recall."

"I think it's harder to accept coming from a forty-three-year-old married man. They think I'm having some kind of midlife crisis."

"Right. Sorry."

"My dad and Danny, my youngest brother, are having the hardest time with it." He shrugged. "And Katie, of course."

I swallowed hard. I didn't like thinking about Kate. I resented feeling guilty about her, because I'd seen Jake first — or at least about the same time she had — and, right or wrong, had convinced myself I had as much a right to him as she did. Of course that was all bullshit. He'd married her, made a commitment to her, and that had changed everything — should have, anyway.

"Do you think they'll come around?"

"I think they're disappointed and shocked and confused and angry." His powerful shoulders moved beneath the navy polo. "I hope they'll come around."

"They love you."

"Yeah, well." His eyes met mine levelly. "It's not always enough, is it?"

No. Unfortunately.

"Did she — Kate — know about me?"

"She does now. Before? No." He gave me another of those clear-eyed, direct looks from beneath his brows. "That's the problem, isn't it? If I'd been able to tell people about you, about us…"

It was too late for this. Too late to keep wandering down memory lane, crashing into the same old dead-end barricades, wondering why we hadn't turned left or right or reversed when we still had a chance.

And yet I heard myself say coolly, "You told Paul Kane about me."

He reddened. "Yes. Inadvertently. And I'm sorry for that, for putting you in his crosshairs. Please believe that I never gave him your name or discussed you. He just knew enough to put the pieces together when I got drunk and maudlin one night. He was very good at filling in the blanks."

"Wasn't he, though?" I brooded briefly. If I were completely honest, there was a part of me still jealous of Paul Kane, still curious about their relationship, still — no matter how much I denied it — angry.

Jake pushed his plate away, wiped his hands on his paper napkin. "We should get going."

I nodded and dropped my crumpled napkin on the paper plate.

♫ ♫ ♫

Sea View Manor was a Spanish-style hacienda with a nice view of the ocean and the green mountains. It was surrounded by a tiled garden filled with ornamental cactus and bougainvillea.

The parking lot was fenced by tall boxwood hedge. On the other side of the hedge was a gloomy-looking hotel, also built in the Spanish style, but by depressed Spaniards.

Jake and I strolled up the front walk lined by yellow-edged agave succulents. Ahead of us, nurses pushed elderly, bent patients in wheelchairs.

"I hope this isn't going to be too much of a shock for the old guy," I remarked.

"Death doesn't usually frighten the very elderly."

I thought about how much cooler I'd been about the possibility of death when I'd figured it was inevitable. Not that it *wasn't* inevitable. As Christie wrote, "Death comes as the end." For all of us.

We were greeted in the breezy main reception area by a crisp young man in Brooks Brothers trousers and shirt who introduced himself as Mr. Vaughn. "Welcome. Mr. Hale is looking forward to your visit. We were surprised to hear he was having company. He doesn't have many visitors." He smiled. "You're not family?"

We denied being family.

"Well, he's quite a character. You'll see."

That sounded promising.

"How is he today?" Jake asked.

Vaughn looked thoughtful. "Today is one of his good days. He's very frail, though. You'll have to keep your visit short."

I asked, "What's wrong with him?"

"His heart mostly. He has emphysema as well. Most people have multiple issues at his age."

I thought of that dapper young man with the constant cig in his smiling mouth.

Mr. Vaughn summoned a young woman in a pastel jumpsuit, who led us down a rabbit warren of tiled and antiseptic hallways to a small room overlooking the garden. There was a hospital bed, but there was also a nice little patio on the other side of a sliding-glass door. Yellow bougainvillea cascaded like a golden waterfall over a low stucco wall. A green hummingbird was dive-bombing its reflection in the glass door.

The nurse or attendant asked us to ring for her when we were done visiting, and she departed.

"And who might you be?" inquired the stooped figure in the wheelchair, turning away from the kamikaze hummingbird.

The years had not been kind to Dan Hale. You could still see the ghost of the fierce young man in the gnarled ruins of the old. Unlike Nick Argyle, who was probably around the same age but still hale and hearty, Hale looked every one of his years. In fact, he looked uncannily like the skeleton in the floor of Cloak and Dagger: prominent bones, sunken eyes, sparse hair.

I felt my chest tighten watching him. I'd never really considered the stark prospect of myself in extreme old age, because I hadn't figured I'd live to an age where I needed to worry about nursing homes or assisted living. If you didn't marry, if you didn't have kids…who looked out for you?

"Jake Riordan. We spoke on the phone. This is Adrien English."

Hale offered a liver-spotted hand, and we shook. "I remember, I remember," he said testily, waving us to a couple of uncomfortable plastic chairs. "You called to talk about Jay Stevens." Hale nodded and kept nodding. He gave a harsh laugh. "Jay Stevens. Kee-rist."

"You remember him pretty well?"

"Oh hell yeah. He and the Moonglows used to play at The Tides." I could see the glow of old pride. "The Tides. That was a club I used to own in Malibu. Best damn jazz club on the coast. Everybody used to come out there, though there wasn't much out that way in those days. Seals. We used to get seals up on the beach sometimes. And sharks." He chortled at the idea of sharks.

"How long did Jay and the Moonglows play at the club?"

"Two years. Near as."

"How did you happen to hire them?"

"Jay contacted me and said they were looking to move out West. They'd been playing the clubs back East for a couple of years, to pretty good reviews. The piano player, Paulie St. Cyr, had lung trouble. He'd been advised to move west to a drier climate, so they were looking for a steady gig in California."

"And you hired them based on that?"

"I had them out to audition. They were good. Very good. And they had a new record. Seemed like they were really going to go places." His face had a melancholy cast to it. "And there was Jinx."

Jinx Stevens. The femme fatale with the pert ponytail.

"Jinx was the singer?"

"Sounded a lot like a young Dinah Shore. Yeah, she did a rendition of 'Every Time We Say Goodbye' that didn't leave a dry eye in the house. Yep, Jay Stevens and the Moonglows used to perform every Tuesday, Wednesday, and Thursday. On Friday and Saturday we had guest bands." You could still hear the old satisfaction. "I got some of the biggest names in the business to come out and play for me. Goodman — *that* was a night — Ella,

Sinatra… We were out in the middle of nowhere, but they all came."

Jake took over. "Sir, they found what they believe to be Stevens's body — his skeleton — buried in the floor of what's left of the hotel where he used to room. According to the preliminary forensics, it looks like a potential homicide. Do you have any thoughts on that?"

Hale started laughing. It was only the threat of disintegrating into another coughing jag that stopped him. "That's exactly like Jay. Turning up when it's too late to do anyone any good."

"How's that?"

It was lost in a coughing fit. I feared he might expire right in front of us. Finally he managed a strangled "Always was a contrary bastard."

Jake asked, "What did you think happened to him?"

The watery black eyes studied him. "Thought he did a flit, if you want to know the truth."

"Would he have left his sister and the band like that?" I asked.

"Footloose and fancy-free, that was Jay."

"Wasn't there a girlfriend?"

It was interesting watching Jake question this very old, very frail man. He took his time, and he was surprisingly gentle — surprising, if you didn't know him.

Hale's mouth moved, but no words came out. Maybe that was nothing more than an oxygen issue, because his voice sounded normal enough — in its creaky, wheezy way. "Kee-rist, I'd forgot about her."

"Would you remember her name?" That was Jake.

"Louise…something. She was a college professor or some damn thing."

"A college professor?"

He laughed wheezily at my surprise. "The ladies all fell for Jay. He was a very hard guy not to like. Even when you wanted to kill him."

"Did you ever want to kill him?" Jake's voice was bland.

Hale laughed again. "Sure. But I didn't." He eyed Jake thoughtfully. "Ex-cop?"

Jake nodded curtly.

"I can tell."

I didn't want him veering off on that track, not least because I wasn't sure if this was painful or not for Jake, and so I asked, "This Louise hired a PI to find him after he disappeared, didn't she?"

His eyes narrowed to squinty lines. "Did she? I don't remember that."

Jake said, "Had you heard rumors that Stevens was suspected of taking part in a number of uptown burglaries?"

"You've been talking to Nick Argyle," Hale said shrewdly. "Argyle was convinced Jay was the Westside Cat Burglar. He was always hanging around threatening to put Jay behind bars…" His expression altered as if something had occurred to him.

"What?" Jake pressed.

Hale reflected. "That might have been partly because of Jinx. I always thought he had a thing for Jinx, Argyle did. Kee-rist, who didn't?" He grinned, a shade of the sharp young blade he'd once been. "Yeah, used to sit there drinking my booze and eating her alive with those beady eyes every time she was on the bandstand. Or maybe it was the thought of locking Jay up and throwing away the key." Another of those scary, hacking cough-laughs.

"So you don't think there was any truth to the rumor that Jay was a cat burglar?"

"Nah."

I was pretty sure that was a lie. I was careful not to look at Jake.

"How did Jay take being suspected by LAPD?"

"Thought it was a big joke."

"He didn't worry about it?"

"Nah." Hale said sardonically, "Jay wasn't a worrier."

"Looking back, can you think of anyone who might have wanted Jay out of the way?"

"Argyle," Hale returned promptly.

"*Argyle?* The cop?"

"Sure." He was amused at my surprise. "He was determined to put Jay behind bars. He thought Jay was laughing up his sleeve at him — and he was, of course."

"Anyone else?"

Hale's black gaze flicked to Jake, and he shook his head. That time I was positive he was lying.

"Was Jay Stevens a very good musician?" I asked.

The rheumy eyes focused on me. "He was; he was." He smiled faintly at a faraway memory. "One hell of a musician. Had a very fluid style. Fun, energetic. He didn't improvise the way Goodman did, but his playing was...engaging."

I remembered Nick Argyle had used the same word. "Engaging."

"Do you think the Moonglows would have made it to the big time if Jay hadn't disappeared?"

"No."

"No?" He sounded absolutely positive, which made me curious. "You said they were good, that people said they were going places." I could see Jake wondering where I was headed with this line of questioning. I wasn't sure myself.

"Music was changing. It was all Frank Sinatra, and I don't mean his swing numbers, or bebop. And then those goddamned bobby-soxers wanting to hear Frankie Avalon or rock and roll. You ever hear that song 'Go Bobby Soxer'?"

"No."

"Yes," Jake said, and I looked at him in surprise. "Chuck Berry," he explained.

"I wish those broads *had* gone. 'Wiggle like a whimsical fish.'" Hale shook his head in disgust. "Those goddamned kids ruined music. It was all jungle bunnies and limeys after that. Even Jinx didn't want to sing the old-fashioned stuff anymore. That's what she called it. *Old-fashioned.*"

"Jinx was leaving the band?"

I couldn't interpret Hale's expression. "Well, she didn't make an announcement or anything. We were going to get married, though. Everyone knew that. And I didn't want any wife of mine on the road. Jay was talking about moving on."

I wasn't clear whether Jinx had been retiring due to the new direction in music or because she planned on settling down with Hale. I looked at Jake. I could see by his expression, he thought we'd hit gold.

"How did Jinx take her brother's disappearance?" he inquired.

Hale began to cough. The spell went on so long, I started thinking we should call someone. Finally he calmed down.

"Sorry. What was the question?"

"How did Jinx take her brother's disappearance?"

"Not good. Not good at all."

"What did she think happened to him?" A thought occurred to me. "Who *did* report Jay missing?"

"Jinx. I told her she was being silly." Hale grimaced. "Turned out she was right."

I said tentatively, "You and Jinx didn't end up getting married?"

"No."

It would have taken a colder resolve than mine to broach that fortress. I went a different direction. "Did you stay in touch with her? What happened to her?"

He stared at me for a long time. "She died," he said at last.

"I'm sorry."

He waved it away. I wanted to ask more about Jinx, but it was obvious he was worn-out.

Jake rose, saying, "This has been very helpful, sir. Would it be all right to contact you with any follow-up questions?"

There was a wicked glint in Hale's eyes. "Sure. Come back. It's nice to get company in this crypt. I don't get much in the way of callers. Even the cops are welcome now."

Jake seemed thoughtful as we stepped outside the nursing-home's front doors.

I said, "What do you think?"

"I think he's pretty lonely, and maybe we'll have better luck next time."

"You didn't think we learned anything useful?"

"We learned plenty that was useful. Mostly between the lines, because what he was telling us was largely a pack of lies."

"He's still in love with Jinx Stevens."

Jake snorted.

"Hey. Call me a crazy romantic. Hale was smitten. He's still got smite marks all over him."

Jake was gazing consideringly at the distant freeway. "The traffic's at its worst now. You want to have dinner up here, or should we start back?"

It had been a good day, a great day, but all at once I was done. Dinner and bed. That was what I wanted. The idea of sitting in a car for another half an hour — let alone two hours or more in traffic — was intolerable.

It must have been there on my face to read, because he said immediately, "No? What's up?"

"Nothing. I guess I'm more tired than I realized." I made a face. "You know when you had me call my doctor to make sure I was okay for traveling?"

The lines of his face sharpened. "So help me, Adrien. If you lied about that, I'm going to strangle you."

"Of course I didn't lie. But he — my doctor — suggested that if a trip was longer than two hours, it might be a good idea to stay overnight." He made a smothered sound and stared skyward as though requesting God to stop him from committing a mortal sin. I forged on. "Would you, er, mind if we found a hotel tonight? I'll pay, obviously."

He put both hands on his hips and glared at me. "You think it's just about the money, do you? What about my time? You realize I'll have to cancel my date for tonight?"

"Your...date?" I regret to say that my shock at the idea was only too obvious, and that was pretty stupid too, because why the hell *wouldn't* Jake have a date? Wasn't I the one who had predicted it'd be all wine, women and — well, wine and song with him for the next decade or so? So why was I stricken at this unsurprising news?

I blinked at him. He stared right back at me, tough and unsmiling, and then a tiny, malicious smile touched his mouth. "Gotcha," he said.

CHAPTER TEN

We booked a double room at the Sea View Hotel, scant yards from the nursing home. The hotel looked older than the nursing home and was not as nicely maintained. Tiles were missing from the roof, and the garden was overgrown. Small things rustled in the vines and spiderwebs glinted between the leaves of cactus. The palm trees were shedding on the walk. Inside, it smelled musty, and the furnishings looked like they dated from the 1920s. This must have been where family stayed when they wanted to visit the old folks. It had an air of funereal efficiency to it like a busy undertaker's.

The shapely receptionist was red-haired and freckled. She wore an eye patch.

Not that there's anything wrong with that.

She couldn't seem to tear her eyes — eye — off Jake. He smiled back at her, a glimmer of the old rakish charm as I handed my credit card over.

"One room, two beds," I said.

Card ran and room keys in hand, we headed across the glassy floor of the lobby.

"Welcome to de Hotel California," I muttered to Jake as we stepped into the elevator.

"'This could be heaven or this could be hell'?"

"A lot will depend on the mattress."

Our room was at the end of a long, dark hallway decorated with sepia photographs of old Santa Barbara. Though supposedly nonsmoking, the room smelled of cigarettes. We opened the windows, and the breeze off the ocean gusted in, rank and salty.

"You want to get room service or go down to dinner?" Jake questioned.

"What do you prefer?"

"Up to you. If you're tired, we can eat up here."

The funny thing was, though I'd felt way too weary for the drive back to Los Angeles, the knowledge that Jake and I were spending the night together was unsettlingly energizing.

"Downstairs, I think."

He nodded, switched on the TV, and stretched out on the bed nearest the window, hands behind his head to watch the news while I called Lisa to say I'd be late getting back and we'd have to put off the trip to the horse farm till Wednesday, after the never-ending cardiac rehab.

"It would serve you right if I let you break the news to your sister," Lisa said darkly. "Where are you exactly?"

Exactly? I didn't think *a hotel room with Jake Riordan* was going to go over well. "Santa Barbara."

"*Oh, Adrien.*" The distress was absolutely genuine. "Darling, that's *too* far. You know it's too far. Why are you pushing yourself so hard? You're going to set your recovery back…"

I lowered the phone and stared at the ceiling, counting watermarks. I could feel Jake watching me. When the irate-fairy voice faded, I put the phone back to my ear.

"So I should be back around…" I looked at Jake, and he silently mouthed, *One.* "One," I concluded. "If you could let Natalie know?"

This unexpectedly set her off on the topic of Natalie who, it sounded, was choosing to spend nights away from the family compound and declining to return phone messages. That wasn't much like Natalie, or at least not the Natalie I'd come to know in two years.

At last I escaped and clicked off. "We are not amused."

"How's she doing?"

I cocked my head. In all the time I'd known Jake, I couldn't remember his asking after Lisa. "She's coming round to the idea that I'm an autonomous adult. Another thirty-five years or so and she'll be fine with it."

He said, "I don't know if you're aware of this. She tried to intercede on my behalf with the LAPD brass."

"She…" My voice gave out. I stared at him in horror.

Jake laughed. "No. I was touched. I was. Especially because I know she'd have preferred Paul to have shot me between the eyes. I'd already made my decision to resign, but…I did appreciate her speaking up."

"She never said anything about it."

I couldn't read that faint smile of his at all.

The nearly empty dining room offered a dramatic view of the ocean. Palm trees stood in black punctuation against the amethyst sky. The water glittered like obsidian spear points. The nursing home was an ominous silhouette against the cliffs.

We were seated right away, our order for drinks taken, and then left to our own devices.

I moved the menu stand out of the way. "I didn't really follow what Hale was saying about Jinx leaving the band. That whole thing about swing music."

"I don't think it had anything to do with swing music."

"I'm not so sure. The thing that I find interesting is, Hale might not have been a solid citizen, but his obsession with big-band and swing music was genuine. World War Two and the 1942 musicians' union strike pretty much spelled the end of swing music, so it was already on the way out when Hale opened The Tides. He fought a rearguard action all the way."

"What's your point?"

"I'm not sure. Obviously he was a guy who took the music seriously."

"You think he and Jinx split up over creative differences?"

"I think it's weird that there's no mention of her death anywhere. She dropped out of sight. Without a trace."

Jake shrugged. "It's not like she was a major player, right?"

"No. But *Kaleidoscope* is kind of a cult classic because it was the first album Paulie St. Cyr made. Same thing with the Moonglows. Paulie St. Cyr's first band. So there's information on them that might not otherwise exist — but nothing on Jinx. It's like she vanished, and no one noticed."

"Someone must have noticed. What about Jay Stevens? What information is there on him?"

"The rumors of his death, mostly. There's not a lot, granted. Compared to what there is on Jinx, it's an encyclopedia."

The waiter brought our drinks: a glass of Salmon Creek for me and a Steam Anchor for Jake.

I sipped my wine. Salmon Creek got a bad rap from wine snobs, but it was actually a steady little performer. Okay, it was not Gun Bun. I'd had worse and paid a lot more for the privilege. "I thought Hale was pretty quick to throw suspicion on Argyle."

"Too quick," agreed Jake. "That was an old resentment surfacing. There was a strong mob presence back in 1950s LA. Mobsters like Mickey Cohen were celebrities. Hell, they used to sign autographs for dimwits. And back in the day, Hale had mob connections. He wasn't in bed with Jack Dragna or the LA crime family, but he was cozy with guys like Johnny Stompanato."

"Delightful."

"Even if Hale wasn't allergic to cops on general principles, he wouldn't have enjoyed Argyle hanging around drinking free booze and planning to throw his main attraction in the slammer." He added absently, glancing over the menu, "A lot of people resent cops."

"Un-be-lievable."

He directed a chill eye at me.

"Kidding. Please don't give me another lecture on how Chief Parker rode into LA on his white horse, reformed the city, and saved Western civilization." Jake came from a long line of law enforcement.

He shook his head. "What are you ordering?"

"Salmon. I'm getting this, by the way. It's my fault we're staying at the haunted mansion."

"There's no fault here."

"Okay, we'll chalk it up to business expenses, and I'll clear this one now."

The waiter finally returned, and I ordered salmon and asparagus. Jake ordered sea bass and another beer.

He leaned back in his chair, stretched out his legs, his feet brushing mine in passing. "Since we're spending the night, maybe we should try to see if we can set up another visit with Hale."

"Okay." I liked that idea. I already had a number of questions I wished we'd had time to ask. Most of them pertaining to Jinx Stevens. "I also got the impression he was fibbing about not having any idea of who killed Stevens. I think he, at the very least, formulated a theory as to who killed him."

"My thought," agreed Jake.

"I think that's bullshit about not believing that Stevens was a thief."

"Maybe. I can see why he wouldn't want to believe it."

"Did you believe him?"

"He's not easy to read. Lying is a reflex with him. That doesn't mean he's hiding anything very important."

"I wonder if the kid sister *was* in on the burglaries. Do you think Nick Argyle might have hung on to any of his old notes or case files? He seems like the type who would."

"Oh yeah? What type is that?"

"Old-school."

His mouth quirked. He said solemnly, "I'll inquire."

The dinner was better than I expected — certainly Jake's appetite was as healthy as ever. We chatted easily, laughed more than I'd have expected. It was easy and companionable. The way it had been between us before things had gone wrong. Before

Kate and the baby. Somehow I'd forgotten how much I enjoyed his company. How comfortable it was with him.

"Did you plan on dessert?" he asked as we were finishing up.

"Dessert?"

"It's a sweet served at the end of a meal."

"I know what dessert is. Go ahead and order something if you want it."

"They've got that coffee-glacé thing you like."

"I don't know if I —"

He said with sudden exasperation, "Adrien, you're probably fifteen pounds underweight. Don't tell me your doctor told you you couldn't have dessert once in a while."

"I have to eat the right things."

He actually laughed. "You could start by eating *something*. So far today you've had half a sandwich, lemonade, a serving of asparagus, a few bites of fish, and a glass of wine. As much as I love your cheekbones, have some goddamned dessert."

Heat flooded my face. "Are you keeping track of what I'm eating?"

"It doesn't require a lot of effort." He handed me the menu. "I'm having the cheesecake."

We had dessert — and it was pretty good, I have to admit — and retired to our room.

I fell back on the bed, comfortably full and pleasantly relaxed. I switched on the television.

"I'm going to take a shower," Jake said.

I nodded.

The door closed behind him. I heard the scrape of shower-curtain rings and then the blast of water.

So what now? I'd only be kidding myself if I tried to pretend I didn't want Jake. That was one thing that hadn't changed — I couldn't imagine it ever would. And I knew from recent experiences that once I started down that road, there would be no stopping. Where Jake was concerned, I seemed to have no brakes. What happened when we ran out of freeway?

The bathroom door opened, startling me out of my thoughts. Jake stepped out wearing nothing but black briefs. I tore my gaze away from the heavy bulge against soft cotton. His body was lean and hard, all muscle and bone beneath brown, smooth skin. His broad chest and long legs were dusted with golden body hair. My mouth dried with the same desire that started my heart pounding and blood pulsing to my cock.

"It's all yours," he said.

"Huh?"

He glanced at me. "The bathroom. It's all yours." He was watching me in the mirror as he set his neatly folded Levi's and shirt on the desktop. He smiled faintly.

My gaze dropped to the pink pucker of skin in his left shoulder — front and back. I put a hand automatically to my own shoulder, which twinged in sympathetic response.

"Matching bullet holes."

His smile faded.

"Good thing," I said. "I'd hate it if my first and only serviceable scar was from heart surgery."

"You really are a nut." He sounded tolerant as he returned to his bed and stretched out once more.

How puzzling was it that I'd been uneasy as to whether I'd have the strength to turn him down, and Jake was making no move at all?

"Did you want to watch something?" I glanced at him, and his eyes were shut. It seemed he was going to sleep.

He shook his head, not bothering to answer.

I turned back to the television. After a while what I was staring at registered. "Hey, this is *The Long Goodbye*."

Jake opened his eyes. "What?"

"This movie. It's Robert Altman's take on Chandler's *The Long Goodbye.* 'Nothing says good-bye like a bullet.'"

"I don't know," said Jake. "Sometimes the words are enough."

I laughed.

He watched the end of the film with me. At the finish, he raised his brows. "One of your favorites, is it?"

"Not really. Interesting, though, don't you think?"

"Pretentious, I'd have said."

I clicked off the remote. "Sure. But still interesting."

If it had been Mel with me, I'd have heard all about the experimental aspects of the film. The cinematography and special effects, the use of theme music and color and contrasts.

"Yep. Still interesting," Jake agreed.

I took my turn in the bathroom. Jake's eyes were open when I got back to bed. He was contemplating the ceiling with grim attention.

"You want the light on?"

He shook his head.

I turned off the lamp between our beds.

The gust of the curtains was a gray shadow in the ocean-scented darkness. It was a lot cooler by the ocean than it was in Pasadena. I crawled under the blankets and told myself I was leaving my shirt on for warmth.

I'd been comfortably drowsy during the movie. Inexplicably, once the lights were out, I was wide awake again.

The desire to be with Jake, to lie in his arms one last time, was like physical pain, an ache in my chest that no amount of heart surgery seemed to heal. And it seemed to be all on one side.

"Jake?"

"Mm?" He sounded on the verge of sleep.

I didn't know if this was a wise question or not, but I needed to ask, and I knew that he wouldn't lie. "Would you have come out if there had been any other way?"

The quality of silence changed, grew alert. No doubt he was probably wondering why I kept poking a stick at this when I had already said it was over between us. No doubt he wished I'd shut up and let him get some sleep.

"There were other ways, Adrien. They didn't work for me anymore." When I didn't answer, he continued. "Don't take this the wrong way. I didn't come out for you. I came out because I had compromised everything that I believed in, everything that was important to me. You were part of that, sure, but it wasn't just about you."

I mulled this over. Did it make it better or worse? I wasn't sure.

He said almost apologetically, "People are complex. They usually have more than one reason for the things they do."

It was a discussion we'd had many times. Motive. Motives were often mixed. And different things motivated different people, so one person's motive for murder might be utterly incomprehensible to someone else.

"If I'd died, you could have —"

"If you had died," he said harshly, "I'd have killed Paul then and there. I'd have blown his fucking brains all over that deck. There wouldn't have been any going forward from that. I don't know what you believe or don't believe. Believe that."

I did. The raw pain in his voice prohibited anything else.

I thought it was time to change the subject. "I got the feeling Hale was lying about not remembering Stevens had a girlfriend. What did you think?"

After a pause, he said, "I thought it caught him off guard. He might not have been lying. Although..."

"Although he was lying about not remembering she'd hired a PI."

"Yeah."

"And I don't see how he could have forgotten that."

"Right."

I smiled into the darkness. Nice to know we were thinking along the same lines. "It's a funny thing to lie about, though."

Jake grunted. I remembered what he'd said about people lying for all kinds of reasons during the course of murder investigations, reasons that often had nothing to do with guilt — at least being guilty of murder. The thing was, given Hale's age and health — well, maybe it was naïve on my part, but I couldn't imagine that the typical, trivial sort of things people lied about would still be important to him.

"I wish we'd got more information on the college-professor girlfriend."

"Newman will have that information."

I rolled over onto my side at this news. "You found the PI Stevens's girlfriend hired?"

"Yep." I could hear the satisfaction across the space between our beds. "Believe it or not, he's *not* retired."

"He's not?"

"Nope."

"When are you going to interview him?"

"Tomorrow."

I felt a pang of disappointment. Clearly I wasn't going to be part of that interview.

As though he read my mind, Jake said, "Newman knows who you are, so I don't think it's a good idea for you to come along until I know what we're dealing with."

"Right."

Bedclothes rustled, and the mattress springs squeaked as he propped himself on his elbow, a pale form facing me in the darkness.

"I contacted him on the pretext of hiring him. Once I meet with him, I'll tell him why we want to talk to him. From what Argyle told me, Newman was always a slippery character, always walking a legal fine line. I'm not bringing you into any situation that I'm not sure of."

"Come on. I'm not —"

"Take it or leave it." He was adamant. "You either trust me to do what you hired me to do, or you do it yourself."

"I understand he might bolt if he sees me. Even if he's not our actual burglar, he's obviously got an interest in the bookstore beyond architecture. Beyond that —"

"Anything beyond that is still my call. Right? I'm assuming you hired me because you think I know what I'm doing and not just because you feel sorry for me."

Astonished at the idea, I said truthfully, "I don't feel sorry for you."

He lay back on the mattress again. "Good. Because I don't feel sorry for myself. Not everything worked out the way I hoped, but I'm moving forward."

"Well…great." I was at a loss. How had we even got on this track? And why did he have to keep making such a point about moving on? It wasn't like I was asking for anything else. *I* was the one who'd said I didn't want to risk… And where the hell did he get that feeling-sorry-for-him stuff?

I was still turning this over and over in my mind when he began to snore very quietly.

I was having another weird dream about Jake and me — something to do with blindfolds and feathers — when someone yelled loudly right next to my ear.

The fragile bubble of that delicious dream burst.

Bewildered and alarmed, I tried to make sense of my surroundings. It was pitch-black, and I was on a lousy mattress in a chilly room that smelled of the damp and the ocean.

"What is it?" I sat up, gasping for breath, heart thundering as though I'd been swimming far, far below the surface. I put a hand to my chest, and I could feel the heavy, frightened pounding of my heart.

Shit. Shit. Not now...

"Sorry." The light blazed on, leaving us both wincing. "Are you okay?" Jake was half out of bed, ready to come to my aid. His eyes looked black, and there were lines carved in his face that hadn't been there when we went to bed. "Sorry. Christ. I didn't mean to startle you."

No, I could believe that. He was careful and quiet in the way he woke me, careful never to startle me awake. Careful even when I was already awake. I waited for my heart to start that old familiar stagger and reel. It didn't. It slowed, still steady, still regular.

No arrhythmia.

Normal.

Jake was still scrutinizing me with that intense, harrowed gaze. It must have been one hell of a nightmare.

"Are you okay?" he asked again.

I quit pressing my hand to my heart — which was probably a large part of what was freaking him out. "Yeah. I am." And I smiled.

He blinked, sank slowly down on the mattress.

"What did you dream?" I asked.

"I-it doesn't matter."

I was silent, and he said reluctantly, "I dreamed he shot you. That I didn't move fast enough, and this time he killed you."

I absorbed that without comment. No question of who *he* was.

"Do you dream that a lot?"

"All the time," he said bitterly. "Nearly every damn night." He rubbed his forehead.

I admitted, "I used to dream about it in the hospital. Not at all now."

Silence.

Jake looked… I'd never seen that bleakness in his eyes. I'd seen wastelands that looked less desolate.

"You saved my life. And you told me not to get on that damn boat. You were very clear about it. 'Don't get on that boat,' is what you said. In words of one syllable, as I recall. I chose to go ahead."

He didn't answer.

"Do me the courtesy of letting me take credit for my own bad decisions, okay? I take pride in my ability to be as big a screwup as the next guy."

"Right."

Seeing the shadows under his eyes, the grooves in his lean face, hurt. For all the times I'd wanted to make a dent in that arrogance, that almighty assurance, I couldn't bear him stricken with regret and self-doubt.

Did he know what I had believed him capable of for those few, terrible seconds? Probably.

"If you'll notice, I didn't waste any time asking for your help."

"I noticed."

He sounded…unutterably weary. Maybe dragging Jake into my problems wasn't fair. Maybe he had already worked out exactly how unfair it was.

I started to ask, but he said, "You're shivering again."

"I'm freezing my ass off over here."

The night wind gusted in, the weighted drapes knocking gently against the wall. I shuddered again and said, "Seriously. Is there room over there for me? I'm cold."

It seemed like it took him time to translate. He shifted over without comment, lifting the blankets, and I scrambled into the warm sheets beside him. He smelled like soap and sleep and bare skin. He smelled familiar. Not the déjà vu familiar of Guy or Mel. Familiar like…the ache in your chest of homesickness, of longing for harbor after weeks of rough seas or craving a fire's warmth after snow — or wanting back something you should never have given away.

My feet touched his, and I felt him jump. "Christ. You're not kidding."

"Told you."

He caught my feet between his and rubbed them briskly. Now *there* was a highly underrated bedroom skill.

"We could always close the window."

I shook my head. "This is good."

He handed over a pillow, and I settled carefully on my side, facing him.

"You're playing with fire. You know that, right?"

I moved my head in negation. "Heart patient here, remember?"

That was deliberately misleading. Sex wasn't forbidden — acrobatics, sure — but non-strenuous intimacy was even encouraged. I could see Jake believed me, though. There was a tenderness in his eyes I could feel in my solar plexus.

His breath was warm against my face as he said, "You know, you can take off your shirt. I'm not afraid of a few scars."

"Take it off? It's all that's saving me from hypothermia."

He made a derisive sound, reaching over me to turn off the lamp. "You really are full of shit, you know."

"I know."

In the safe darkness, we moved into each other's arms, his hold protective and careful.

"Are you still in a lot of pain?"

I shook my head. "No. Coughing isn't a lot of fun. Or sneezing. Or laughing."

Not that I'd been laughing a lot of late.

His hands moved over my back. "I can count your ribs."

"It's the new math."

He continued to rub my back — small, soothing movements — and I stopped feeling self-conscious about my shoulder blades and ribs. It felt…nice. Nice to be held again. Nice to be touched by someone who wasn't a doctor or a nurse or a therapist. I hadn't even let myself consider how much I was missing this. How much I missed Jake.

I shifted, getting comfortable, and he moved to accommodate the sharps and angles of my body. "The worst thing is, I like to sleep on my side, and I can't right now."

It made sleep difficult. Usually. Usually it made sleep difficult, but right now, finally warm and relaxing beneath that light touch, I was getting drowsy again.

He said softly, "This is the first time you've let me hold you since…"

It took me time to answer. "It's not that I don't want it. It's that I want it too much."

"That's not the problem you think it is."

"I wish that were true."

It seemed he had no response to that. I was sliding into sleep when his lips brushed my forehead. He whispered, "I never met a more obstinate son of a bitch than you, baby."

$$\int \int \int \int$$

I woke to the dozy knowledge that I was pain free, comfortable, and had a considerable case of morning wood. And that it was being dealt with, with exquisite efficiency. I cracked the window shades of my eyes. Jake knelt over me, the head of my cock in his mouth.

I raised my head, mumbled, "What are you doing?"

He paused the proceedings long enough to utter, "If you don't know, I must not be doing it correctly."

I gulped a laugh, dropped my head back on the spongy pillow, and then, as he resumed, caught my breath. "*Jesus.*"

"Mmm?"

"Don't stop." And that was a definite plea.

He spared another breath to order, "Lie back and take it easy, then."

It was only too easy to take. And keep on taking. Not fair to Jake, though it seemed a bit late for protest, even if I'd had it in me. I arched, instinctively pushing into that wet heat. Whimpered as he sucked harder. Dizzily, I thought that with that mouth action, he should have played the clarinet. His lips were tight, velvety, warm, all at the same time. Talk about embouchure. He sucked and pulled my cock like he was playing a slow, sweet piece of music. Instead of producing warm waves of sound, lilting shocks of pleasure rolled through me from the tips of my toes to the prickling ends of my hair. Oh yeah, he was most definitely playing my song.

And in a minute I'd be singing along so loud, they would hear me out at sea. Me and the mermaids. Fireworks danced behind my eyelids, the muscles of my legs tightened, and all the will in the world couldn't keep my hips from thrusting hard in this extremity of pleasure.

The percussion section in my chest was going a mile a minute, and I didn't care, didn't care if I blasted into pieces, flew apart, as the crescendo swept through me, and I surged up and shot long jets, the silvery extended notes of pleasure that went on and on, and Jake took it all, swallowed it down verse and chorus.

I sank into the peaceful release, closed my eyes, and drifted away like music on the breeze.

♫ ♫ ♫ ♫

A hand closed on my shoulder. "Time to roll," Jake said quietly.

My eyes flew open. I'd fallen into a much-deeper sleep than I'd intended; I'd meant to close my eyes for a few minutes and then give Jake relief of his own for that blissful and unexpected release. He was already dressed again, looking remarkably fresh and uncrinkled in body, soul, and outerwear.

"What time is it?"

"Eight. If we're going to get in to see Hale again, we ought to get over there early."

"Right." I yawned so widely, my jaw cracked. I sat up, remembering my first awakening. I threw Jake an uncertain look. He was looking through his wallet. He looked like always. Which was reassuring. And disappointing.

But that was what I wanted, right? Anything else would have felt like pressure, wouldn't it?

I pushed up from the mattress and went into the bathroom to shower, barely looking at my reflection — when I remembered that I hadn't weighed myself. Hadn't weighed, hadn't taken my temperature. My heart rate was okay — at least until I realized I didn't have my morning meds either.

"Jake."

He looked up quickly at my tone as I stepped out of the bathroom. "What's wrong?"

I explained what was wrong, getting more breathless and panicky by the second, not helped by the fact that he had turned away and was opening and closing the battered dresser drawers. What the fuck was he looking for in the middle of my medical emergency? Gideon's Bible?

About to acidly inquire, I stopped as he pulled out a phone book, flipped through it, and said, "Phone your doctor and tell him to call a prescription in to Rite Aid. I'll go pick it up while you finish dressing."

There.

Simple. Easy. Why all the uproar? I sat down on the foot of the bed and put my face in my hands.

"Now what?" He crossed to the bed. Stood over me.

I couldn't answer. I was literally mute with relief — and embarrassment at how obviously I'd come unglued.

"Adrien?"

"Nothing." I jumped up and went back in the bathroom, locked the door.

"Don't lock the door," Jake ordered clearly on the other side.

I bit back the immediate and stupid comment that sprang to mind, and unlocked the door. I splashed cold water on my face, got myself under control, and exited the bathroom.

Back to the room, Jake stood gazing out the window at the ocean. He glanced around without comment.

I phoned my doctor, and Jake went to get my prescription. I took my shower and dressed, and when he arrived back at the hotel, we went to breakfast like calm, civilized folk.

In contrast to the night before, we had remarkably little to talk about over the oatmeal and scrambled eggs. He seemed preoccupied.

After breakfast we walked back across the parking lot to Sea View Manor.

At the front desk we asked after Dan Hale, and the silver-haired receptionist got a certain pained look on her face.

"Are you family?"

"No," I answered. "We were here visiting yesterday."

Somehow I knew even before she spoke. "I'm so very sorry to inform you that Mr. Hale passed away during the night."

"What happened?"

"Old age." She smiled sympathetically. "He was nearly ninety, you know."

"He seemed…" I stopped. Frankly, Hale *had* seemed pretty infirm.

"I know," she commiserated. "It's always such a shock." Clearly it was rarely a shock around Sea View Manor; this was the politic thing to say.

"Thanks," Jake told her.

We turned away.

A thought occurred to me, and I turned back to the desk. "Did Hale have any family left?"

The receptionist pursed her mouth. "I don't know that he did. He was a widower, and I don't believe they had any children."

"Who paid for his care?"

"Oh. Well, I really couldn't say."

"Could we talk to whoever is in charge?"

She hesitated and punched a button on her phone and requested the presence of Mr. Vaughn.

Mr. Vaughn, in another Brooks Brothers ensemble, appeared gracious and apologetic. He praised us for brightening Mr. Hale's final day. We asked about Hale's immediate family, and he got the same cagey look the receptionist had.

I said, "Yesterday you asked if we were family, which seems to indicate Hale *had* family, even if they didn't visit often."

"I really couldn't say."

"Who could?" Jake asked.

Mr. Vaughn looked disconcerted.

"Who's in charge here?" Jake pushed less politely.

Dr. Sawyer.

Mr. Vaughn retreated, and Dr. Sawyer, trim and dark, entered the fray. Sawyer came prepared, having already heard what we were after. He was apologetic but firm.

"I'm afraid that's confidential information, gentlemen."

I remarked mildly, "Is it that much of a deep, dark secret?"

"No, of course it isn't," Dr. Sawyer said with a hint of irritation. "However, the family values their privacy."

"So Dan did have family left?"

Dr. Sawyer looked chagrined. He recovered at once. "I'm afraid I've revealed as much as I'm prepared to. If you'll excuse me, I've patients to attend."

He strode off, his white coat flapping.

"Now what was that about?" Jake's gaze met mine.

"Hale lost everything after The Tides went under. I guess it's possible he managed to recover financially, but he never opened another club. He doesn't turn up on the Internet as the owner of any other successful business endeavor."

"So?"

"This place must be fairly expensive. It's Santa Barbara, for one thing. Everything's expensive. So, assuming Hale wasn't paying for all this, who was?"

I could see the gleam of approval in Jake's eyes. "Very good." He gave me a "hold that thought" and went back to the reception desk.

When he rejoined me a few seconds later, he was smiling.

"What?"

"Memorial service on Thursday. I have a hunch it'll be very interesting to see who turns up to say good-bye to Dan Hale."

CHAPTER ELEVEN

The drive back from Santa Barbara was unremarkable — except for my inadvertently pissing off Jake.

We were passing through Carpinteria when I got up the nerve to say, "You know, once the renovation on the other side of the building is done, I'm planning to rent out the top level to writers or students looking for a quiet space to work or study. If you wanted to set up shop, you'd be more than welcome. Rent free."

I was staring out the side window when I made this offer. He didn't respond for so long that I turned to look at him and saw his face was ruddy with emotion. I looked closer and saw that the emotion was anger.

His hands were white knuckled on the steering wheel.

I wasn't sure where I had gone wrong, but I clearly had. As I started to question, he cut me off, his voice unnaturally even, which only served to emphasize how mad he was.

"Christ. You really are your mother's son."

My mouth opened. No words came out.

"You better hurry up and figure out what the hell it is you want, Adrien."

"Sorry?"

He risked a quick look from the highway, and his tawny eyes were bright with anger. "I've never known you to play games, so I'm going to assume you truly are confused and not deliberately jerking me around."

"*Jerking you around?*" I practically stuttered.

"Let's start with climbing in bed with me last night. Or the fact that you've hired me to look into this bullshit case."

I echoed disbelievingly, "Bullshit case?"

"You say it's over between us, okay. That's not what I want, but I can accept that there's too much water under the bridge.

You're probably right. You know more about this kind of thing than I do, and you sure as hell should know more about what it is you want. So it's over. I'd like to stay friends with you. I think you want that too. For that to happen you need to respect the boundaries."

My heart was racketing around my chest like a ricochet gone wild. It took a couple of hyperventilating breaths before I managed to say, "Speaking of mixed signals, what was this morning's blowjob supposed to be? Taps?"

I could see the muscle moving in his jaw.

"I wanted to do that for you," he said in that too-level voice. "I wanted to do that for myself. I wanted one last time with you."

My throat closed off, and I turned to stare back out the window at the sand and water flying by in sunlit flashes of anguished blue and gold.

Finally I got control of my voice. "You're right. I didn't think." I swallowed. "I guess... I don't want you to go."

It took a lot to admit that. I could have saved my breath. He shot back, "I don't think you know what you want. Which...fair enough. You've had your share of trauma for the year. Just... don't push me anymore."

I snapped, "You got it."

The rest of the drive was made in silence. There was plenty to say, but what was the point? I'd made my mind up, right? I was finally, for once in my life, doing the sensible thing.

When we finally reached Cloak and Dagger, I scrambled out of the car.

"Can you let me know how it goes with Newman?"

I got a curt "of course."

The Honda was starting to roll forward, so I managed to push the door shut without slamming it, and away he went. Places to go and people to do.

I walked into the bookstore; the bells on the door jingled cheerfully. A tall, bony, sallow woman in her late forties looked up and delivered the kind of glower that old-style librarians and German nuns used to great effect.

"Uh, I'm Adrien." I barely managed not to apologize for it. "I own this place."

"Ms. Pepper." She didn't smile. I think maybe the scowl lessened a fraction.

"Welcome aboard, Ms. Pepper." She had a grip like a stevedore.

I walked past the customers cowering in the aisles and hunted Natalie down in my office.

"Hi," she whispered. We were evidently on speaking terms again. After a day of Ms. Pepper, even I was probably a welcome relief.

"Who is that?" I whispered back.

"Naomi Pepper."

"I know. Where did she come from?"

"The agency sent her."

"She's scaring the customers."

"She scares me."

"We have to get rid of her. What were they thinking? She's like…she's like having a gorgon for a Walmart greeter."

Natalie made frantic shushing motions, although if we were any quieter, we'd have been communicating by telepathy.

"We *can't.*"

"Why can't we?"

"I guess she was the only qualified person willing to work here."

Two tiny murder investigations and everyone treated us like plague house.

I opened my mouth and then closed it. I wasn't in position to insist. "Does Elphaba know anything about books?"

"Does it matter?"

She had a point.

I went to the doorway and peered out. "Why are all the lights on in there? It looks like a prison yard after an attempted escape."

"Ms. Pepper felt it was too dark."

I thought it over. "I'll be upstairs," I informed her sotto voce.

"Coward."

"I have a note from my doctor."

"*Oh*. Do *not* let Mr. Tomkins out of your rooms. Ms. Pepper doesn't like cats."

I nodded my dismayed understanding.

As I slunk up the stairs, I noticed the music was not on, which added to the general study-hall atmosphere. Did Ms. Pepper also not like music?

Upstairs, I greeted Tomkins — who expressed himself at length on what he thought of such tomcat behavior as staying out all night — changed the clothes I'd been wearing for two days, forced down another of those ghastly protein-shake things — and tried to think of what to do with the rest of my day.

I really didn't see what more I could learn on my own. The case was simply too cold, and I had read all I wanted on jazz, swing, and early Malibu.

I wondered how Jake's meeting was going with Harry Newman.

I wondered what the hell had been up with Jake on the drive back from Santa Barbara.

I wondered why I couldn't stop thinking about Jake.

I got out the manuscript for *A Deed of Dreadful Note* and worked on it for a bit. My agent and editor were going to be delighted at how early this thing would be arriving on their desks. I'd never turned in anything this fast. Then again, I'd never had this much time on my hands before.

Unfortunately, that was what it felt like. Too much time on my hands.

Lauren dropped by late afternoon to invite me for a swim at the house in Porter Ranch.

"What was that?" she asked of Ms. Pepper when we got outside.

"That's Ms. Pepper. She's the new bookstore assistant."

"She told me to lower my voice when I asked for you."

"I hope you lowered your voice."

"I did."

♪ ♪ ♪ ♪

When I got back around four thirty, I looked to see if Jake had called yet, but the answering machine was disconcertingly blank. Even Lisa seemed to be preserving radio silence.

At five I could hear the familiar sounds of Natalie's closing up shop. I thought it was quite a commentary that the shop seemed noisier after it closed for the day than it had during business hours with Ms. Pepper manning the front desk.

Finally, at six, the phone rang. I jumped to get it, trying not to acknowledge that I hoped it was Jake. It wasn't. It was Guy.

It seemed he had decided to forgive me. He chatted about how his week was going, and I gave him a vastly edited version of my own week.

"Are you sure you're not overdoing things?" he asked tentatively.

I squelched the instant flare of resentment. It was a reasonable question — and he hadn't even heard half of what I'd been up to.

I still felt queasy when I remembered how easily I'd forgotten my meds. Thank God for Jake.

I blinked at the mental echo of that thought.

"I'm pacing myself."

"Right. Well, you've got a second chance. You don't want anything to jeopardize that."

I was beginning to be very tired of people telling me how lucky I was. "I know. I'm conscious of that. I'm doing everything I'm supposed to. Scout's honor."

We talked a bit longer, but as glad as I was that we were back on good terms, I found myself strangely stumped for dialogue.

When I finally hung up, there was only a short time to prepare for Partners in Crime, the writer's group I hosted at the bookstore every Tuesday evening. The fact that I could contemplate having the group meet was proof of how much progress I'd made. Even the week before the mere idea of critique had exhausted me.

Jean and Ted Finch showed up early to set up the chairs and table and set out the snack foods. The Finches were married writing partners, but they looked unsettlingly like brother and sister, which reminded me of Jinx and Jay Stevens. Except Jinx and Jay had really been brother and sister.

Hadn't they?

Now there was an angle I hadn't considered before.

"How are you feeling, you poor baby?" Jean asked, to my embarrassment, giving me a big hug.

"Good," I assured her. "Better all the time."

"You look good. Much better than any of us expected. You got a little sun, I see."

Ted looked up from moving chairs into a wide circle. "Have you solved the mystery of the skeleton in the wall yet?"

"I haven't. And he was in the floor. Not that it makes a difference."

Ted and Jean looked at each other and twinkled.

I added, "And if Avery Oxford finds a body in the wall of his newspaper office, I'm suing you both." We all laughed merrily. "Seriously."

Avery Oxford was the protagonist of their appalling first novel, *Murder, He Mimed.* He was a thirtysomething, sharp-tongued, self-satisfied twit who bore a strong physical resemblance to me, right down to his slender build, silky black hair, and bright blue eyes. He even had a tough cop friend named Jack O'Reilly. Alarmingly, Jean and Ted recently claimed to have found representation for the book. I tried to comfort myself that whoever had agreed to such a thing was probably even now in rehab and that I had nothing to worry about.

The rest of the group started to file in, and I was assured several times how surprisingly healthy I looked. I took it as a compliment, although I had to wonder at what I'd looked like before.

Paul Chan, once Jake's partner in homicide, was the last to show up. He was a paunchy, middle-aged detective, and that night he was chewing stick after stick of Juicy Fruit gum, leading me to believe he was once more trying to quit smoking. From the point of his arrival, the discussion veered away from writing and publishing back to the skeleton in the floor.

Chan confirmed that the body was presumed to be Jay Stevens and that the investigation was proceeding along those lines.

"Who's in charge of the investigation?" I asked.

Chan named the detective who I'd spoken to previously. He'd left a message that morning saying the construction site had been approved to be reopened.

"Alonzo isn't part of the investigation?"

"Alonzo?" Chan looked cautious. "Not to my knowledge. It's strictly CCHU."

"Is that so?"

His look was inquiring. I let it go. It was good to know that I had recourse, but I wasn't sure I wanted to risk antagonizing Alonzo. With Jake gone, my only friend at LAPD was Chan.

At the break, Chan asked awkwardly after Jake.

I thought of my last conversation with Jake. "Hard to read," I said shortly. "You should give him a call."

"I did," he said, surprising me. "Right after it all went down. I heard a rumor that he's moving." His brown eyes met mine.

It wasn't exactly an accusing look; even so, I felt myself coloring. "He's been offered a job in Vermont."

"Vermont? What would Jake do in Vermont? He's a California boy, born and raised. All his family is here."

"Maybe that's the point," I said wearily.

When the meeting broke up at last, I headed straight upstairs in the hope that Jake had called.

The answering machine was empty of any calls.

♪ ♪ ♪ ♪

I spent an undisturbed night, so perhaps the trouble with Harry was over.

The next morning, Wednesday, I weighed myself. Halle-fricking-lujah. I'd finally gained a pound. I took my temperature. Perfect. Heart rate also normal. Incision looking good. I studied myself in the mirror.

"It looks like you're going to live."

The guy in the mirror smiled sheepishly back.

♪ ♪ ♪ ♪

"Let's talk about Friday's cardiac-rehab session," Dr. Shearing said in the tone of one who would brook no arguments.

"I wasn't here on Friday."

"*Exactly,*" she said with satisfaction. "One week into cardiac rehab and you've already started playing hooky. Do you understand why that sends up flags for your recovery team?"

"Not really. I'm sure people —"

"Patients," she interjected in that kind, all-knowing way that made me long to hit her with the crystal angel paperweight on her desk. "There's an element of denial —"

"Patients," I corrected, "occasionally have to miss rehab."

"Occasionally emergencies crop up," she conceded graciously. "What was your emergency, Adrien?"

I opened my mouth to tell her it was none of her damned business, though that was bound to create more problems than it solved. "To tell you the truth, I went out with a friend."

"That's *excellent*," she praised, as though I'd managed to mostly stay within the lines of my coloring book. "I'm very glad to hear that you're making an effort to reach out to friends and family again. That's very encouraging. *However*, I'm sure if your friend realized how important cardiac rehab is to your recovery —"

"I missed once last week," I interrupted. "I was here Monday, and I'm here today. I'll be here Friday. I'm committed to my recovery. I want to get well."

"You still sound a *wee* bit defensive," she observed. "However, you're much less angry than our last session, and that's *very* good news."

I sighed.

"Fear, depression, and anger are very common after cardiac events…"

And they're off! I kept a polite expression on my face while her mouth galloped along yards ahead of her brain.

Why did they call heart attacks and surgeries cardiac *events*? Why not cardiac incidents? *Incident* far better captured the sinister connotations.

I realized that Dr. Shearing had stopped and was waiting for an answer.

"Sorry? I missed that."

She summoned her patience. "I said perhaps this friend would be willing to act as your support partner?"

"I don't think so."

"We never know until we ask."

"Sometimes we do."

She gave me a chiding look. "I'm going to give you your first homework assignment, Adrien. I want you to invite someone — you can choose anyone you like — to accompany you to our session next Wednesday."

"Does this count toward the final?"

She allowed herself a very small smile. "Indeed it does."

I nodded. It sounded to me like an excellent time to transfer to woodshop.

♫ ♫ ♫

"How much longer, Lisa?"

"Call me 'Mummy,' Em," Lisa instructed gently, eyes on the rearview.

Emma's eyes met mine. She shoved a french fry into her mouth and chewed without comment.

Lisa sighed.

We were once more on the road to Chino, having stopped briefly to supply Emma with lifesaving McDonald's french fries. Other than that, it had been an uneventful trip. I hoped it stayed that way. Or at least that the only event would be the purchase of a horse for Emma.

"Are you seeing Jake Riordan again?" Lisa asked over Jacqueline du Pré's performing Elgar's Cello Concerto in E Minor.

I glanced back at Emma, who was now managing to eat french fries while holding her nose as we passed yet another dairy farm.

"Natalie told you I went with him to Santa Barbara."

"Was it a secret?"

"No."

"You're a grown man, Adrien," she said, and I almost fell out of my seat. "I'm not going to tell you what to do."

"Why, thank you."

"*Are* you seeing Jake Riordan?"

"No. He's...helping me with the situation at the bookstore." She didn't comment, and I added unwillingly, "He may be moving."

"*Jake?*" It was the closest I'd ever heard to her sounding dumbfounded.

I nodded, gazing out the window.

"Why is he leaving?"

I looked at her in surprise. "He got a job offer in Vermont."

"*Vermont?*" She asked quite sharply, "Are you thinking of going with him?"

"No."

I thought she might have something to add to that, but by then we were turning off for Osseo Farms.

At the farm, Lisa and I stood watching in the paddock as Adagio was saddled and Emma mounted. Karin Schultie led horse and rider to the larger arena, and Lisa and I followed.

We leaned against the tall white fence, watching as Emma rode the gelding around the arena.

"You see the difference in his three gaits? See that? He really is a beauty."

Lisa eyed me resignedly. "I suppose. He does have a pretty face."

I ruthlessly suppressed my smile as we watched Emma, solemn faced, make another pass around the enclosure.

"I'm glad you get along with her so well," Lisa remarked.

"She's a great kid."

"Yes." She sounded unexpectedly melancholy.

"I'm not competing with a memory. Em never had a big brother before."

"I suppose that's true."

I glanced at her still-flawless profile. "Can I ask you something?"

"Of course, darling. We have no secrets from each other."

"Er — right. Anyway, kind of a funny question, I know, but why is it that I call you *Lisa* and not *Mother*?"

Lisa's gaze locked onto my own. "Did you want to call me *Mother*?"

"Now? No. I mean, it doesn't matter. I'm not — I'm curious…"

"Your father taught you to say *Lisa*. He thought it was very funny, and it was. You said it with the exact same inflection he did, but in your baby voice." To my alarm, tears filled her eyes. She turned her profile to me, staring out once again at the arena. "And after he died, I liked hearing it. That…echo."

"Oh." I swallowed hard. Had to ask, didn't I? Now she was wiping hastily at her cheeks.

I looked quickly out to where Em continued putting Adagio through his paces, still with that set and serious expression on her face.

At last Karin walked out, and Emma reined in. They returned to the paddock. We followed, rejoining them as Emma swung down from the saddle.

Karin raised her eyebrows in inquiry.

I said, "Well, Em? What did you think?"

Emma parroted, "He's got lots of suspension, and presence and great reach." Then any attempt at dispassion flew, and she hugged me. "Oh, Adrien. He's *wonderful*. I *know* he's the right one."

I thought with a pang that one day she would be telling me this about some unworthy asshole boy. At least she was probably right about Adagio.

"Okay, but remember what I told you about show jumping. Adagio is a classic Arabian. Lots of spirit, lots of stamina. The best jumpers are heavier. They've got that solid bone structure to absorb the impact of landing on their front legs."

"I don't care about show jumping. I love him."

I looked at Lisa, and she closed her eyes in pain.

"Jumping aside, we're not going to find a better horse for her."

"We haven't even looked."

"Sometimes when you find the right one, you know it." I said coaxingly, "If she's not interested in show jumping, there's less opportunity for her to break her little neck, right?"

"How you can joke about that…"

Emma and I waited while Lisa struggled inwardly. She said at last, "If I don't do this, you're simply going to go around me and buy this wretched animal yourself, aren't you?"

"Yes." If I had to hock the bookstore to do it.

She opened her eyes and pinned me with a blue look as fierce as the flame of natural gas. "Very well. I will do this," she said tightly, "if you promise to attend *every bloody session* of your rehab. No more sloping off to play detective. You're there every day, and you're participating fully."

Emma clung to me, gazing up hopefully.

"Deal."

Emma squealed in delight and ran to Adagio.

My mother looked at me and shook her head.

∫ ∫ ∫ ∫

When I got back to Cloak and Dagger, Natalie drew me into my office and informed me Ms. Pepper was unhappy with our business hours.

"What's that mean?"

"She feels we should be opening earlier in the morning and staying open later in the evening."

"She's probably right about that. We don't have the coverage."

Natalie took a deep breath. "Ms. Pepper is happy — well, she didn't actually say *happy* — but she's agreed to work the extra hours."

"You mean she'd be here *more* often?"

Natalie nodded.

I swallowed. "Let me think about it."

"Don't think about it too long."

"What's that mean?"

"I don't know. Only...don't antagonize her."

"Did you ask the agency if they've found anyone else yet?"

Her hands fluttered in alarm. "*Shhhh.*"

"Nat, I think we were better off before...her."

More hand fluttering. "The thing is, I'm afraid the agency sent her as a test for us."

"Come again?"

"I think she's a spy for the agency."

"I think you've been hitting the espionage shelves again."

"We have a terrible reputation with all the agencies in the city. They claim our employees don't get their breaks and are frequently murdered."

"That's ridiculous. Only one employee was ever murdered."

"I'm telling you what our reputation is."

"I don't care about our reputation. We have to get rid of her." I added hastily, "The usual way."

I left Natalie chickenheartedly filing in my office and went upstairs. A message was blinking on the answering machine. I checked the number. Jake. Instantly my spirits rose.

I called him back. He didn't pick up.

"Come on, Riordan."

I contemplated ringing him again, but more than one message was going to look desperate. Hell, it might look like I wasn't respecting the boundaries.

I went into the kitchen and opened the fridge. There was plenty of food there. My family was doing their best to keep me stocked in vegetables and fruits and lean meats. Somewhere around here was a cookbook. If all else failed, there was a copy of the *Nancy Drew Cookbook* downstairs. Even I could probably whip up Casserole Treasure or 99 Steps French Toast.

Or I could open a can of salmon. I had the can opener in hand when the phone rang.

I jumped for it — even Tomkins looked impressed with my spring. I saw the number flash up as I lifted the receiver.

"*Hey.*"

"Hey." Jake's voice was neutral. "Talked to Newman."

"I thought I'd hear from you sooner." I heard that and winced. "How did it go?"

"Interesting."

"Good interesting or bad interesting?"

"He'll talk to you if you're willing to pay for the privilege."

"Seriously? How much?"

There was a pause. "For some reason I didn't anticipate you being thrilled by this news."

"Why not? I want to talk to him."

He said delicately, "You're usually more concerned with your cash outlay."

"Oh. Well."

"So here's the deal. It's five hundred bucks —"

"Five *hundred* bucks?"

"You heard right. Plus the price of lunch. He'll meet us Friday afternoon at the Formosa Café. You can ask him whatever you like, and he's promised to answer to the best of his ability."

Friday. Cardiac rehab. Shit. I'd given my word. I closed my eyes. "What time Friday?"

"Up to you."

I opened my eyes. "How about two?"

"Sure. I'll set it up."

A crazy thought went through my mind, and I very nearly asked him if he'd go with me to cardiac rehab. He was guilty enough about my getting shot that I was pretty sure he'd agree, but talk about failure to respect the boundaries.

Apparently I had all the steadfastness of an alcoholic making his New Year's resolution.

Jake said, "Hello? Did you swoon away at the thought of spending all that money?"

"Er, no. Do you think Newman's really got anything to tell us?"

"I think so, yes. From the few crumbs of information he doled out, I think he's definitely got a story to tell. I don't know if it's worth five hundred bucks, and if you'd like, I could try negotiating with him."

"What kind of crumbs did he dole out?"

"Nazi treasure."

For a few stunned seconds I couldn't come up with an answer.

"Did I lose you?" Jake inquired.

"For a minute I thought I heard you say Nazi treasure."

"I did."

"No damn way." I was totally disgusted. "That's got to be one of the oldest scams in the book. The guy's a con artist. If he doesn't have anything better than that, tell him to forget it."

That surprised a laugh out of Jake. "Not the reaction I expected."

"It's ridiculous."

"I don't know. It's not impossible."

"Yes, it is. *Hidden Nazi treasure?* Puhleaze. Newman saw us coming a mile away. I can't believe you, of all people, are considering for one minute that this might have credence. The bastard's playing us. Or trying to."

"He was looking for something in the bookstore."

That stopped me in my tracks. "So he does admit to trying to burglarize the bookstore?"

"He does. He seems pretty forthright. I get the feeling he's decided five C in hand is worth more than all the legends of Nazi treasure in the bush. Or hidden in the floorboards, in this case."

I considered. If Newman had confessed to burglary, maybe there was more to this than I thought. "Did you think he was credible?"

"I did. Yeah."

"All right. Let's do it."

"Okay. I'll set it up." Clearly about to sign off.

I interjected quickly, "Jake?"

"Yes?"

"Are you going up to Santa Barbara tomorrow for Hale's funeral?"

The hesitation was loud and clear. "Yes."

"Could I come along?" I heard the diffidence in my voice. Knew he heard it too.

"If you want to." He added in that same neutral tone, "You're spending a lot of time traveling in cars this week. Do you think that's a good idea?"

Obviously Jake didn't want me along or he'd have suggested it himself. Not even counting the argument on the way back from Santa Barbara, it had probably been a total pain in the ass having me along the last time. Besides the genius of having forgotten my meds, there was the fact that I couldn't seem to stop picking over the bones of our failed romantic past.

"Probably not." I tried to sound good-humored about the whole thing, because I was damned if I was going to confirm his belief that my head was screwed on backward. "You'll fill me in on everything?"

"Of course."

"Good enough. I'll talk to you…maybe tomorrow?"

"Talk to you tomorrow."

He rang off, clearly too busy to sit around shooting the breeze with me.

I replaced the receiver.

Tomkins *meowed* at me.

"No way," I said. "I'm the one who set these boundaries to start with. This is *exactly* how I want it."

Really, what the hell was my problem? Maybe I'd been hanging around Emma too much. I seemed to have developed a mild case of little girl.

The phone rang. I picked it up.

Jake said, "I've got to leave at six in the morning to get up there in time for the funeral, which would mean picking you up at five forty-five. Can you manage that?"

Inexplicably, I had to work to get that one word out. "Sure."

"Okay. I'll see you then."

He disconnected before I could thank him.

CHAPTER TWELVE

Jake was, as always, on time.

The car pulled up outside the bookstore Thursday morning at the crack of dawn, I slipped inside, and we glided away from the curb.

"Morning." His gaze was on the rearview. He was dressed for success — or a funeral — in a well-cut dark suit, a crisp white shirt, and a black and blue botanical silk tie. He looked great, and he smelled great. For the first time I noticed he wasn't wearing his wedding ring anymore.

"Morning."

Sparing me a glance, he commented, "Your nose is sunburned. Find someone to swim with?"

"Lauren drove me out to the house yesterday."

"It turns out Argyle was right. Newman was hired by a college professor by the name of Louise Reynard to find Stevens after he disappeared."

"Is Reynard still alive?"

"No."

"Shame."

Conversation languished. I admitted knowing that Jake didn't particularly want me along had an inhibiting effect on my normally cheerful self. I resolved to annoy him as little as possible.

We left Pasadena sleeping in the cool morning smog and merged onto the I-210 West, already busy even at this early hour.

As the odometer racked up the miles, Jake threw me another quick glance, his dark brows knitting. "What's the matter?"

"Me? Nothing."

"You sure? You've barely said a dozen words since you got in the car."

"Still half asleep, I guess."

"Why don't you put the seat back and sleep?"

"I'm okay, thanks."

He let it go.

$$\int \int \int$$

I hadn't been to as many funerals as Jake, though I'd been to more than I liked. This was my first at eight o'clock in the morning. It seemed indecently early. The sun was barely over the yardarm, and the fog had yet to burn off as we stood in Santa Barbara Cemetery, overlooking the ocean.

Politicos, war heroes, and Hollywood stars all kept each other company in those misty fifty- some acres of grass and trees and stone. John Ireland, who played many a hard-boiled bad guy in films, rested there — as did Vera Hrubá Ralston, who insulted Hitler after winning the silver in the 1936 Olympics. Ronald Colman and Laurence Harvey — Kenneth Rexroth, the poet and essayist who believed in transcendent love. Supposedly Rexroth's was the only grave to face the ocean, which was the kind of trivial information my brain stored by the bushel.

Maybe the early hour explained the lack of attendance. The only other fellow mourner was a woman in an expensive dark pantsuit, Audrey Hepburn sunglasses, and a dark hat. She stood across the freshly dug grave from us. It would be hard to say who was more curious: her or us.

The service was generic and short. As the pastor read from Psalms, my attention wandered. It was probably one of the most beautiful graveyards I'd seen: acres of palm trees and ornate tombstones — and that spectacular view of the ocean with the silver and green morning tide rolling in.

Unobtrusively, I studied the woman across from us. It was hard to tell what she looked like beneath the hat and the sunglasses. Despite her trim figure, she wasn't young. Maybe midsixties.

…As far as the east is from the west,

So far has He put our transgressions from us.

The Lord has established His throne in heaven,

And His kingdom rules over all.

Bless the Lord, all you His angels,

You mighty in strength, who do His bidding.

A pretty innocuous send-off for Dan Hale. In the back of my mind I kept hearing Martha Tilton singing, "We kiss and the angels sing and leave their music ringing in my heart…"

When the pastor had finished his reading, he asked if any of us would like to share our personal memories of Dan Hale. We unanimously declined.

That was pretty much it. The pastor offered up another prayer. Jake bent his head, his expression sober. He'd had a lot of practice at gravesides, and I knew he was taking as careful stock of the woman across from us as I was — only less obviously.

The service ended, the woman placed a bouquet of red roses on the casket, shook hands with the pastor, and walked away. Poised as a fashion model on the runway, she picked her way through the gravestones and wet grass.

Jake started after her. I put a hand on his arm. "Jake, I think that's Jinx Stevens."

He threw me a startled look, nodded. He caught up to her quickly.

I heard him say, "Ms. Stevens?"

She stumbled in the grass, and he reached to steady her. "I'm sorry?" Her face was unreadable behind the glasses. Her voice was alarmed.

I joined them as he stated in that calm, authoritative way, "Excuse me, ma'am. You're Jinx Stevens, aren't you?"

She opened her mouth. I was sure she was going to deny it. I think Jake's cool certainty — the cop vibe — undid her. The strong, fierce line of her body seemed to soften. She seemed smaller, older.

She answered in a husky contralto, "Stevens was my maiden name." She didn't offer her married name.

Jake introduced himself and me.

"You're private investigators?" The alarm was back. "Who are you working for?"

I said, "Actually, he's the PI, and he's working for me."

"Working for *you*?"

Jake reiterated, "We just want to ask you a couple of questions, ma'am."

"About?"

"Jay Stevens. Your brother."

There was another inward struggle. I wished she'd take off the damned glasses. "What about him?"

I tried to break it gently, but her attitude was hard to read. "Did you know that Jay's body was recently recovered?"

The impenetrable black glasses faced me. She said at last, "English…you own the bookstore where they found him."

The business owner in me felt obliged to clarify. "He wasn't in the bookstore, but…yes."

Jake said, "So you did know his body had been recovered?"

"I knew."

Yet she had made no attempt to claim his body. That seemed peculiar by any standard.

"The police have been asking for anyone with information on Stevens to come forward." Jake reverting to form.

She said stiffly, "I don't have any information on Jay's death."

"But —"

She cut me off. "I know what you think. Just take it for granted, you're wrong."

Few people are able to take that for granted.

Jinx added, "I loved my brother. I never loved anyone more. But my life now is complicated."

Oh. *Complicated.* I didn't say it. I left it to Jake to say. "Okay. We can respect that. What can you tell us about Jay?"

"I don't understand?" The black shades turned his way. "Are you — Why do you want to know? Surely after all this time? Fifty years?"

"There's no statute of limitations on murder."

"Murder." She repeated the word, but not as though she was shocked or surprised by it. More...trying it on for size. "It *was* murder?"

"You must have suspected that something bad had happened to him. You went to the police after he disappeared."

She nodded. "Yes. I knew Jay didn't run out on us. That was never his style." She considered us. "How is this your business? You're not the police."

"No. But the police are giving me a hard time because your brother's remains were found on my property. I hired Mr. Riordan to look into his death."

"What can you possibly hope to discover after all this time?"

I shrugged.

"How will it change anything?"

"I don't know if it will change anything."

"So it's simply curiosity?"

I didn't have a real answer for her. Curiosity *was* part of it, but it wasn't the only reason I wanted answers. Nor was I genuinely afraid of police harassment. I looked at Jake. He seemed to be waiting for my response too. "I guess I feel a responsibility to Jay."

"*Why?* Why should you?"

"Because what happened to your brother was wrong. Because murder is wrong. And…I know about it. And knowing about it, it would be wrong to walk away."

"You're a real weirdo," she said.

She turned to walk away, but she was headed for the chapel, not the cemetery gates. We followed her through the pines and majestic cypress, past the small though elaborate family mausoleums. Jake said under his breath, "Every once in a while I think you'd have made a good cop."

Inside the chapel, it was dark and cool and private. Jinx slid into a pew and began to pray. Jake stood at the back, leaning against the wall, waiting patiently. I sat down in a nearby pew and looked around. The chapel was built in 1926 and designed by George Washington Smith, a Santa Barbara architect who was interred in one of the walls. I studied the surprisingly contemporary ceiling frescoes — the garlands of lilies and peonies, the nuns and monks with their candles and serene faces.

Jinx finished her prayers and stood up. She said to me, "All right. I'll tell you what you want to know. It's all over now anyway."

I glanced at Jake. He raised his eyebrows but said nothing.

We followed her outside. The fog was lifting. It was going to be a beautiful day.

Jinx lit a cigarette, took a few impatient puffs. "I adored Jay. Everyone did."

Not everyone, clearly. I didn't point that out.

She added, "But he was a…a scamp. Like the song. *Exactly* like the song."

"Song?" Jake inquired.

I offered, "From *Lady and the Tramp*. 'He's a Tramp' by Peggy Lee."

"That's it. We used to do that number." Jinx's smile was reminiscent. She took another quick, almost-guilty drag on her cigarette.

"This was back when you were singing with the Moonglows?"

"That's right. We used to play a regular gig at Danny's." She glanced back at the cluster of trees sheltering Hale's plot. "Danny owned a club in Malibu called The Tides."

"We talked to Hale right before his death. You were engaged at one time, weren't you?"

Another one of those flashes of alarm. "You talked to Danny? When?"

"Monday."

"What did he say?"

"For one thing, he told us you used to be engaged."

"That's true," she said reluctantly.

"But you didn't marry. What happened?"

She said with a saucy spark of the girl she must have been, "It's a woman's prerogative to change her mind."

"You must have had a reason for changing it."

"Yes." She stared at the blue haze of ocean. "There was quite an age difference between us."

I couldn't help noticing that she was only in her sixties, quite a bit younger than everyone else who'd turned up in the case so far.

"If you don't mind my asking, how old *were* you back in the day?"

"Seventeen."

"Jeez."

Her smile was wry. "I looked older. I *was* older. We grew up faster in those days, for all the vaunted sexual experience kids boast about now. I'd grown up on the road. Jay — well, we were all the family we had left — but yes, technically, I suppose I shouldn't have been anywhere near The Tides."

It was a guess based on the fact that she was the only mourner at Hale's funeral; I said, "Even if you didn't marry Hale, you must have still had feelings for him. You paid for his treatment at Sea View Manor. You paid for this funeral, didn't you?"

Shock — or maybe anger — flared. "How did you know that?"

"Is it confidential information?"

"It most certainly *is*."

"We're not planning to share it with anyone."

Jake interjected, "What did you think happened to your brother all those years ago?"

"I thought…" Jinx's voice faltered; then she said steadily, "It's true that I believed he was dead. I was afraid — but it's not as though I had any idea or suspicions. It was only fear."

That was so obviously a lie, it wasn't even worth responding to.

"Can you think of any reason at all why someone would have wanted your brother dead?"

She shook her head. "I always assumed it was some terrible accident or misunderstanding."

It had taken her fifty years to talk herself into believing that — and she still wasn't sold.

Jake inquired, "Do you remember a police detective by the name of Nick Argyle?"

"*Nick Argyle.* My God. I haven't thought of Nick in years." She gave a throaty laugh, dropped the cigarette to the path, and ground it out with the pointed toe of her shoe. "Is he still around?"

"Hale and hearty," Jake said.

"Get a load of that. He must have been older than any of us, except maybe Danny." She still had that sentimental curve to her mouth.

"Did you know Argyle believed your brother was a criminal? He had a theory that Jay was a cat burglar and that you were his accomplice."

She gave Jake a long, direct look — or seemed to. It was hard to tell what was going on behind the shades. "Did he?"

"He did. He said for a period of about two years, you and your brother pulled off a series of high-profile cat burglaries in the Los Angeles west side."

Jinx gave another of those husky laughs.

"I notice you're not denying it."

"Sure. Well, it was true."

"You admit it?"

"You're the one who brought up the statute of limitations, and it's long expired." She added flatly, "Not that I want that information leaked."

"Do you think your brother's death had something to do with your sideline in burglary?"

"No."

She said it too quickly. And why not take what was an easy out? Either she already had her own suspicion as to who had knocked off Jay, or she intensely disliked that idea for other reasons.

"You don't think any of your brother's criminal associates...?"

"No. My brother didn't have criminal associates. We worked alone always."

"Who fenced the goods?"

"He's long gone. An antique dealer in Chinatown on Chun King Road. His name was Turkey Lancaster."

I repeated. "Turkey?"

She shrugged. "It was so odd, I never forgot it."

Jake said, "I heard a rumor that your brother might have been killed because he knew something about valuable World War Two artifacts."

She stiffened. She was fast on the recovery, though. "No."

"You never heard anything like that?"

"No." Unwisely, she added, "I'd be the first to know, right?"

"What do you think happened to him?"

"That hotel was a dump. Dopers, whores… Believe me, you've no idea. There were scumbags there who would have robbed Jay blind in a second if they could've got away with it. I always thought that it must have been something like that. A robbery that went wrong."

"Were you living there too?"

She shook her head. "I was living with Dan."

At seventeen. Terrific. Speaking of statutes, that was statutory rape right there. One thing was for sure. Jay Stevens might have been a charmer, but he was one hell of a guardian for a young girl.

She looked at her watch. "I'm sorry. I've got to go. If I spend any longer, it's going to cause comment."

With whom? I wondered.

Jake asked, "Is there a private number where we could get in touch with you?"

She was shaking her head. "I'm sorry. No."

"You're not going to claim your brother's body?"

"I've had fifty years to come to terms with the idea that my brother is dead. That…that shell you found is not my brother. And Jay would understand my decision."

Her chin rose challengingly. Neither of us argued.

Jinx walked unhurriedly down the asphalt drive, past the Celtic crosses and stone monuments. As she disappeared into the shade of the tall trees, Jake ordered, "Wait here."

He went after her, moving fast but unobtrusively through the manicured grass and flat grave markers. I doubt if she had any idea she was being followed.

He was back a short time later with the license-plate number of her black limousine.

"Well done," I approved, rising from the stone bench where I'd been waiting.

He tucked the slip of paper into his pocket. "Not a bad morning's work."

"She's married. She's wearing a wedding ring."

"She could be widowed."

"True. Either way she's worried about someone finding out about her connection to Hale."

"She's a woman of affluence and position now. You can tell by the clothes and the car."

"And the attitude."

His mouth curved. "That's the attitude of privilege. You have it too."

"*I* have it?"

"You're more gracious about it, but you were born to it. And you have nice manners. But you're definitely used to getting your way."

"*I'm* used to getting my way?"

He frowned and looked around the graveyard. "Is there an echo out here?"

It took me a second to catch on — the bastard was laughing at me. "Hey, they're hiring at the Comedy Club, Riordan."

"I'll keep my day job."

That reminded me of a couple of things, and my smile faded. "Jake? Listen…"

We were headed back to the parking lot ourselves by then. He glanced at me.

"You're right. I mean, what you said in the car when we were driving back on Tuesday. I don't know what's wrong, but I'm all over the map right now. I know I'm not being fair to you."

He seemed to be waiting for me to say something else. When I didn't, he said, "Here's what I believe. Based on what I know of you, I don't believe you allowed yourself to think much about what happened between us for the last two years. So you're trying to deal with it now — along with trying to come to terms with getting shot, and heart surgery, and the fact that I want back in your life. And the truth is that, in addition to not trusting me, you're angry and you're hurt by what went before."

He sounded as cool and clinical as a lab technician discussing a suspicious slide.

"Not bad, Dr. Freud," I retorted. "What treatment do you suggest?"

Bewilderingly, he put his arm around my shoulders and pulled me over to him as we walked. I was so nonplussed that Jake — *Jake* — was hugging me in public (if you were willing to count a graveyard), I missed half of what he replied. Sure, it was merely a casual hug, a hug between buddies, but there was a time, and not long ago, when he wouldn't have touched me in anywhere resembling public with a ten-foot pole.

"…then there's Guy and Mel and who knows who else," he was saying. "If it was only a matter of giving you time to work through it, I'd give you all the time in the world. If you think I don't know I owe you that —"

"You don't owe me," I said irritably.

"But I don't think it's that."

"So you're leaving?"

He said carefully, "It's not an ultimatum. I think it's the best move for a lot of reasons."

I shrugged off his arm. Stopped walking. "What if I ask you not to go?"

He stopped too. "Is that what you're asking?"

"Jesus, Jake. You say you're not giving me an ultimatum, but… you are. I told you I didn't want you to go." I shook my head. "Don't you get it? I can't think clearly about this with the threat of you leaving hanging over me."

"Is that what it feels like?" he asked slowly. "A threat?"

"That's what it feels like, yeah. You said you'd give me time, but it feels like you got fed up after five minutes and decided to walk. I can't promise you—" I stopped, tried again "—that I can let go of everything that happened between us. As much as I want to. As much as I feel like I should. You've called it right. I'm angry, and I guess I am hurt. I want to trust you…but I don't even trust myself anymore. All I know." I had to stop again. I took a deep breath, steadied my voice. "All I know is, I can't… face you leaving right now."

He looked pale beneath his tan. "All right." His voice was gentle.

"And I know it's not fair. I know you've got this great job offer, and I know you're losing the house and your family's flipping out. I know —"

"Baby, you win. You can take the brass knuckles off." His smile was crooked, though the tone was still uncharacteristically gentle. "We'll leave it for now. Okay?"

The relief was staggering. I felt almost giddy. Not once had it occurred to me that he would concede. "Okay."

After that we couldn't change the subject fast enough.

"The logistics of the thing puzzle me," I said when we were in the car once more and on our way back inland.

"Which thing?"

"Stevens was killed and buried under the floor of his room. That requires foresight. At the very least it requires hammer and nails. Not what you'd expect to find lying around in the average jazz musician's bedroom."

"Not exactly the kind of thing you bring when you come calling either."

"You'd have to plan ahead."

"You think someone went to the hotel that night planning to murder him?"

"Doesn't it seem that way to you?"

"The whole thing feels hinky — and has from the first. Why hide the body?"

"Well, that's not unusual, is it?"

"No. It's unusual to hide it under the floor."

"He obviously couldn't move Stevens's corpse out of the hotel without being seen."

Jake was following his own line of thought. "He'd have to rip up the floorboards, lower Stevens down. But that would work. Building standards were a lot looser back in the day. There would have been room for a body between the joists. He'd have to hammer the floorboards back down again. That wouldn't be a quiet process."

"Maybe it wasn't a quiet hotel."

"Even so."

"There's something else that's been bugging me. The construction crew found a bunch of dead rat skeletons in the attic. In the walls, under the floor."

"Nice."

"Too many to have died naturally."

"And you think there's a connection?"

"Both the attic and the third floor were sealed up at one point. I think that explains why Stevens's body was never discovered. I think there was some kind of infestation of vermin, and that part of the building was closed off."

"You think there was construction going on around the time Stevens was killed?"

"I wish there were a way to know for sure. It would explain a few things. It might even help narrow down potential suspects."

"Well, it's pretty clear who Jinx Stevens thinks killed her brother."

"Dan Hale."

"'It's all over now anyway,'" he quoted.

"What would Dan Hale have to do with Nazi treasure?"

He shrugged.

It was a quick drive back to Los Angeles. No side trips today.

As I got out of the Honda, Jake said, "I'll pick you up tomorrow at one thirty for the appointment with Newman."

"Thanks."

I opened my mouth to… I don't know. Say something. It felt like we had crossed some bridge.

He nodded crisply. "Later."

And that was it. He was gone.

I walked inside the bookstore, nearly bumping into a customer coming out.

I apologized and took a closer look at the tall, skinny young man with long blond hair and a goatee. If it hadn't been for the John Lennon specs, I could almost have mistaken him for Warren.

He was staring at me as though I should know him.

I looked closer. Recognition dawned. "*Angus?*"

CHAPTER THIRTEEN

"So when I got your letter, I thought I'd come home."

"Did you want another?" I nodded at the empty plastic cup on the table between us. We were sitting in the indie coffeehouse down the block from Cloak and Dagger. Angus had already had two ice-blended blueberry drinks. Judging by how thin he was, they were the first things he'd had to eat in a while. He made me look robust. Heck, he made Jay Stevens's skeleton look robust. "Or would you like a bagel or a sandwich or something?"

He shook his head. "Did you mean it? About my having my job back if I wanted it?"

"I meant it." If I hadn't been sure before, I was now. The kid had obviously had a rough time of it. He looked years older beneath the mahogany tan. "We're going to have to figure out what your legal status is."

"What do you mean?"

"I mean that you were cleared of involvement in Kinsey Perone's murder, but you might have been implicated in the deaths of Karen Holtzer and Tony Zellig. I don't know. I'll talk to Jake."

"That asshole Riordan?" he said, energized by loathing.

"That's the guy. If you have a problem with that —"

"No problem," he said, instantly cowed.

"Have you been in Mexico the whole time? What did you do for two years?"

Angus said hopelessly, "Whatever I could. I worked as a mason, as a houseboy…I picked fruit." He sounded exhausted, as though he'd done all of it in the last hour.

"Why didn't you come home?"

"There was nothing to come back for. Wanda didn't want me anymore. My family didn't even want to talk to me."

"Where are you staying?"

He looked at me, his sad eyes meeting mine, flicking away, darting hopefully back.

I sighed, studying him, drumming my fingers on the table as I tried to think what to do. "Okay, listen. I'll loan you a sleeping bag and an air mattress, and you can stay in the bookstore till you figure out something better. I'll pay you to be my...I don't know. Night watchman, I guess."

His breath caught, and he looked like he was going to burst into tears.

"In the daytime, you can have your old job back, but...you need to pay attention to this. My sister — my stepsister — is now also working in the bookstore. You need to...I don't know. Be careful of her."

He looked puzzled, and I didn't blame him. "Forget it."

He nodded.

I rose. "Let's go talk to Natalie and get this settled."

"Um, Adrien?"

"Hmm?"

"I guess I *would* like a sandwich."

∫ ∫ ∫ ∫

The Formosa Café started life as a trolley car on Santa Monica Boulevard in West Hollywood. The last time I'd had lunch there, Paul Kane had broken it to me that he and Jake were lovers — and had been for at least part of the time Jake and I had been together. Indigestion and the Formosa were now synonymous in my mind, and probably always would be.

It was still a great place, though, with a lot of history, and it was hard to imagine a more suitable setting for meeting the old PI Harry Newman.

Newman was already seated and enjoying cocktails and hors d'oeuvres when we arrived.

He smiled unrepentantly as I sat down across from him in the red leather booth and said, "How are the folks back in Milwaukee?"

He offered his hand, and we shook. "Can't blame a guy for trying."

"No, that's generally left to the courts."

He laughed. "I like you, English."

"I'm so relieved." I made more room for Jake on the leather bench. Our eyes caught, and he gave me that wry twitch of his mouth.

"Let's order," Newman said, "and I'll tell you everything you want to know."

He'd been busy familiarizing himself with the menu while waiting for us to show. When the waiter arrived he requested another mai tai to go with his calamari. Then he ordered a rib-eye steak and wasabi mashed potatoes. The most expensive items on the menu. Jake went, predictably, for the Kobe-beef burger. I went for the salmon.

"You're not drinking?" Newman said suspiciously. "I don't trust a guy who doesn't drink."

I ordered a glass of red wine and sparkling mineral water. Jake ordered a mai tai.

"A mai tai? I've never known you to drink mai tais."

"This is the new me," he said. "See what a fun guy I am?"

"By the way," Newman said, "I believe you have something belonging to me."

"Like what?"

He pointed to the impossibly black strands coyly arranged on his head.

"The rug? It makes a great cat toy."

He choked, but our drinks arrived then and he launched into his tale.

"You want me to start at the beginning? For me, the beginning was Louise Reynard."

"That was Stevens's girlfriend?" I asked. "The one who hired you to find him after he disappeared?"

"You got it. She taught art history at Immaculate Heart College. Pretty girl. Woman, you'd say. Hair the color of dark molasses and big, wide eyes. Very French looking. She used to always wear these silk scarves." His index finger made a twirling motion next to his neck. "In fact, her grandfather had fought in the French Resistance, which is where the story really starts, I guess."

Jake said, "She wasn't a nun?"

"A nun?" I repeated.

"Immaculate Heart was a Catholic college. My mother went there."

All this time and it hadn't occurred to me there might have been a heavy dollop of Catholic guilt in Jake's sexual hang-ups.

"Definitely not." Newman took a sip of his drink. "Stevens was a thief. A high-class cat burglar." He paused. When we expressed no surprise, he continued. "One night he robbed a house somewhere in Los Angeles. He never did tell Louise the location of the house or the name of the man he ripped off, so don't ask. If she'd known, she'd have gone straight to the fuzz after Stevens disappeared."

Instead she'd gone to Jinx Stevens, and Jinx had waited to go to the police. Not that it mattered if Jake was right and Stevens had been dead, already placed under the floorboards.

"Stevens only got away with one item that night, but it was a prize. A carved gold cross studded with rubies and agates and pearls. He didn't know exactly what he had, but he knew it was old, and he knew it was special. So he made a sketch of this cross, and he took it to a college art department that seemed safely out of the way, and that's how he met Louise. He was looking for information on the cross."

"And she just happened to recognize this cross?" I was skeptical.

"You betcha. Right away. Louise knew *exactly* what he had. The Cross of Rouen."

He was gazing at us expectantly. When neither of us spoke, he said, "That's a place in France."

"*Je ne comprends pas.*"

"The Cross of Joan of Arc."

"Uh…" I looked at Jake. He looked blank. "You mean the Cross of Lorraine?"

"No."

"I've never heard of the Cross of Rouen."

"Well, the story I heard, it was the cross belonging to Joan of Arc. However, that's sort of beside the point."

"It is?"

"The point is that the Cross of Rouen was a priceless national artifact, and it was supposedly carted off by the Nazis during World War Two."

"Supposedly?"

"Yep. Louise knew that this cross had disappeared when the Nazis occupied Rouen. Naturally she wanted to know how Stevens had got hold of it. She took it kind of personal, seeing that her grandmother died during the war, and her grandfather fought in the Resistance."

"Stevens wouldn't tell her?"

"No. Well, he promised he would tell her eventually. He said it was complicated."

"He had an accomplice," Jake commented.

"Sure he did, although he told Louise he didn't." Newman took another sip of his mai tai. There was a thin line of pink foam on his mustache. I watched it, fascinated, as he spoke. "Here's the thing — and you can take it for what it's worth, but I guarantee Louise believed this to be the truth — Stevens told her he was going to give her the cross to return to the French people on behalf of her grandparents."

Jake and I exchanged looks. "That wouldn't go over very well with the accomplices."

Jake was more cynical — and practical. "Why would he?"

"That's the funny part of all this. According to Louise, she and Stevens fell totally and completely in love at first sight. Not only was he going to give her the cross, he was going to go straight for her." He snorted at what he read in our expressions. "I know, I know. But she believed it till the day she died, and I'll tell you something else. She was a smart lady. Educated, sure, but she had street smarts too. She was nobody's fool. And like I said, a good-looking dame."

"When Stevens disappeared —"

He cut me off. "Louise suspected foul play from the first. See, Stevens disappeared the very night he was supposed to bring her the cross. When he never showed, she went straight to Stevens's sister and then Dan Hale. Of course they both denied having any idea about what she was talking about. She always believed they were both in on it. On stealing the cross, I mean. Hale claimed Stevens took off for greener pastures. The kid sister did eventually go to the police to file a missing persons report."

"Did Louise believe Hale and Jinx killed Stevens?"

"She thought it was not inconceivable. Hale, in particular, was a pretty rough customer, for all the surface polish. She also thought there was another possibility." He waited for us to connect the dots.

I said slowly, "That whoever Stevens stole that cross from figured out who took it and came after him?"

"Very good." To Jake, he said, "Bright boy."

"Like a shining star."

I got sparkling-mineral-water bubbles up my nose.

"Right," Newman said. "Because whoever had that cross sure as hell had no business having it. Louise thought this ex-Nazi war criminal might have come looking for Stevens. See, aside from the considerable monetary value of that cross, having the thing found in his possession was tantamount to a confession. You can see there would have been considerable incentive to get it back and silence the thief."

"Oh yeah."

Jake said, "But Stevens never told Louise where he recovered the cross?"

"No. But she had a theory about that."

Louise sounded like a girl with a lot of theories. I liked her. "What happened to Louise?"

"Breast cancer. She died ten years ago." It was clear he'd been fond of Louise.

Jake asked, "What was her theory as to the identity of this Nazi war criminal?"

"She believed him to be a friend of her grandfather. A Wilshire Boulevard art gallery owner by the name of Guilliam Truffaut." Newman said, "Truffaut was supposed to be another former member of the French Resistance. In fact, he'd built quite a reputation for himself as a slayer of Nazis."

"Did you talk to Truffaut?" I asked.

"I talked to everyone." Newman shook his head. "You won't understand this, and I can't quite explain it myself, but there was something about Louise that… You found yourself doing things, taking chances you'd never have dreamt of before."

"I've known a Louise in my time," Jake said.

A Louise?

I looked up, surprised. Jake was staring right at me. My heart skipped a beat — absolutely nothing to do with repaired valves.

The waiter arrived with our meals, and the extraordinary moment ended.

After our plates were set in front of us and the waiter had gone, I asked, "What did Truffaut have to say when you interviewed him?"

"He denied everything and threatened to sue me." Newman shrugged. "Dead end."

"Did you believe him?"

"No. No, I didn't. But I never quite believed he killed Stevens either, although Louise remained convinced of it. Me, I always figured Dan Hale did Stevens in for trying to pull a double cross."

I thought this over. "If Hale had killed Stevens, wouldn't he have had possession of the Cross of Rouen? He seems to have died close to destitute." I viewed Newman over the rim of my glass. "You already figured that out, which is why you tried to search the bookstore."

Another of those unrepentant smiles. "Knew it was going to be my last chance. Like you say, if Hale had the cross, he'd have had the money to save that club of his — that was the only thing he ever really cared about. Well, and maybe Jinx Stevens ran a poor second. That doesn't mean Hale didn't kill him, though. Just that he couldn't find the cross. Stevens could have hidden it."

"Why did you wait so long to try to search the bookstore? Renovations started in May."

He admitted ruefully. "I only noticed what you were up to a couple of weeks ago. I'd sort of forgotten about it, you see? Fifty years is a long time."

More than my lifetime. More than Jake's lifetime. Yes, I did see.

"Was there anyone else you suspected in Stevens's disappearance?"

"Well, yes and no. Stevens was living with a bunch of dope dealers and thieves and whores in that hotel. It's not impossible someone there might have knocked him off. Hell, someone might have knocked him off for his clarinet. Or his hat."

Jake said, "The only problem with that theory is, it's doubtful that kind of lowlife would know where or how to dispose of a valuable art object. It would have surfaced by now."

"Probably."

"You said you talked to everyone. Did you ever talk to the cop in charge of the case?"

"Argyle? Yeah. But he always insisted Stevens had skipped. I never did believe that. No one ever saw Stevens leave the hotel that night."

"Is that surprising, though? It was pretty much of a roach motel by then, wasn't it?" I sampled the salmon.

"Plenty of people saw Stevens getting visitors that night. I don't know why they'd have missed him leaving."

And of course, Stevens hadn't left.

"What visitors did he get?" The sauce on the salmon was sweet. Not something I cared for. I pushed my plate aside.

"Hale, Jinx Stevens, the piano player from the band…"

Jake took my plate, slid his over. Absently, I picked up his burger. "Paulie St. Cyr?" I questioned and took a bite.

Newman nodded. "That was it. Paulie St. Cyr."

The burger was pretty good. "If the Cross of Rouen was hidden in the building, someone would have found it by now. I guarantee my contractors would have uncovered it. They've been through the entire structure — and dismantled half of it."

"I figured that much." He chuckled. "I'm no fool. I know when to cut my losses."

"What happened to the sketch of the cross?"

"Wondered if you'd remember to ask about that." He reached into the pocket of his red Hawaiian shirt and pulled out a folded paper. "This is a copy. Louise kept the original. Look it up in the art books. You'll see it's genuine enough."

"Thanks." I took the sheet, unfolded it, and studied it. Jake leaned over to look.

It was a cross fleury, similar to the fleur-de-lis. The arm ends were carved in gem-studded flowers. The top arm passed right through the body of a dove, and the bottom fleur had a deadly-looking point at the top. Even in this rough black-and-white sketch, it was impressive.

I met Jake's gaze. I could see what he was thinking. Plenty of motive for murder right there.

"Is there anything else you can tell us?" I asked Newman.

"Nah. If you think of any more questions, I'll be happy to answer them. We could have lunch again."

We left him enjoying chocolate volcano cake for dessert.

"What do you think?" Jake asked as the valet opened the passenger door to the Honda.

"I think he's telling the truth. I think he was in love with Louise Reynard."

He glanced at me. "Same here."

He tipped the valet, took his keys, and slid behind the wheel. He slammed shut the door and said, "So that's it. You found Henry Harrison, and you know what he was searching for. Satisfied with that?"

I felt a jab of alarm as I looked up from the sketch of the cross. "We don't know who killed Stevens. We don't know what happened to the cross."

"You don't seriously think we're going to find this Cross of Rouen?"

I didn't, no.

"I don't know. Look how much we've found out already. We're halfway there."

Jake's head moved in denial. "Here's what I think happened. I think Hale killed Stevens. I think the sister knew that, which is why she didn't marry him. I think Stevens stowed the cross somewhere, maybe a locker in Union Station or someplace like that, and one day it'll turn up, but we aren't going to find it. And

I don't think we're ever going to be able to prove that Hale killed Stevens."

"If Jinx thought Hale killed Stevens, why did she pay for his medical care and his funeral?"

"Maybe she loved him anyway."

I couldn't think of a reply to that. At last, I said, "I'm not ready to give up."

Silence.

Jake said carefully, "I...don't see this going anywhere."

"Maybe not." Probably not. I nerved myself for rejection. "Will you give me a little more of your time?"

He expelled a long breath. "It's your dime."

I'd felt close to him in the restaurant. Physically close, yes, sitting with our thighs and shoulders brushing, but emotionally close too. In tune. Now I couldn't read him. Did he want me to give up? Why? Or was I missing the obvious?

"One more week?" I stared out the window at the valets busily trotting back and forth, shouting friendly insults to each other.

I could feel his gaze. "One more week," he said brusquely and turned the key.

CHAPTER FOURTEEN

It looked as though Jay Stevens had not held the attention of the CCHU for long. When I arrived back at the bookstore, the construction crew was at work once again on the other side of the building.

Over the buzz of sanders and the machine-gun rattle of drills, I could hear Natalie and Angus bickering quietly in the back of the store. I took a sec to enjoy the blessed normality. Lights were mellow, music was playing, customers were grazing peacefully. All was right in my world again.

I settled with my laptop in my office, where I could work and keep an eye on the kids.

I had found a site listing art treasures that had gone missing during World War II, when Natalie tapped on the door frame.

"Come," I said absently.

"Can we talk?"

"Oh God. Please keep in mind that I'm a sick man."

She sniffed. "You look pretty healthy these days."

I felt pretty healthy too. I still got tired faster than I liked. I still found myself needing the occasional nap. My chest still felt like it was liable to separate when I laughed or coughed or sneezed. But overall, I did feel better than I'd felt in a long time. I even felt...younger.

"Is this about Angus?" I did my best to look forbidding.

It didn't appear to work. Natalie wrinkled her nose and said, "He's kind of weird."

This from the woman who was considering plighting her troth to Warren — *plight* being the operative word.

"I've got two words for you."

Her chin rose.

"Ms. Pepper."

"Oh."

"Do not scare him off, or there will be hell to pay. With interest."

She made a face and departed.

I turned back to my laptop and the missing treasures of World War II.

There was plenty to read on the topic of Nazi plunder, and it was easy to get distracted by the many, many stories of families — often Jewish, though not solely — that had their art collections confiscated by the Third Reich or had to sell their valuables far below their worth to fund their escapes from arrest and execution. Then there was the systematic despoliation of museums and galleries and churches. The Nazis had stolen everything from the paintings of old masters to religious artifacts — and everything in between — and by the end of the war, they had amassed hundreds of thousands of priceless artworks and antiques. Some of those objects had been returned to their rightful owners; shockingly, most of them were still lost or hidden in private collections. Some of them were even in public collections; museums and galleries fighting to hang on to their sometimes-innocent — sometimes not — acquisitions.

The Cross of Rouen was one of many, many such items.

Its provenance was sketchy. According to legend it was the cross Joan of Arc had carried into battle. It seemed unlikely to me that she would have carried anything quite so valuable into battle — especially because there should surely have been an amazing mythology about how this gem-studded gold cross had come into her possession. There was nothing. According to historical accounts, the cross had been taken from her after her capture by the Burgundians, yet it was reputed to have been the cross held up for her to see as she was being burned alive at the stake in Rouen.

So much for the history of the cross. That there had been a Cross of Rouen was inarguable. There were several photos — all black-and-white, unfortunately — of the thing in its original place of pride in Rouen Cathedral. The cathedral had been bombed twice during World War II, though it was sometime during the Nazi occupation of Rouen that the cross disappeared.

Tap, tap on the door frame.

"Yo?"

Angus sidled in, looking downcast.

I knew that look of old. "How are you settling in?" I made myself inquire.

"She doesn't like me."

"She'll get over it."

He looked more downcast than ever.

"Don't take it personally. She's having boyfriend problems."

Angus brightened.

He departed, and I got back to researching the Cross of Rouen.

Generally I liked research, but I was finding it hard to concentrate — and not only because I was being interrupted every twenty minutes.

I didn't understand Jake's reluctance to continue with the case. Was he regretting his promise not to leave town? Was he worrying about what would happen if he didn't grab the job in Vermont while it was available? He wasn't alone in that. I too was worried that I might cost him this job — and for no good reason.

Was there a good-enough reason to prevent his making a new and successful start somewhere else?

I swore under my breath and reached for the phone. Jake didn't pick up his cell. I tried the house.

"Hello?" a woman's voice answered.

Heart thumping, I replaced the phone.

So…Kate was still at the house. That was the most logical explanation. And there were plenty of logical reasons for her to be at Jake's house — not least of which was that it was technically her house too.

Face it. The problem was not Kate or the fact that Kate was at the house. The problem was my own instant and panicked reaction to hearing her voice.

The problem, as illustrated by my reaction, was that I still didn't trust Jake. My instinctive response was…not healthy or productive. And how the hell was there any chance for us if I couldn't trust him?

No, this wasn't about Jake. Or at least it wasn't *just* about Jake. Part of the problem — maybe most of the problem, by now — was me. My inability to accept the fact that, yeah, I might get hurt again. Might get my heart ripped out and fed to me for lunch.

These days I was on a vegetarian diet.

§ § § §

In the evening Lauren and I went to the house in Porter Ranch to swim, and when I got home, I fixed supper for Angus and myself and then spent the hours before bed researching Guilliam Truffaut.

There was a wealth of information on him. He'd been born in Paris and had worked with moderate success as an artist before the war. When the Germans occupied Paris, Truffaut had joined the French Resistance and fought with great cunning and courage to free his country from Nazi tyranny. According to several articles, he had been betrayed twice, was captured, and tortured, both times escaping through his own resourcefulness and ingenuity. After the war he had immigrated to the States, where he had married a wealthy Angeleno socialite and opened a successful art gallery. He became a well-known figure in Southern California art circles and society. He had one child, a daughter by the name of Evelyn.

That was the official bio. It made for impressive reading, I had to admit. In the sixties, near the end of his life, he'd authorized a biography called *Le Coeur du Courage*.

Truffaut had capitalized shamelessly on his war-hero status, but why not, if it were true?

That was the question. If it *were* true, what had he been doing with the Cross of Rouen in his possession?

And if it weren't true, it was one hell of a story for Jay Stevens to make up. In fact, I couldn't believe Stevens would or could make up such a tale. It was too fantastic too — by all accounts — outside the realm of everything Stevens knew. Every lie rested on some building block — no matter how thin — of recognizable truth.

Besides, why should Stevens lie? What would be the incentive for such a lie? He'd come by the cross somehow. He didn't pretend that it was honestly. So why lie about where he'd stolen it?

Shocking though it might be to those who had known Truffaut as successful businessman, loving family man, patron of the arts, and former war hero…it looked to me like Stevens's story was true.

And if it were true, it was one hell of an incentive for murder.

I drank a glass of pineapple-orange juice and considered the possibilities while Tomkins practiced his typing skills on my laptop.

"Hey, go find another mouse to play with." I lifted him off the sofa and put him on the floor. He *meowed* at me. I *meowed* back and started Googling Evelyn Truffaut.

She wasn't hard to find.

It turned out that Evelyn was the child of a second marriage. The first Mrs. Truffaut had died in a car accident in 1960. Truffaut had remarried that year, and little Evelyn had come along eight months later. Supposedly, she was a premature baby, but Jake wasn't the only cynic in the secret clubhouse. Evelyn had been seven when her famous papa had gone to meet his maker — and his former pals in the Resistance.

Truffaut's gallery had closed after his death. Evelyn had opened her own gallery and boutique — Truffauts and Trifles — in Beverly Hills.

It was by appointment only.

Luckily I knew someone with both the commanding presence and the impeccable credentials to get me past the strictest security.

I picked up the phone, dialed the number I knew by heart. A woman answered.

"Lauren," I said, "can I speak to my mother?"

♪ ♪ ♪ ♪

It was a jolt to realize I'd totally forgotten that I'd agreed to see Mel on Saturday. It had so completely slipped my mind that I didn't remember until he showed up at the bookstore to pick me up for a day of swimming and sunning at the Porter Ranch house.

I was listening to Ella Fitzgerald and finishing the last pages of *A Deed of Dreadful Note* when Natalie knocked on the door.

"It's open."

She stepped inside. "Do you have a date?"

"A date? No." As I tried to decipher her expression, realization hit me. "Shit. Is today Saturday? Is Mel downstairs?"

She nodded.

I swore again and put the laptop aside.

"Do you want me to tell him you're not feeling well?"

"What? No, of course not." I considered it hopefully for a second and then said more firmly, "Of course not. Send him up."

She vanished, and a few minutes later Mel was inside the apartment we used to share and checking things out with the keen interest of someone visiting a museum.

"Holy moly. Does this place bring back the memories."

I pulled a T-shirt over my head and called from the bedroom, "I'll be right there. I lost track of time."

"You've still got the grape leaf stenciling I did in the kitchen."

"Uh…yeah."

"And this is the Tabriz carpet we bought at the flea market when we first moved in."

I stared at myself in the mirror over the dresser. My cheeks were flushed, and my hair was standing up in spikes. "You brought this on yourself," I told my reflection.

"Did you say something?"

"I'm talking to the cat."

"I thought you didn't like cats."

"I don't."

"I recognize *this*. This is that half-moon table from your grandmother's ranch."

I stepped inside the bathroom to get my swim trunks, and when I stepped out again, Mel was standing in the doorway of the bedroom that had once been ours. He was smiling meaningfully at me — a smile I remembered as well as he remembered the table.

"You haven't kissed me hello."

I remedied that — probably with more efficiency than enthusiasm, although he didn't complain.

"You look *great*." He cupped my face between both his hands. I'd forgotten how much that irked me. "About one hundred percent better than you did last week. You've got a healthy flush in your cheeks. You don't look as gaunt. Your eyes don't have that haunted look."

Sure. Now they looked hunted. In fact, I probably had the same expression Tomkins did when Natalie tried to kiss his nose.

"You're starting to look like your old self. I admit I was worried that first day. You looked so frail."

"We should probably get going." I smiled politely and freed my face.

"Are we in a hurry?"

"Uh…yes. I'm supposed to be back here in time for…supper at my — Lisa's."

He looked crestfallen, and I felt a flash of guilt at the lie. "I thought we were spending the day together?"

"We are. Mostly."

"I thought we'd have dinner. I had it all planned. Made the reservations and everything. I was going to take you out to the Tam for dinner."

The Tam O'Shanter Inn on Los Feliz Boulevard was where Mel and I had celebrated each anniversary after we had moved in together.

"You always loved the trout," he added.

I said lamely, "I didn't realize."

"Well, I mean, you could call Lisa, right? Tell her you have other plans? Surely she wouldn't mind if she knew we were going out?"

"The thing is…I still get really tired. I don't have a lot of stamina yet."

"It's just dinner. You have to eat."

"So everyone keeps telling me. How about I see how I'm feeling at the end of the day? If I'm up to it, I'd love to go to dinner."

He was a good sport about it, waiting patiently while I grabbed towels and suntan lotion and fretted over other things I might need.

"I've got a cooler full of drinks and snacks," Mel said as we went downstairs.

I bade good-bye to Natalie, who called, "Now don't overdo it, Adrien."

For once it didn't annoy me.

♫ ♫ ♫

The house in Porter Ranch was a two-story pseudo-Tudor affair of cream-colored stucco and artfully placed black half timbers. It possessed steeply pitched roofs and a quantity of pretty windows. There was a cobblestoned driveway and large front and backyards that were meant to emulate English-cottage gardens. A deadly-looking black, wrought-iron fence — suitable for displaying decapitated heads — framed the tiled swimming pool. When I was growing up, my friends and I called the place Somewhereshire.

Mel parked in the circular front drive, and we went inside to change. Even though I'd been out to swim with Natalie a couple times, this was the first time in two years I'd felt compelled to explore the house. Because this place too was full of memories for Mel, and he was curious, I found myself wandering the empty rooms in his wake.

"Looks different without the furniture, doesn't it?" he commented.

I agreed. It hadn't occurred to me before what a beautiful house it was. Seeing it utterly empty was like seeing it for the first time. Seeing the possibilities of it unfettered by memories.

The kitchen had blue granite countertops and glossy barn-wood floors. The hardwood floors were in the dining room too, which offered a spectacular view of the large garden and wild mountains behind the house. The other rooms had plush ecru carpet and fresh white paint over the decorative moldings. A gorgeous set of Palladian windows looked over the front garden.

I went upstairs and checked out the master bedroom with its built-in bookshelves and fireplace. There was a sunken marble tub in the adjoining bath.

"Why haven't they sold it yet?"

"It's haunted."

Mel looked at me and laughed.

We wandered back downstairs, and I headed for the room at the back of the house that looked over the pool. If I lived here, this would be the room I chose for my office. I stared out the window at the pool, sparkling in the bright summer sunlight.

Mel slipped his arms around me.

"How's your dad?" I asked.

"Better each day." He said, suddenly serious, "You're going to think this is crazy, but this is the first time it's occurred to me my parents are...mortal. I never thought about it. And it kind of brings my own feelings of mortality home. Kind of a punch in the gut."

I studied him curiously.

I'd had plenty of time to get used to my own mortality, so Mel's epiphany struck me as...belated, at best. The truth was, his was probably the normal mind-set. Most people probably took it for granted they would outlive —

"You have a funny expression," he observed.

I opened my mouth. Closed it.

His smile was uncertain. "What's up? You look like you saw the ghost you mentioned earlier."

"It's nothing."

Nothing but the realization that I might have to deal with outliving people I loved. Something I'd always comfortably assumed wouldn't be a problem for me.

Something I didn't want to think about.

Maybe Mel saw the trouble in my face, or maybe he had been waiting for me to shut up long enough to make his move. He reached for me, and we tumbled awkwardly to the plush carpet in the spacious, empty room.

I wasn't prepared, and so it hurt quite a bit as my torso twisted, and I reached to brace myself. I was focused on that, on not damaging myself — and not yelling my pain — when it occurred to me that if I didn't want things to progress, I needed to speak up. Mel was kissing me with unexpected passion. I could feel his erection, and to my surprise, my body was responding eagerly, which was a relief. You never knew, did you? But everything seemed to be in working order.

Except that we were working for something I didn't want. Or at least my brain didn't. My body had other ideas. One idea in particular.

I tore my mouth away from his, gulped. "I don't think —"

"You don't have to," he said. "This happens naturally."

He reached for the hem of my T-shirt and pulled it up.

"Wait," I said, but I was too late.

He froze at the sight of my carved-up chest.

"Oh my God," he said. It was horrified and heartfelt. I felt his erection wilt against my thigh.

"Sorry." I yanked my shirt back into place. "I should have warned you."

Mel drew back, sitting cross-legged on the carpet, staring at me.

"Oh my God," he said again.

"Well, what did you think? That it was a flesh wound?" I heard the sharpness in my voice and tried to modulate my tone — his disquiet was genuine, but so was my hurt and embarrassment. "It was open heart surgery."

"I know." He looked ashamed. "I wasn't expecting…"

"You saw your dad after his surgery, right?"

"Right. I mean…right."

What the hell *did* he mean? I straightened my T-shirt, which didn't require further straightening, annoyed that my fingers were shaking. There was probably a bit of frustration in there too. A month was a long time when you were used to having it.

"I'm sorry," Mel said quickly. "It's not…it doesn't mean I don't still want you. You're still…"

"Beautiful?" I mocked.

He pulled himself together — it took visible effort — and reached for me again.

"Come on, Adrien. That's not fair. It was a jolt, that's all. I'd forgotten."

He eased me back, and I let him kiss me. I needed it now. Needed to feel desirable again, to feel that I was still wanted. My ego required stroking, a little TLC.

He was sweet and contrite and reassuring. I tried to relax into it, but it was taking more effort than was conducive to pleasure. And I could feel Mel's tension like a wire stringing him together. His erection was still a no-show, and my own wasn't any perkier.

Eventually I pushed him back. "Stop."

He let himself be pushed away, sitting back on his heels. I stared at him. The simple truth was, I didn't want him. I wanted Jake. I wanted Jake at that instant like some wild thing wailing for the moon. I wanted him so much, I could have cried. I wanted him now, and I wanted it to be three years ago when I had loved him without fear, when I hadn't realized he could hurt me enough to cripple me, destroy me.

Mel looked back at me with, I'm sure, his own fair share of confusion.

"I'm sorry. I'm afraid I'm going to…hurt you. Are you sure your heart's strong enough for this?"

"No," I said bitterly.

I was speaking philosophically, but he lost color.

"Bad joke," I said. "It's a major turn-off for you, isn't it? It would be for anyone."

"No. Of course not. I'm afraid of...doing you harm." He swallowed. "Terrified, actually."

"Yeah." I dredged up a smile. "It's okay. Bad timing. Let's leave it."

He nodded with alacrity and jumped to his feet. "Yes. Look, why don't we swim, and I can...can get used to it."

If a sound escaped me now, it would be something close to a howl, so I clenched my jaw tightly, so tightly, I'm surprised my teeth didn't go out of alignment.

I nodded.

Mel waited for me to speak. I made a herculean effort to say calmly, "Give me a couple of minutes, and I'll join you out at the pool."

"Okay."

He stopped in the doorway, hesitating. "Is — are you —"

"Five minutes," I said desperately.

He turned and left. I heard the slap of his bare feet going down the hallway. I pressed the heels of my hands to my eyes, pushed hard.

When my vision was clear, I stared up at the frosted-glass lamp fixtures overhead.

From in the pool yard, I heard the springy creak of the diving board and the splash of water.

Holy moly.

CHAPTER FIFTEEN

"Adrien?"

I looked up from the laptop screen, focused on Angus's uneasy expression. He blinked nervously behind the specs. "Hmm?"

"She's crying."

I almost made the unforgivable mistake of asking who. I caught it in time.

"Okay."

He ducked out of my office again, and I sighed. It was Sunday morning, the day after my date — my first and last — with Mel. We had managed to get through the rest of our swim date. I wasn't faking it when I told him I was exhausted as we went inside to change back into our street clothes. He had said all the right things, but I knew he was as relieved as I was that the day was over. We'd talked film noir like our lives depended on it on the drive back to Pasadena, and when we'd arrived at long last at Cloak and Dagger, he'd promised to call — although the next few weeks were going to be pretty busy getting ready for the fall semester.

I said I'd look forward to it, and I'd gone upstairs and gone straight to bed.

All the same, things looked brighter today. There was no denying that I was getting stronger and feeling better all the time, and a scarred hide was a small price to pay for being alive.

Accordingly, I stuffed my squeamishness back in the box and went out to the book floor, where Natalie was crying soundlessly into the Dell Mapbacks.

I took a soggy copy of *Armchair in Hell* out of her hand. "Can I take you to lunch?"

She nodded miserably.

We went to Mijares Mexican Restaurant and settled on the back patio with a pitcher of El Presidente margaritas and a basket of homemade tortilla chips and salsa. Three baskets of chips, if we wanted to get technical. The Zone diet had apparently veered into the danger-zone diet.

"It's over," Natalie announced as she demolished the last of the tortilla chips.

"You and Warren?"

Her mouth quivered, though she kept crunching bravely as she nodded.

I wisely kept my opinions to myself. "What happened?"

It was a bit confused. The gist seemed to be that Warren — miracle of miracles — had the good sense to recognize that they wanted different things out of life and each other.

There seemed to be a lot of that going around these days.

"I'm sorry, Nat."

"No, you're not." She glared at me.

"Let me rephrase. I'm sorry this hurts you."

She picked up a chip. Her tears fell in the salsa as she dipped the chip. "He's seeing someone else. He's been cheating on me for *weeks*."

"Who with?" It was hard enough to believe he'd ensnared Natalie — let alone that he could lure another doe into the tar pit.

"Right before the band broke up the last time, they hired a female drummer. Jet."

"What kind of a name is Jet?"

"*Her* name. She has tattoos over her arms. *Both* her arms. Like she's the illustrated woman. And she has a stud in her tongue."

"Owth."

She stared at me and started giggling. This was followed by more tears, then a recital of all Warren's good qualities — both of them — then more tears. We ordered lunch, and I kept plying her with margaritas. When she had talked herself dry but was nicely lubricated, I paid the bill, steered her out to her car. It was still a few days too early for me to drive, but I figured we were safer with me behind the wheel than Natalie. I drove back to the bookstore and put her to bed upstairs.

"What?" I said grouchily when I caught Angus staring at me as I gathered up the invoices Natalie was supposed to have paid that morning.

"Nothing."

"*What?*"

"You just seem…different."

"I am different. I'm an imposter. I killed Adrien two years ago and buried him under the floorboards. My real name is Avery Oxford."

He seemed to think that was unreasonably funny. When he'd stopped guffawing, he said, "You seem the same but…older."

"Uh-huh. I hope you're not counting on a pay raise anytime soon."

"Not *old*. Old*er*. Or more…"

"Wiser? Mature? Worldly?"

He was grinning. "Yeah. All of the above."

"That's what I thought you meant." I held up the invoices. "I'll be in the office taking care of these. Yell if you need help."

"I got it."

To my relief, he did seem to have it. He was catching up quickly, and he was already proving an enormous help to Natalie while I was out of commission. Next week I'd probably be able to start working a few hours a day, and for the first time ever, we'd be adequately staffed.

I felt positively cheerful as I paid the week's invoices.

Tomkins jumped up on the desk and nearly knocked over the can of Tab I was nursing. I saved the precious elixir. "You know, you're well enough now to be reintroduced to the wild. If I let you stay any longer, you're going to lose your survival skills."

He stared at me with those huge green-gold eyes. Moon cat eyes.

"Come on." I rose, scooped him up, and carried him over to the side door. I opened the door, set him outside. He slipped back inside, wound his sinewy self around my shins, and *meowed*.

"Don't give me that. You're supposed to be a feral cat."

"What are you doing?" Angus looked up from reshelving the day's strays.

"Reintroducing him to the wild."

"I don't think he wants to go."

"If you want to go, now's your chance. If I buy you a collar and a license, you're here for the duration."

"Are you talking to me?" Angus asked.

"Don't tempt me."

Tomkins rubbed his face against the blue denim of my Levi's. After a few seconds more, I let the door to the alley swing shut.

Come to think of it, his survival skills had never been all that hot.

♪ ♪ ♪ ♪

When we closed for the day, I cautiously woke Natalie and had Angus drive her home in my Forester. She went out, hand to her head like Ophelia considering the cool sanctuary of the river.

When at last they had departed and the building was quiet once more, I gave in, went upstairs, and called Jake.

I hadn't heard from him since our Friday lunch with Harry Newman. Not that I'd expected to; I certainly didn't imagine he was spending his weekend chasing this cold case when he'd already stated he thought it was a waste of time. And the parameters I'd set made it difficult for him to call me for any other reason.

"Riordan."

"Hey."

"Hey." His voice warmed fractionally.

"Is this a bad time?"

"No. What did you need?"

"What are you working on?"

"My stalker case."

"You mean the case where you're working for the stalker?"

"That's the one," he said tersely.

No wonder he was ready to hang up the PI gig.

"It turns out Guilliam Truffaut has a daughter. Evelyn. She runs an art gallery in Beverly Hills. I've got an appointment to go see her Tuesday. Would you want to come along?"

"How did you manage that? I can't even get her to answer my phone calls."

"Lisa arranged it. So you did know about the daughter?"

"Believe it or not, once upon a time I did actually solve a number of police cases without your help."

He sounded sardonic but amused. I said, "I know. Sorry. It's just that I'm bored."

"You sound down. Everything okay?"

How did he do that? How did he know? Because there was nothing in my voice. I was pretty sure of that.

"Yeah. Pretty much. Just...tired of being tired. I've decided to keep the cat."

"He seems like a nice little cat."

"Yeah. I'm not sure he could make it on his own anymore."

"Why should he? By the way, I did the checking you asked. Your boy Angus is in the clear. His Blade Sable playmates didn't incriminate him." He added, "That doesn't mean he wasn't involved."

"I know. I think he's learned his lesson, though. He's not a bad kid. And I think these two years have been good for him in a way."

"Uh-huh."

"Thanks for checking."

"Sure."

"So about Tuesday…"

"What time?"

I told him, he agreed. I rang off reluctantly.

A second later the phone rang.

I picked up. "Listen, if you're not doing anything this evening, why don't you stop by on your way home?"

An unfamiliar male voice said, "I'll stop by, all right, and I'll bash your ugly face in if you don't leave my mother alone."

"I'm sorry?"

"You heard me. Stay away from my mother."

Admittedly not a threat I get a lot.

"I think you've got the wrong number."

"No, I've got the right number. And I've got your address too. Don't forget it." It was hard to slam down a cell-phone receiver, but he clicked off forcefully.

I stared at my own phone receiver and dialed the code for call return. I'd gotten a lot of mileage from that through the years — people have this innocent belief in their invisibility when it comes to phones, the Internet, and license plates. That day was no exception. The phone rang, picked up, and the same male voice announced, "Chris Powers."

"Hey there, Chris. Are you aware it's a felony to make threats over the phone?"

To give Powers his fair due, he got over his shock within a split second. "Try it, asshole. I dare you. My lawyers will have you for lunch." He clicked off again.

I did what any red-blooded American male would do. I called my big, ex-cop ex-boyfriend.

"What's up?" Jake answered.

"Did you run Jinx Stevens's license plate?"

"I did. I was going to talk to you about that."

"Maybe you should talk to me about it now. I've got a guy by the name of Chris Powers threatening me with bodily harm if I didn't leave his mom alone. I can't think of anyone besides Jinx Stevens who would fall even remotely into the moms-I've-harassed-lately category."

"That would be Chris Powers, the son of the late Bruce Powers."

"*Senator* Bruce Powers?"

"That's the one. Jinx a.k.a. Jane Powers married the senator back in 1967. She didn't drop out of sight so much as reinvent herself."

"No wonder she didn't want to come forward and identify her brother's remains. No way would she be able to fly beneath the radar."

"No. Furthermore, the son is an uptight prick with his own political ambitions. He's married to one of Terry Robinson's daughters."

"As in Terry Robinson, the right-wing, evangelical extremist?"

"Nice to know you do keep up on current events, even if you don't watch much TV."

"People like Terry Robinson are one reason I don't watch much TV." I mulled over these latest revelations. "Okay. So it turns out Jinx Stevens has a past someone might be willing to kill to protect."

"Except that her brother was killed in fifty-nine. Eight years before she'd even met the senator."

"That we know of."

"You've been reading Raymond Chandler again, haven't you?"

"This would be more like Ross Macdonald, but you're right. It does sound like that kind of convoluted Byzantine plotting. Can we talk to Jinx again?"

"I'm going to try to interview her again, yes. *I'm* not having a lot of luck getting past her social secretary."

I didn't miss the emphasis on *I'm*. I said only, "It looks like Jinx — or Jane — confided in her son. He knows who I am and where I live."

Jake said ominously, "Yeah? Don't sweat it. He won't be bothering you again."

"I'm not worried. Don't tangle with some rich right-winger on my account. I'll see my mom against his mom any day of the week."

He didn't laugh, and I said, "Seriously, Jake. I'm not worried about this. I called you because it's a development in the case. I'm wondering exactly how much Jinx told Powers. She could have spun it all kinds of ways and still avoided telling him anything concrete about her past."

"True."

I hesitated. Tried tentatively, "Did you want to —"

"*Shit*," he exclaimed. "Gotta go. I'll talk to you Tuesday."

Dial tone.

I sighed.

$$\int \int \int$$

Monday morning's weigh-in indicated I had gained another half pound. If I kept it up, my jeans would stop falling off me and I'd no longer resemble a scholarly gangbanger. Temperature, blood pressure, heart rate: all normal. My morning routine was becoming so automatic, I no longer thought about it.

I popped my pills, shaved, and thought about getting a haircut.

The day's e-mail brought a note at last from Todd Thomas saying he'd love to get together with the old gang. It seemed clear to me his reading comprehension left much to be desired. He did offer a couple of amusing reminiscences of life on the road with the Moonglows.

Otherwise it was an uneventful day. I finished the manuscript for *A Deed of Dreadful Note* and sent it off by e-mail to my publisher.

I missed Jake — which was funny because I'd managed to go two years barely thinking of him at all. It seemed like from the moment I'd decided we had no future, I'd been unable to get him out of my mind. What was that about?

After breakfast on Tuesday, I went for morning walk. It was hot and smoggy even that early in the morning. The city was noisy, busy, but I felt less threatened by it. More able to cope with whatever the day brought.

In fact, I was looking forward to the day — and to seeing Jake.

When I got back to the bookstore I could hear Natalie and Angus laughing, and my spirits rose. I settled down at the computer and tried a search for "Jane Powers." I found a wealth of info on her. Granted, the bulk of it pertained to the last twenty years. Back in sixty-seven, when she had first popped up on the radar, the media wasn't quite as intrusive or aggressive in its pursuit of political figures. And Jane had not been a political figure. She had been the lovely and self-effacing wife of a political figure. Smart girl that she was, she'd done her best to stay out of the limelight — the best that one could do if one had her heart set on marrying a US senator.

According to the official bio, she was born in New Haven, Connecticut. She had been orphaned at an early age. She had lived with relatives and moved around a lot. She had put herself through college — Scripps, a college for women in California — graduating with honors in '66.

I admired the shrewdness of it. The bare facts were accurate and verifiable. The real story was in all that was left out. Putting the pieces together, I guessed that after her brother went missing,

Jinx had left Dan Hale — I concurred with Jake that it looked on the surface like she had believed Hale had been, at the least, partially responsible for Jay's disappearance — and dropped out of sight. During those missing years, she had attended Scripps College.

Senator Bruce Powers's younger sister was also a student at Scripps and had provided the intro. After marrying Powers, Jinx had proved the perfect political wife: beautiful, intelligent, charming — and very much in the background. Literally. She was literally smiling in the background of nearly every photo of Bruce Powers.

In '69 she had delivered a set of photogenic twins: Christopher and Charlotte — and helped secure her husband's reelection. The Powerses were the perfect political family, a California dynasty.

I was deeply engrossed in the tale of Charlotte's messy divorce when Jake arrived — shortly before Lisa was due. Which was good, because I wanted time to warn him that she was accompanying us on this jaunt to Beverly Hills.

"Hi," I said, coming out to meet him. Jake smiled, a white flash in his tanned face. He was wearing tailored slacks and a sports shirt in a deep forest color that brought out the green in his eyes. He looked relaxed and handsome and successful. I was happy to see him; it felt natural to move to kiss him hello.

I instantly realized my mistake. Kissing in public? Kissing in front of Angus and Natalie and for all the world to see? I was already pulling back, trying to make it look like I'd sort of lost my balance and weaved forward, when he stopped me — hand on my shoulder — and kissed me.

Just a casual graze of mouths. Just a taste of him. Just as though we had been kissing each other hello in public for years.

I had to reach back to steady myself on the sales desk.

"Hi," Jake returned.

Instinctively I looked around, expecting... Natalie was smiling as she flipped through a stack of sales receipts, Angus had his back to us as he spoke to a customer, the customer wasn't paying attention — no one was paying attention. No one thought anything of that kiss. That casual brush of lips that could never have happened five weeks earlier.

No one seemed to notice what felt like one of the most important moments of my life.

Even Jake was looking at me like he was about to ask if I was feeling all right.

The shop door bells jangled, and I looked over expecting to see Lisa. Instead I got a gander of Detective Alonzo's smiling face headed our way.

"Well, well, well," he greeted us jovially, his gaze zeroed on Jake. "It's the Hardy Boys. Dick and Peter."

"Ugh," Natalie said. It could have been her hangover talking, though it did nothing to defuse the situation.

Alonzo's broad face took on a dusky hue, and his shoulders bunched up with defensive aggression. "I got more questions for you, English." To Jake, he said, "And you step one inch out of line, Riordan, and I'll bust your ass. You're not a cop, remember? You don't get to hide behind your shield now, and you don't get to use your authority to cover up for your little playmates anymore."

It was like waving raw steak in front of a grizzly. Jake's head snapped up, his expression cold and dangerous. His body went relaxed and alert — the way a fighter readies himself. I could see in a flash exactly how it was going to play out. Jake was going to pulverize this asshole — boyishly enjoying every minute of it — and then he was going to get thrown in jail for assaulting a police officer and lose his license and probably go to prison, where he would die in a massive riot because he couldn't control his goddamned temper...

I moved to meet Alonzo, smiling my best and most practiced smile. "Whoa, Detective. Did you hear what you said? And in front of all these witnesses?"

I think it was the smile that stopped him cold. You didn't expect to be greeted by smiles when you were doing your best impression of the Incredible Hulk.

"You walked in here and, without provocation, insulted me and Mr. Riordan — and then threatened us."

Alonzo had been so focused on Jake, so intent on his goal of getting Jake to throw that crucial first punch, I didn't believe it had occurred to him that these people standing around were technically witnesses. Recognition didn't calm him down any, and I had to wonder how he'd passed the academy psych test. Maybe his antipathy for Jake was an anomaly.

Or maybe not. I remembered something Jake had said when Alonzo was investigating Paul Kane: that Alonzo hated fags, hated intellectuals, and hated being wrong. Put it all together, and he was one boiling mess of resentment and frustration. On top of that, he was ambitious, and he believed Jake had kept him from solving the kind of homicide case that made careers.

So I guessed it was reasonable that he hated my guts — nearly as much as he hated Jake's.

Unfortunately he was the kind of guy who didn't know how to reverse when he found himself in deep shit. He kept spinning his wheels, digging in deeper. He came toward me, saying, "The hell I did. Nobody is going to give a damn what your family says."

Jake's hand fastened around my upper arm like a vise. I expected to be tossed out of the way any second, so I kept talking. "Come on. I already know the Stevens's case is closed. I got a call from the detective in charge of the case at the CCHU. This is harassment, and we all know it. Everybody in this room knows it. You can stand here and rant and rave, but you're not going to provoke the reaction you want."

Alonzo stopped again. He was nearly in arm's reach of Jake now — and how they both dearly wanted me to shut up, move out of the way, and let them at it. I could feel it in the tension of their bodies. They were practically quivering with it. And yet...

and yet…Jake was listening, waiting, and watching — he wasn't going to throw the first punch. He was still in control. The grip on my arm was more purposeful than punishing.

Even Alonzo was still in control enough to take a step back and say, "Oh yeah? We'll see. We'll see if it's over."

The first step was the hardest. Having managed it, he began to retreat toward the door, jabbing his finger at Jake as he said, "I'm not forgetting you, Riordan. Not for a minute. This is not over."

"It *is* over," I said. "I'm going in my office now to call your boss and file a complaint. It's over, and we all know it."

He was less than complimentary as he slammed out of the store.

"My gosh," Natalie exclaimed. "Is he *crazy*?" Over her shoulder, I could see Angus's horrified face.

"*You're* going to file a complaint?" Jake queried. He still had hold of my arm. Belatedly, it dawned that he had not been planning on throwing me aside; he'd been trying to restrain *me*. "That's a new one."

"Believe it. I'm sick of this juvenile male posturing. There's a reason we have laws, and there's a reason why police, more than anyone, need to be respectful of those laws."

There was a line from *The Lady in the Lake* I could have quoted him: "Police business is a hell of a problem. It's a good deal like politics. It asks for the highest type of men, and there's nothing in it to attract the highest type of men."

When Jake recognized that he had failed to live up to his responsibility to uphold that law, he had resigned. He had had the honor and the courage to step away. Not every man had that in him; I thought probably very few men did.

"Yeah, but you've never…" Jake said slowly, disbelievingly, "Are you trying to protect me?"

"What if I am?" I said shortly. "What about it? Can't it go both ways?"

I couldn't tell if he was amused or offended. He seemed at a loss for words. At last he said simply, "Sure it can, Adrien. Thank you."

CHAPTER SIXTEEN

"Have you ever been to London, Jake?" Lisa asked.

"No," Jake replied.

"We're thinking of spending Christmas this year in London."

Jake's eyes met mine in the Forester's rearview mirror. We were on our way over to Truffauts and Trifles in Beverly Hills. Lisa was riding up front, while I sat in the back and recovered my equilibrium after my showdown with Detective Alonzo. Once the adrenaline had faded, I felt drained. Proof that I was still a ways from my usual self.

I said, "I haven't committed to Christmas in London. I haven't committed to Christmas anywhere."

My mother was clearly amused. "Darling, Christmas happens whether you commit to it or not. Why not spend it in London? We had a lovely time in London when you were ten." She confided to Jake. "He was *such* a wee imp."

"I bet."

What a shame Jake was an excellent driver. The likelihood of us all being wiped out by a semi anytime soon was scant, no matter how hard I wished it.

"What do you think about Christmas in London, Jake?" Something had happened to change Lisa's attitude toward Jake, and I couldn't figure out what it was. It was as though she had decided, out of the blue, to call for a cease-fire. She wasn't grilling him, exactly, though her idea of chitchat would have made an SS officer quake in his shiny boots.

"I like Christmas with the family."

I stared out the window as a *Variety* billboard flew by. What would Christmas be like for Jake this year? Would his family have come around by the holidays? I thought of how desperately I'd wanted to spend Christmas with him two years earlier.

I wondered what I'd be doing for Christmas if Lisa took everyone overseas for the holidays. I glanced forward, and Jake was watching me in the rearview mirror again.

I smiled faintly. His mouth quirked in response.

"I can't leave the store unattended for that long."

Lisa made a small sound of impatience. "I don't see why. You've hired that boy back. Surely he can handle the holiday trade?"

"We're a lot busier than we used to be. That's why I'm expanding the bookstore."

She bestowed on Jake the smile that usually turned strong men to puddles. "If you haven't noticed how *obdurate* my darling son is, let me warn you now."

He grunted.

"He's supposed to be developing a more healthy lifestyle. The doctors are adamant about that. I haven't seen much sign of it so far."

"Speaking of healthy lifestyles, if you don't want me to fling myself from this speeding car, you'll stop discussing me like I'm not here."

A muscle moved in Jake's cheek. Either he was keeping himself from saying something he'd regret, or the bastard was trying not to laugh.

"Of course, darling." Those arched eyebrows spoke volumes. She confided to Jake, "Naturally, like all men, he's sensitive about his health. I imagine you're strong as an ox?" She didn't actually pat his muscles or ask to check his teeth, but I did get the impression she was trying to determine his market value.

Jake seemed focused on the traffic — which, granted, was heavy.

Lisa sat up straighter in her seat. "This junket should be amusing. What's our cover story?"

"Cover story?" Jake questioned.

I said, "I can't think up a suitable cover story for asking if someone knows whether her father was a Nazi war criminal. I think we're going to have to wing it."

"*Hm.*" My mother sounded very much like Emma when Emma did not approve of the vegetables on her dinner plate.

Jake's eyes found mine in the rearview mirror. "I've got interesting intel on our friend Harry Newman."

"What's that?"

"Nick Argyle said that Louise Reynard never confirmed hiring Newman."

"Are you serious?"

He raised one broad shoulder. "According to Argyle, there's no confirmation that Newman was ever working for anyone but himself."

"Where does Reynard fit in? *Was* she Stevens's girlfriend?"

"That part of the story appears to be true. She did evidently convince Stevens's sister to go to the police —"

"*If* Jinx is Stevens's sister."

"What? Where did you come up with the idea that she might not be?"

"It's probably crazy, but it occurred to me the other night that just because Jinx and Jay said they were brother and sister, doesn't prove that they were."

"Ah," Lisa said. "*Crime passionnel.*" She was powdering her nose.

"So you're theorizing that Jinx and Jay were married, and she killed him in a fit of jealous rage? Why would they pretend to be brother and sister?"

"Because she was underage. Because if she were his wife, he could have gone to jail for statutory rape, but if she were his sister, he was only guilty of being a lousy big brother."

"I admit it's an interesting theory. Where does the Cross of Rouen fit in?"

"She took it, sold it, used the money to go to college, where she met and married Senator Powers."

"Are you talking about Jane Powers?" Lisa inquired.

I nodded.

"Darling, that's ridiculous. I've known Jane for years. She's no more capable of murder than I am."

"I think anyone is capable of murder, given the right set of circumstances."

Astonishingly, she said, "Killing, yes. Murder, no. I would *certainly* kill to protect my family. Could I commit cold-blooded murder? No." She looked at Jake, smiled sweetly, and snapped shut her compact.

∫ ∫ ∫ ∫

Eve Adams-Truffaut was tall, thin, and auburn haired. She looked remarkably like Katharine Hepburn, something she was undoubtedly aware of as she affected Hepburn's boxy, mannish style of dress, a vaguely '40s hairstyle, and a certain educated drawl.

The gallery itself was the perfect background for her: stark, elegant, immaculate. According to what I'd read on their web site, T&T specialized in eighteenth- and nineteenth-century European antiques, art, and collectibles. Furniture, clocks, sculptures, paintings, silver, glass, chandeliers — I loved antiques, and for the first few minutes after our arrival, I was in danger of forgetting why we were at the gallery.

"A very fine Italian opaline and crystal chandelier. All original glass. Circa 1902." Eve languidly steered us through the long and spacious showroom with white walls and floor tiles the color of old blood. "A steal at thirty-five thousand dollars."

"Lovely," my mother murmured.

"Or this perhaps. A French nineteenth-century belle-epoque gilt-bronze chandelier decorated with leaves."

"That *is* nice," I admitted.

"A mere nineteen thousand six."

Jake made a pained sound behind me.

"It's rather small," Lisa objected.

"We'll call it nineteen thousand," Eve said carelessly.

We moved on to the paintings, which were upstairs. The staircase leading to the second level was wide and steep, but I experienced no distress climbing it. Granted, I didn't run up.

The gallery was another long white room, though ornamental shutters blocked out harmful sunshine. Strategically placed lights threw dramatic shadows on the paintings lining the walls.

"Ernesto Ricardi. Oil on canvas. *The Chess Game*. Signed. Sixteen thousand five hundred."

"Is that an Atkinson Grimshaw?" I asked, moving past to a small green and gold oil of a moonlit harbor.

Eve followed. "John Atkinson Grimshaw. Yes. Eighteen seventy-nine, oil on canvas. *Moonlight at Whitby*."

"Beautiful." It was classic Grimshaw. Glowing window lamps, shiny, wet streets, sparkling moonlit water, luminous night skies. It looked mysterious, haunting, magical.

Eve's sherry brown eyes glinted. "Do you like it?"

"Very much."

Jake must have thought it was time to intervene on behalf of my ailing wallet. "Have you heard of a piece called the Cross of Rouen?"

Eve considered. "I don't believe so. What is it?"

"A cross," Jake said too patiently.

"You mean an actual cross? Such as a crucifix? *Not* a painting?"

"Right."

"Are you in the market for such a piece?"

"Yeah." He just didn't look like a guy in the market for a crucifix.

"Is it an original?"

Jake looked at me. I said, "I'm sure it is."

"Really?"

I said, "To be honest, it's a fifteenth-century religious artifact plundered by the Nazis during World War Two. It's made of carved gold and studded with rubies and agates and pearls."

"Oh? We only handle eighteenth- and nineteenth-century works."

Jake and I exchanged another look. She was too blasé to be anything but serious.

"The legend is that the cross belonged to Joan of Arc. She was supposed to have carried it into battle."

"That doesn't sound very practical."

"It's only a legend, but the cross itself existed," I assured her. "I've seen photographs of it in art-history books and on the Web. It was kept at Notre Dame Cathedral in Rouen. It disappeared during the Nazi occupation."

She made a moue with her mouth — not a bit like New England Kate Hepburn. "A lot of things did. They turn up now and again. I could put feelers out."

Since she seemed to have no qualms about such details like returning or making restitution for stolen cultural assets, I said, "Had you really never heard of the Cross of Rouen? Because we'd heard from a fairly reliable source that your father might have had possession of it for a period of time."

"Oh my God," Eve exclaimed. "Daddy was a Nazi war criminal, blah, blah, blah."

The three of us gaped at her. She gazed back as placid as a cow in a field of buttercups.

"Then you have heard the rumors?"

She raised her slim shoulders in a distinctly Gallic gesture. "But of course. In fact, one reason my mama closed the original

Truffaut Gallery was there were too many questionable pieces among the inventory."

"Questionable pieces? You mean...items were correctly identified as those stolen or forcibly sold during the occupation of France?" Lisa inquired.

I looked at her in surprise. Meeting my gaze, she said, "I saw a wonderful program on Lifetime, darling. It was all about a book called *Nazi Looted Art*. It was fascinating."

"It is fascinating," Eve said in that polite, slightly bored voice. "However, it was very embarrassing for my mama. So she closed the gallery and sold off most of the inventory posthaste."

"You're saying your mother believed your father was an escaped Nazi?" That was Jake going straight for the legal jugular.

Eve scrutinized him reflectively. "Among other things. The family joke is that my father murdered his first wife so he could marry my mother."

That was some familial sense of humor. Whom was she related to? The Borgias?

"What does your mother think?"

"Mama passed away nine years ago, but I don't think she would have been utterly confounded to learn it was true. My father was...an original."

I couldn't help remarking, "So were Vlad the Impaler and Adolf Hitler."

"Don't be bourgeois, darling." Lisa gave me a chiding look. To Eve, she said, "So if your father had this priceless religious artifact in his possession, and someone nicked it, would it be reasonable to assume your father would be willing to kill to get it back?"

Most people would be shocked by such a forthright question. Eve didn't bat an eyelash. "From what I know of my father...let me simply say that nothing would surprise me." I could believe that, since not that much *did* surprise her.

She moved past us to straighten the Grimshaw painting on the wall. When she stepped back to examine it, she planted her Gucci loafer on Jake's instep. "Sorry." She smiled charmingly. "I suppose you're hoping I have a certain special recollection of my father? That I can tell you I remember seeing him acting suspiciously one dark and stormy night? But I was only seven years old when he died. I thought he was wonderful."

"Naturally," my mother returned.

Eve tilted her head, eyeing the painting critically from the other angle. She said absently, "To say that my father would be willing to kill is not to say that he *did* kill. I think many people would want to kill in those particular circumstances. Would they kill? I don't know. I can tell you, my father had a very strong sense of self-preservation — I imagine that could have been a determining factor either way. For what it's worth, my mother didn't believe my father was a Nazi. She believed he did what he had to do to survive, but that there was no malice intended, no philosophical or political agenda. He simply wished to live and prosper. You can hardly blame a man for that."

I thought you probably could. I thought if anything, it made it worse to go along with atrocities if you didn't believe in the cause that motivated them. But she was not asking our opinion. Life was different on her planet.

♪ ♪ ♪ ♪

While Jake and I waited in the car for Lisa, who had remained inside to complete some suspicious transaction, we talked it over.

"Aside from the fact that she's living in Cloud Cuckooland—"

"Oh yeah," Jake agreed. "She's telling the truth. As far as she knows it."

"If Truffaut did kill Stevens — and I can totally believe that he did — what happened to the cross?"

Jake said, "Mama Truffaut sold it off when she closed the gallery."

I leaned forward against the front seat. "That makes sense. I don't believe Eve was prevaricating — even when she should have been prevaricating. I don't think she'd ever heard of the Cross of Rouen. And she probably forgot about it five minutes after we walked out the door."

"It confirms Stevens's story as far as where he found the cross — which seems to confirm Newman's story. I don't know how he'd have found out about the cross otherwise."

"So he *was* hired by Louise Reynard, regardless of whether she admitted it to Nick Argyle. Why do you think she denied it?" I asked. I couldn't seem to tear my gaze from the crisp, precise line of the hair against the back of his neck. It was a strong neck, but somehow there was something boyish and almost vulnerable about his nape. I had the strange desire to lean forward and kiss it.

I resisted.

"He didn't say she denied it, just that she never confirmed it. She might have been afraid of getting Stevens in worse trouble."

"She did go to the police, though, once he went missing."

"Yes. Argyle told me she made a nuisance of herself once Stevens disappeared."

I said, "I didn't get the feeling Newman was lying."

"Neither did I."

We fell silent as Lisa returned to the car with a small, rectangular, brown-wrapped parcel.

"What's that?" I asked uneasily.

She was busy with seat belt. At last, she looked over her shoulder. "It's either a housewarming gift or a Christmas present."

"You haven't decided?"

"*You* haven't decided," she said. "Or you don't realize you've decided."

$$\int \int \int \int$$

"Did you want to stay for dinner?" We were back at Cloak and Dagger. Jake had parked the Forester, let Lisa and me out, and was climbing back into his S2000.

He said awkwardly, "I can't. I'd like to. Rain check?"

"Sure."

"I'll call you." His eyes met mine. "We need to talk."

My heart sank. "Oh."

I knew what he was going to say. The case was closed. As closed as we were likely to get it. We both knew it. The most likely scenario by far was that Guilliam Truffaut had come looking for his missing property at the Huntsman's Lodge — and had decided to leave no witnesses. How he'd known to look for Jay Stevens was something we would probably never know.

And if the case was closed, there was really no reason for Jake to be calling me all the time or staying for dinner — or anything else.

"Anyway, you've got your writing group tonight, right?"

I'd totally forgotten. The weird thing about convalescence was my internal clock seemed to be off. I couldn't keep the days of the week straight.

"Right."

"I've give you a call Thursday."

"*Thursday?*" I reddened at the giveaway tone of voice. Jake didn't seem to hear it. "Thursday," I reaffirmed stalwartly.

He caught my arm as I started to turn away. I glanced back. "Behave yourself."

"It shall be so." I walked away to open the side entrance for Lisa, raising my hand in farewell as the Honda rolled away with a purr of its well-tuned engine.

∫ ∫ ∫ ∫

I flexed my culinary muscles that evening and made chicken salad with walnuts and black olives, which I ate on whole-wheat toast and washed down with a glass of low-fat milk. It seemed to me that I was getting the hang of this healthy-living stuff, and if everyone would stop giving me a hard time over working too hard and having too much stress in my life, I'd be back to normal in no time.

I was restless and dissatisfied after the writing group had departed. I put a DVD into the player. Tomkins made himself at home on my lap while I watched *The Dark Corner*. It was a 1946 film-noir gem directed by Henry Hathaway and starring a feisty Lucille Ball and painfully bland Mark Stevens. The film has art thefts, troubled PIs, and sinister Germans. The last time I'd seen it was several years ago with Mel, but the memory brought no pain. It was distantly pleasant, as though it had happened to someone else.

The cat purred as I stroked his soft, soft fur.

I wondered how Jake planned to tell me what we both already knew. Probably as carefully as possible. I couldn't help my instinctive dread at hearing the words *we need to talk*. The last time he'd said it — but no. Those weren't the words.

"I need to talk to you."

That was it. How could I forget? And he'd told me Kate Keegan was pregnant, and he was going to marry her. That he wanted the marriage to work, wanted it to be a real marriage. That it was over between us.

It had been Christmastime, and I could still remember the scent of cinnamon and pine whenever I thought of that afternoon. Christmas carols had been playing, and outside, the window-shoppers had walked past talking and laughing, cars had flashed by carrying evergreens, and life had gone on in a blur...

CHAPTER SEVENTEEN

Jinx — Jane — Powers was not happy to hear from me; however, she did take my call.

"I didn't realize you were Lisa English's son," she said in that smoky, smooth contralto. She sounded peevish, as though I'd deliberately played a trick on her.

"I didn't know you were Chris Powers's mom," I returned.

She had an expressive voice. I could hear the unease. "Do you know Chris?"

"Not exactly. He called threatening to bash my face in if I didn't stop picking on you."

In the silence between us, I could hear Natalie and Angus bickering on the book floor. I listened. It didn't sound serious. I took a sip of Tab.

Jinx Stevens's exasperation carried all the way from Santa Barbara. "Chris shouldn't have done that. He's overprotective."

"He's something, that's for sure. Why? That's the question. It's not like I was pestering you for another interview. What's he so worried about?"

"Clearly you know exactly what he's worried about." She was no-nonsense now. "My son has political ambitions, and there are things in my past that might prove embarrassing to him."

"He doesn't think having Cat Woman for a mom is a selling point with the neocons?"

Natalie carried in a box of battered paperbacks and shoved them on the already-crowded shelf. There was a Dell Mapback on top. *The Blackbirder* by Dorothy B. Hughes. Now *that* was a very collectible book. I automatically reached for it.

"What do you want?" There was no anger in Jinx's voice, only a vast weariness.

It occurred to me that she had lived with the threat of blackmail and exposure for half a century. A long time to bear that burden. No surprise she was tired. I wondered if she ever secretly hoped it would all come out and she could stop worrying. Or maybe she'd been worrying about it so long, it was second nature, a part of her.

"Look, if you didn't kill Jay, I have no —"

"*Kill Jay?*" If she was acting, she'd gone into the wrong segment of the entertainment industry. "Are you out of your goddamned mind?"

"If I'm off base here, I apologize, but it occurred to me that you and Jay might not have been brother and sister."

I had to hold the phone away from my ear. One thing for sure, she could still hit those high notes. Her vocal range was as clear and strong as ever. When she had wound down at last, I said, "I apologize. I'm very sorry. That was way out of line."

"Where on earth would you get such a crackbrained idea?"

"I write mysteries. I get crackbrained ideas."

"I loved my brother. I adored him. He was my hero."

"Please don't scream at me anymore. I have a theory. Another theory. Would you like to hear it?"

"No." But she didn't hang up.

"My theory is that you thought you knew who killed your brother — and that's why you left Dan Hale."

Silence.

"I think you loved Dan Hale nearly as much as you loved your brother, but Jay's murder was something you couldn't forgive. Or forget."

"You're wrong." It was the jaded, world-weary tone again. "I forgave Dan long ago."

I blinked. So in the end it was this simple?

"Hale confessed?"

"No. He never did. We never spoke of it after the night I accused him and walked out."

She gave another of those heavy sighs. I had the brains not to interrupt.

"That was a terrible night. The worst night of my life. I didn't see Dan again for nearly twenty years. By the time we met again…neither of us had any desire to dig up those memories. What was the point? We had both moved on. Nothing could bring Jay back."

"If Hale never confessed, why were you so sure he was guilty?"

"There was no other possibility. I knew Jay hadn't skipped town."

"What about Guilliam Truffaut?"

Another of those ringing silences. She said as precisely and carefully as though she were picking the letters out of alphabet soup, "How do you know about Guilliam Truffaut?"

"I spoke to Harry Newman."

"Who?"

"Harry Newman. The PI Louise Reynard hired after Jay disappeared."

"I…I'd forgotten. How strange. Yes, Louise did hire a private investigator. She was desperate to find Jay. She believed from the very first that something terrible had happened to him." Jinx's laugh broke off sharply. "Then you know everything."

"Not really. I'm not sure why you were so convinced Hale was guilty. I'd have put my money on Guilliam Truffaut. The guy who stole the cross in the first place. Did you know he was suspected of murdering his first wife?"

"*W-what?*"

"That's according to one of his biggest fans. Not a nice man, by all accounts."

Jinx seemed to think this over. "Jay did say we needed to be careful. That we might have bitten off more than we could chew that time."

"The way it sounds, Truffaut was a traitor to the Resistance, maybe even a Nazi collaborator. And if even half of his war experiences are true, he had the necessary skills, ruthlessness, and resources to commit murder and hide the body of your brother. Plus, he had the strongest motivation of anyone I've come across yet. If word got out about his having the Cross of Rouen in his possession, he'd have been facing a lot worse than a prison stretch for theft."

The line was live, although she wasn't speaking.

"Why did you think Hale killed your brother?"

"Because he threatened to."

"Hale threatened to kill Jay?"

"Yes. And he went to his hotel that night. I know because Paulie — Paulie St. Cyr — saw him arrive as he was leaving."

"Why was Paulie St. Cyr there?"

"He was picking up musical score sheets. He didn't speak to Danny, though he did see him go up."

"But that's pretty circumstantial. Why did Hale threaten to kill Jay?"

"Because of that goddamned cross. Jay wanted to turn the cross over to Louise. She was practically insisting on it. Her grandmother died in a concentration camp, and her grandfather had also fought in the French Resistance. In fact, her grandfather was a great friend of Truffaut's."

"He knew Truffaut?"

"Not in the Resistance. At least, I don't think so. They met here. And naturally they became close. Louise wanted to give the cross to her grandfather to return to the French people. She wanted to unmask Truffaut. Reveal him for the traitor she believed he was."

I was getting lost. "Wait. How did Hale know about any of this? Was he involved in the burglaries too?"

"Yes. Danny was our silent partner. He set up the jobs, and he arranged for a fence to move the stuff we stole. Once we hooked up with Danny, we did very well. Much better than we'd ever done on our own. Then Jay fell for Louise, practically overnight, and somehow she convinced him of this crazy idea she had about turning the cross over and going straight. And Danny was furious. *Of course.* It was the biggest haul we'd had and he desperately needed the money to keep the club afloat. He couldn't believe Jay was considering handing over the cross — let alone giving up our burglary sideline. They argued and argued over it."

"If Hale killed Jay, what happened to the cross? He'd have sold it, right?"

"Yes. If the cross was where he could get at it."

"But the cross *would* have been there, because Jay was taking it to Louise that night. Where else would it be?"

"I don't know. It wasn't found in his room at the hotel obviously. I had to accept that Danny had followed through on his threat."

"I don't think Hale killed your brother. I think he told you the truth. I think he went to the hotel that night to have one last shot at talking Jay out of giving up the cross."

"So who…?"

"I think Guilliam Truffaut killed Jay and retrieved the cross. I think that's why the cross never surfaced again. Guilliam was the one person who would know better than anyone why that cross couldn't be sold to anyone."

I could hear her breathing; it sounded like she was trying not to cry. I didn't blame her. If she had loved Hale as much as I thought she had, it would be pretty hard to face knowing she had ended their relationship for nothing.

Not that Hale had been any prize — and she'd done all right for herself with the senator — but in blaming him for her brother's death, she'd wronged Hale. Badly. Betrayed him.

Why? Why had she been so quick to believe the worst of him?

"You were at the Huntsman's Lodge that night," I said. "Was there construction going on?"

"There was always construction going on. The place was falling down around their ears. I remember one thing. They were putting poison out for rats. You could smell the dead rats in the attic."

I guessed that explained why no one had paid attention to the smell on the third floor. It sure explained why Jinx was living with Dan Hale and not her brother.

I said, trying to work it out for myself, "The thing I still don't understand is, you loved Hale. I don't know why you wouldn't trust him when he told you he didn't —"

"You've never been afraid," she said harshly. "You're like my own kids. You've been protected and pampered all your life, and you don't know what fear is. Not real fear. Not gut-wrenching, piss-your-pants, do *anything*… You know what it is? It's a dark tide sweeping in and pulling you out into the deep. Way out. And you go with it even when you know you should fight, even when you know the end will be your destruction, because you're too afraid not to. You'll trade your soul for one day, one hour, one minute more of safety. It's why people do the things they do — that dark tide dragging them along like an undertow."

She was still talking. I didn't hear the rest of it. I was thinking about the war, and how people closed their eyes to the terrible things around them, did terrible things themselves — Guilliam Truffaut was perhaps that kind of villain. Or perhaps another kind. And I thought of Paul Kane and of the dark, remorseless tide that had nearly taken me and Jake on the *Pirate's Gambit* only a few weeks earlier.

I thought how Jake had swum in that dark tide for most of his life, and yet somehow kept from going under.

And I thought how naively, a few seconds earlier, I had said to her, *"You loved him. I don't know why you wouldn't trust him."*

I put the phone down softly.

§ § § §

I had only been to Jake's house in Glendale once before, but I found it without too much difficulty. I guess I had been paying attention that day.

I parked on the opposite side of the shady street. It was a nice house, well tended and in good repair. There was a FOR SALE sign planted squarely in the tidy lawn.

Parked in the driveway was a small blue pickup truck. The bed was loaded with cardboard boxes, potted plants, and a couple of framed pictures.

I went up the brick walk, and the screen door banged open. A tall, slender woman with red hair and green eyes walked out holding a cardboard box.

I moved back, and she gave me a long, measuring look. I think I'd have known her for a cop even if I hadn't realized who she was.

"Hi. I was looking for Jake."

She continued to assess me; she called over her shoulder, "Jake. It's for you."

She moved past me down the brick walk and disappeared around the corner of the house.

From where I stood, I could see through to the dismantled dining room and the glass door — open — leading onto the brick patio, where Jake was sliding open the screen. He walked through the dining room. I saw by the way his shoulders stiffened that he'd recognized me before he reached the entranceway.

I said, "I don't have to ask if it's a bad time. I should have called."

"What are you doing here?"

"I need to talk to you."

I need to talk to you...

"The phone still works as far as I know." He shoved the door screen open, and I stepped inside. "Out back will be better." He turned to lead the way.

I followed him out into the tidy square of the backyard. A hose lay glistening in the grass like an emerald snake spilling water sluggishly into the yellow roses lining the wooden fence.

"I was going to call you," Jake said. "You'd better sit down."

I didn't like the expression on his face. I sat down on the nearest wooden patio chair.

A sleek German shepherd puppy came gamboling from around the side of the house, a blue rubber ball in its mouth. He had a reddish black coat and one tipped ear. He trotted right up the brick steps and dropped the ball on my feet, gazing at me expectantly.

"Hey, where did you come from?" I stroked his head, looking up at Jake. "Is this the puppy from Nick Argyle's ranch?"

He nodded.

"I didn't realize you'd gone up to Ojai again."

"I've been there a couple of times talking to Argyle."

"You like that old copper." I tugged gently on the pup's silky ears. "You didn't say anything about buying this little guy."

"Yeah, well. I thought I'd get him trained and give him to you for your birthday."

I didn't know what to say. I couldn't keep a dog. Where the hell would I put him? And this was going to be a *big* dog. The oversize paws on my knees told the story. And yet, as I gazed into those shiny-button, laughing eyes, I felt myself smiling back.

"And if I'm wrong and you don't want him, I'll hang on to him." A reluctant smile tugged Jake's mouth. "He grows on you."

I picked up the puppy — ouch, fat little bastard — and leaned back in the chair. He proceeded to frantically lick my chin. I lifted my head out of reach. "All the way over here, I was trying to think what to say. It turns out I have the worst timing in the world. Maybe you should tell me your news first."

The screen door slid open behind us. Jake turned as Kate said, "I guess that's everything."

They were both calm and controlled, but it was obvious how much in pain they were, and I realized exactly how bad my timing was.

She was staring at me, and Jake said quietly, "Kate, this is Adrien."

"Adrien. Well." Her tone was flat. "We meet at last."

I nodded, putting the puppy down and belatedly rising. I didn't know what to do or say. Not something covered in any etiquette book I'd read. Why the hell hadn't I thought of this? What was I doing intruding here?

"I'll walk out front with you," Jake said to Kate. He gave me an indecipherable look, and they went inside.

The puppy picked up the blue ball and dropped it on my foot in reminder. I picked it up, forgot, and threw. For a racked instant I thought I'd snapped the wires holding my sternum together. The puppy tore off down the yard barking like a demented a squeak-toy.

After what seemed like a very long time, Jake came back. He walked to the edge of the patio and stared out at nothing.

I said, "I should have called first."

"You said that."

He continued to stare out unseeingly at the clipped and trimmed yard and the puppy galloping up and down the grass, the ball in its mouth.

"I'm sorry, Jake."

He didn't seem to hear.

"Is there anything I can do?"

Probably not, since I didn't currently exist.

The puppy dropped the ball on the bricks and looked up hopefully. Jake bent automatically, snatched up the ball, and threw it. Hard. It slammed into the wooden fence with a force that sounded like it cracked the board.

I rose, went inside the house, rummaged around until I found the bottle of Wild Turkey. There was a shelf half full of clean glasses in the cupboard. I poured a stiff drink and brought it out to the patio.

He looked at the glass, looked at me. His brows rose. He took the glass and tossed back the bourbon.

"Another?"

His grin was crooked. "Thanks. No. I don't think drinking tonight would be a good idea."

"Do you want me to go?"

"Yeah."

I nodded, turned away. As I reached the screen door, he said, "Adrien, no. Don't go."

I came back and leaned against one of the wrought-iron posts propping up the metal patio roof.

He threw the ball to the puppy a few times more. "You know what I thought the first time I saw you?"

"No."

"Point of no return."

"Huh?"

"I *knew*. I knew from the second I laid eyes on you, everything was going to change."

I'd had a similar feeling. Granted, I'd expected the change to have something to do with a lengthy prison sentence.

"I don't even know what it is about you. Why I couldn't forget you. I tried. Believe me. You're smart enough, but you're not a genius. You're funny, but you're no comedian. You're beautiful, but —"

"All this flattery is going straight to my head."

He didn't smile, still preoccupied with his own mordant thoughts. I thought of the words of the Renaissance philosopher Michel de Montaigne. "If you press me to say why I loved him, I can say no more than because he was he, and I was I."

I said, "You know what I thought the first time I saw you?"

The hard smile he gave reminded me of that first time. "You were scared to death."

"I was. And I never wanted anything as badly as I wanted you."

The smile faded. His eyes were wary, waiting.

"And I still am. And I still do." I drew a breath. "And if you haven't changed your mind —"

We met halfway.

There were faded squares on the bedroom wall where pictures had once hung. An empty drawer thrust out of a tall dresser as though sticking its tongue out. The king-size bed was minus any quilt or comforter.

The sheets were a pale yellow like fading sunshine. There was nothing in the room to remind me that it had ever been Kate's — and nothing to remind me that it was still Jake's. It was a room in transition — like a hotel room, like a waiting room.

We sat on the edge of the bed, side by side, and undressed each other with tremulous fingers, careful and slow. I didn't believe we had ever been this tentative — not even in the very beginning. Perhaps especially not in the very beginning. We gave each other plenty of time for second thoughts, for a change of heart. We were polite with the buttons and respectful of the zippers. And all the while we watched each other's face, eyes locked.

The somber darkness in Jake's eyes hurt my heart. In that moment I would have given him anything in my power.

He undid the last button, pushed the shirt back off my shoulders. He glanced down at my chest.

"Ugly, isn't it?"

I heard the rough intake of his breath. "Is that what you think?"

"Oh it is," I said easily. Somehow I knew the ugliness didn't frighten him any more than it frightened me.

He bent his head and kissed the curve of my neck, said against my flushed skin, "Nothing about you could be ugly to me." I shivered despite the warmth of the room, the heat of our bodies. He pushed me back in the smooth used sheets, and he kissed the lowest point at my sternum, working his way, his mouth nuzzling up that tender pink ridge — stinging and soothing at the same time. It tickled and made me want to laugh. It melted my guts and made me want to cry. I tried to hold still, not wriggle away, finally relaxing as his mouth nibbled and kissed its way beneath my jaw and at last found my mouth. We kissed long and hungrily.

Passionate kisses, the intoxicating exchange of breath and saliva — and something more intimate — something there was no real name for, like a spark catching between us and taking light.

How had I forgotten this? How had I been satisfied with anything else? Guy...Mel...it was like choosing celluloid kisses over the real thing. The real thing was raw and powerful and dangerous...but it was the real thing. Had I really believed I could make do with safe substitutes?

Jake tasted of bourbon and sorrow. I opened my mouth to his tongue, the rough velvet push against my own — claiming me as I was claiming him. This sultry afternoon, wooden blinds knocking against the wall, the hum of bees outside the window, the distant buzz of a plane off to faraway places was merely another link in the chain. There seemed a strange, sweet continuity in this tentative, cautious coupling, and yet it somehow felt like the first time as we made love in the wreckage of Jake's dreams.

It *was* the first time. The first time we were together with no secrets and no restrictions. It was us naked…in every way.

We kissed until we were out of breath. Jake lifted his head. He said, "I'd given up. What made you change your mind?"

"I guess I finally caught up on my sleep."

He didn't smile.

I stared at him, at the silver-gold at his temples, the tiny lines at the corner of his eyes, the stern but tender line of his mouth. It had to be the truth from now on. "Because nothing could hurt worse than never seeing you again. I can't do it. It's breaking my heart."

Though my vision blurred, I could feel his gaze like a caress, like a kiss against my eyelids, lingering at the corner of my mouth. He spoke so quietly I had to strain to hear, "You remember asking me if I'd ever begged?"

I wiped the corner of my eyes, sniffed. "Is this about to get kinky?"

"Do you want it to?"

"Mmm." I hastily wiped my nose. "Maybe. I read this thing about silk scarves and feathers once. I wouldn't mind trying that one of these days."

His mouth quirked. He said gravely, "I'll keep that in mind. No, this was a conversation we had where you said you thought I'd never begged for anything in my life."

"And you said you did beg once — and you got what you asked for." I waited, wondering if I was going to like what I was about to hear.

Jake said, "When your heart stopped on that fucking boat." The sudden fierce glitter in his eyes had to be a trick of the light. "I begged then."

I couldn't think of a thing to say. It was the last thing I'd expected. Almost the opposite, in fact, of what I'd expected.

"I've never been that afraid. Not even close. I worked over you, and I called you every name in the book." His face twisted. "I cried. And then I begged. You're damn right I begged. I promised — not that I had anything worth promising — but I was willing to give *anything* for you to be able to walk away from that." His smile was the rare one, the wide and unguarded one. "And you did."

I caught a ragged breath. Sat up so fast, we nearly head-slammed each other. "Jesus, Jake. If that's true, why the hell can't you *say* it?"

He looked confused.

"If you *do* feel that way, then why have you never said it? It would have helped. Because to *not* say it at this point feels like you have some reason for not saying it, that you're making some point by not saying it."

He was shaking his head. "I don't know what you're talking about. Of course I — what do you think this is about?"

"Knowing and believing are two different things."

He was looking at me like something had been lost in translation.

"Why can't you say it?" I hardened my voice. "Because I'm telling you, you *never* have. I'd have remembered."

He stared at me with disbelief. Then he lunged forward, pushing me flat in the pillows once more. He leaned over me, his mouth a brush of lips away from my own, his breath warm on my face.

"*Love* you? Of course I love you. Baby, I fucking worship you."

We moved into each other's arms, a tangle of warm, bare limbs on rumpled sheets. He was holding me so tight, it hurt. As we rocked together, I could feel his heart pounding away beneath supple skin — pulsing faster than my own — I could hear his harsh, quick breath.

"Are you scared?" I whispered.

He gave a shaky laugh. "Maybe I am."

He gathered me close, rolled so that I was on top of him. I sat up, straddling him, running my hands down his broad, muscular chest, feeling the crisp silk of his body hair, feeling the points of his nipples stiffen. He sucked in a sharp breath.

"I like that."

"I can tell." I found his cock — or it found me — rising long and thick, leaking excitement, the sharp, pungent smell of sex wafting between us. I was already erect and pulsing in needy discomfort. It had been way too long; flying solo was not the same. I rubbed our cocks together, finding that tidal rhythm, that ancient meter, long, slow strokes like the crest and fall of waves.

Pleasure built like an underswell, that turbulent, kinetic energy swirling up, whirling to the surface. I moved my hand faster. He bucked against my haunches sending a frisson of delight though the network of nerves and muscles. One big hand stroked my back, caressed all the way down my spine, smoothing over the curve of my ass and tracing its way to the tight knot of warm, dry skin between my buttocks, gently probing.

I groaned. "Yes. There. Please."

I massaged our cocks more frantically as he pushed harder against the tight opening. Long, sensitive fingers with blunt tips. He poked through that instinctive resistance, moving back and forth in an exquisite tease.

"Like that? That what you want?"

That shivery, sweet friction. No one touched me the way Jake did, with that easy, unshockable expertise as though he knew my every secret desire.

I wriggled and strained against him, wanting more. I could hear the sounds I was making, embarrassing, frantic noises as

I squirmed and rubbed. Only with him could I let go like this, permit myself this…

I could hear the rush of his breathing, feel the slippery leak of excitement and need between us, seed pearls easing the friction between our moist, sweaty bodies. He was panting now, thrusting hard into my hand, his finger doing unspeakably enjoyable things to me.

Oh, it had been far, far too long for both of us.

I tensed, felt my thundering heart pause and consider. Release came in a tidal wave, roaring in from the bottomless deep, rushing forward in a shining wall and knocking down every remaining barrier, every doubt and fear…sweeping away all resistance. Sea swelter pulsed sweetly, slickly on Jake's skin.

I slumped forward as Jake came with an inarticulate cry, squeezing the air out of my lungs as he clutched me tight, orgasm ripping through him seconds later.

ʃ ʃ ʃ ʃ

I woke to the sound of gnawing as though giant rats were chewing through the walls.

They were not my walls. This was not my room. I turned my head, and Jake was lying beside me, his eyes shut, his lashes dark crescents against his cheekbones. He was breathing slowly, evenly, but I knew he wasn't asleep.

I said, "Your dog is chewing the legs off this bed."

"He's your dog."

Was he? It seemed that he was. "What's his name?"

"That would be for you to decide."

I thought about it, stared up at the ceiling fan moving air languidly around the room. "Scout," I said dreamily.

Jake snorted.

"What's wrong with that?"

He shook his head, eyes still closed.

"Scout, stop chewing the bed," I ordered.

Scout sat up, the one ear tilting drunkenly.

"You shouldn't have done that," Jake said.

He was proved correct about thirty seconds later.

"Get off the bed," I ordered.

Scout laughed his puppy bologna-breath into my face. I turned my head toward Jake. "He's not very well trained."

"I'm sure now that you're taking over, he'll shape up in no time."

"Get off the bed, Scout," I ordered.

Scout circled twice and folded up on my legs. He looked at me from under his eyelashes.

$$\int \int \int \int$$

The next time was more urgent — and yet easier. It was getting familiar again.

Hands ranging possessively, relearning, caressing, reassuring. "I love you," Jake whispered. "Are you strong enough for this?"

I made myself comfortable. Said over my shoulder, "Sure."

"Would you tell me if you weren't?"

I grinned. "Maybe. I can't think of a nicer way to commit suicide."

"That's good. I can't think of a more pleasant way to commit murder."

Maybe it wasn't so funny given recent history, but we'd always shared that black sense of humor.

Like the Boy Scout he had been, he was always prepared. Very rarely we had done foolish things, but generally he was even more careful and cautious in this way than I was. How had he managed it with Kate? How had he explained the ongoing need for protection between wedded man and wife? Or in his fear had he risked her life and health? No, I didn't believe he would do that. So...more lies. Complicated and involved lies.

I didn't have it in me to judge him.

The oil he used was scented, flowery, and for an uncomfortable instant Kate was in the room with us, between us. But once his hands were stroking, circling, pressing, I forgot about her again. Ten months, twice a week — occasionally three times — what a pity they hadn't come up with word problems like that in geometry class... It had only been a taste, the beginning.

"Nice," I said as my body relaxed beneath that delicate invasion.

He sank into me, and we started to move together. It was tender and bruising and invigorating. The pulse of cock seeming to echo the beat of our hearts, we were so close together I couldn't tell where he stopped and I began. When release came this time, it was in delicate shock waves, echo after echo.

In the aftermath we lay together, relaxed, peaceful. It felt as though something off-kilter had slipped back into its track. The world seemed stable again. Steady and balanced and poised. Which, considering what had brought us to this, was extraordinary.

He linked his hands with mine, brought our hands to his mouth, and kissed my fingers.

I smiled. Such an old-fashioned, courtly gesture. Poor Kate. How would she survive losing him? It had nearly killed me the first time. Nearly killed us both, really. The sun was moving across the sky, and the shadows on the ceiling looked like wings.

$$\int \int \int \int$$

Afterward we talked in fits and snatches.

"Will you open your office in the bookstore when the renovations are complete?"

He said lazily, "If the price is right."

"I might be able to sweeten the deal."

He smiled, rolled onto his side so that we lay facing each other. Reaching over, he tucked a strand of hair behind my ear.

"So what's this about you developing a more healthy lifestyle?"

I made a face.

"What's that mean?"

"I don't know. Everyone's trying to make this big deal about stuff."

"What stuff?"

"Like me living over the bookstore." I rolled on my back, frowned moodily at the ceiling. Now the shadows looked like hands pressed in prayer. "The fact that I haven't had a vacation in three years."

"Since we were at the ranch."

"Right." I slid my gaze his way.

Jake was watching alertly. "What's entailed in this healthy lifestyle?"

"Exercise. Diet. Medication."

"There must be more to it than that."

"Stress management. Lots and lots of sex."

"Uh-huh. What else?"

"Various scenarios have been discussed." I said tentatively, "Apparently the house in Porter Ranch is mine, if I want it." I waited to see what he'd say. This was a fantasy I had never been unwise enough to let myself entertain. I couldn't believe I was suggesting it now.

"The one with the swimming pool? Do you want it?"

"It's too big for me on my own."

He said casually, "Not an issue now, is it?"

"Are you sure?"

"Up to you. You're the confirmed bachelor. I like domesticity."

"Confirmed bachelor?" Mildly startled, I reflected on that.

"You like your space. Physical and emotional."

"I wouldn't mind...you."

His smile was a mix of affection and skepticism. He added pragmatically, "The house sounds like a good idea. Not too far from Pasadena. Just far enough from Chatsworth. Pool for you. Big yard for the dog."

"And the cat."

"And the cat."

"Natalie could move into my apartment above the bookstore. I think that would simplify things for her and Lisa."

"It's worth considering."

I smiled, closing my eyes. Wait till Dr. Shearer got a load of my cardiac-rehab partner. She'd waxed long and loudly on her disappointment with me that morning.

I opened my eyes. "What was it you were going to tell me?"

Jake looked blank.

"When I arrived here today, you said you had something to tell me."

He tensed. Closed his eyes and opened them. All at once, he looked years older. "Christ. I forgot. How the hell did I forget that?"

"You've had a few things on your mind."

The expression in his eyes was bleak as they met my own. "It's bad news."

"Tell me."

"Harry Newman is dead. He was shot to death."

CHAPTER EIGHTEEN

"It has to be a coincidence," I insisted.

We were sitting on the sofa in the living room eating scrambled eggs. The sofa was one of two pieces of furniture. The other piece was a large, relatively new flat-screen TV.

When Jake didn't respond. I said, "Newman didn't exactly walk the straight and narrow. He could have pissed off the wrong people or stumbled into something."

"I think it's a pretty big coincidence. Newman wasn't technically retired, but he wasn't working any cases either."

"But everybody's dead."

"Not everybody."

"Mostly. Besides, I thought we were in agreement that Truffaut was the most logical person to have killed Stevens?"

"Truffaut made a very good suspect. And a convenient one, since he's not around to argue," he agreed. "But I wasn't ever entirely sold on Truffaut as our perp."

"This is news to me." I started to put my plate down, caught his expression, and picked up my fork again.

"Truffaut had motive, sure. And he probably had means. Though we have no idea of his movements the night Stevens died."

"It's not in Argyle's case notes?"

"Argyle had no information on Truffaut or the Cross of Rouen."

"How could that be, if he talked to Louise Reynard?"

Jake's voice was colorless. "Louise Reynard might not have confided that information. With Stevens gone and his sister and her lover denying everything, it's not something she could prove — and it might have been dangerous for her to try."

"Okay. Chris Powers is our culprit."

"And that conclusion is based on what?"

I tried to read his expression. "There's something you're not telling me."

"You said it. We're running out of suspects."

"We've still got Chris Powers. He's got the strongest motive at this point. He's planning to run for office, and his mother's history is pretty shady. It could be a problem on the campaign trail."

History. Reputations. Good names. Did people still kill to protect those things?

Blackmail simply didn't seem like the motive it once had in these days of reality TV and tell-all memoirs.

"How would Powers know about Newman?"

"Jinx could have told him."

"How would she know?"

"She knew about the PI Louise Reynard hired. I mean, she says she'd forgotten, but how could she? If we want to consider all the possibilities, *Jinx* had as much motive as anyone."

Not that I believed that. She had cried on the phone that morning. Cried when she realized Dan Hale hadn't killed her brother.

Scratch Jinx.

As though reading my mind, he said, "Did you believe her when you talked to her on the phone?"

I nodded.

Jake said patiently, "So even if Jinx did remember Louise hired a PI, she might have forgotten his name. Fifty years is a long time, and they've been busy years for her. If she did know about Newman and feared a revelation on his part, why wait till now to get rid of him?"

"I don't know. We'd have to ask her. Look, I freely admit I don't believe Jinx killed Newman. I'm sure she didn't kill her brother — because she believed Dan Hale killed him. And if she didn't kill Jay, she had no reason to kill Newman. That still leaves her son. Chris Powers has plenty of motive, and he threatened me."

"Chris Powers has an alibi."

"What?"

"He's got an alibi. Newman was gunned down Saturday morning when he went for a bike ride. Powers was sailing with friends at the time of Newman's death."

"He could have hired someone."

"True."

I could see he didn't buy it. He had already worked this out.

"The motive can't be the Cross of Rouen, or it would have shown up by now."

"The motive is the same thing it's always been."

I picked my glass of orange juice off the floor. Sipped it. Considered. "I guess I'm more tired than I thought, because I'm not following this. I thought we were agreed that Stevens was killed for the cross?"

"We were. Newman's death changes everything."

"And you won't consider the idea that it was a coincidence?"

"I know it wasn't."

I was getting a very bad feeling. "Okay. So the motive for Newman's death is…fear of exposure? Somehow, as he reviewed the case, he figured out who killed Jay Stevens? He obviously wasn't above a little bit of friendly extortion. Did he try to blackmail someone?"

"I think so. That's my guess. I don't have any proof."

"I don't believe Eve Truffaut cares enough about her father's reputation to commit murder to protect it. So that leaves Chris Powers — who apparently has an alibi. Who else is left?"

Scout padded over, snuffling my orange juice and nearly knocking the glass over. I steadied it. My head jerked up, and I stared at Jake.

"No way. Why?"

"I don't know why. At least…I'm not certain."

"You're sure he's our guy? Why?"

"Because the only person I told about Newman was Nick Argyle. Hell, I showed him a photo and said Newman was trying to break in to the bookstore. I practically hand-delivered him."

I swallowed hard. The orange juice had turned sour in my stomach.

"I don't think so, Jake. Argyle's not the type. He was a good cop. You can tell —"

"No, you can't tell," he said harshly.

I could see how hard this was for him. He liked Argyle. Maybe identified with him.

"This isn't making sense to me. If he killed Newman, he killed Stevens. Stevens *had* to have been killed for the cross, and I don't believe for one minute that Argyle would have stolen that cross. I don't care how valuable it was. He wasn't — isn't — that type."

"No. He wasn't that type."

I didn't get his tone of voice at all. "Do you think in his obsession to put Stevens behind bars —"

I stopped and reconsidered that obsession. I remembered Dan Hale saying how Argyle was at the club all the time, his eyes eating alive Jinx — or someone — on the bandstand. I thought about Argyle — seemingly unmarried and living alone — the house with no photos, no woman's touch.

I sat up straight. "Jesus. Argyle's gay, isn't he?"

His voice was quiet. "I don't know. I think so."

"He was in love with Jay Stevens."

"I don't know that either. Clearly he was obsessed with him."

"Even if you're right, why kill him?"

Jake shook his head.

I remembered Argyle saying that Louise Reynard had never confirmed hiring Newman — he'd tried to discredit Newman. There had to be a reason for that.

I remembered something else. Something that, strangely enough, seemed even more significant: Alonzo's butting into an investigation that was not his own. Butting in for his own personal reasons. Argyle had stated Louise Reynard made a nuisance of herself after Stevens disappeared, but why would she be a nuisance to Argyle? He was working robbery-homicide. He wouldn't have been in charge of Stevens's disappearance. Shouldn't have. And yet there he'd been. The whole time.

I said, "Without Newman we're never going to be able to prove any of this."

Scout bumbled up with those big feet and sat down, leaning against Jake's leg. Jake absently scratched him behind his ears. "Yes, we are."

I didn't like the sound of that. "Meaning what exactly?"

"I don't know why Argyle killed Stevens, but he killed Newman to cover up the first murder. If he was willing to kill twice, I don't see him stopping there. He's not about to — can't — risk discovery now."

"Quit trying to spoon-feed it to me. Tell me whatever the hell it is you're thinking."

"Argyle called me this afternoon, not long before you arrived, and told me he thought he'd figured out where Stevens might have hidden the cross. He wants to meet tonight."

"Where?" I asked with foreboding.

"The Tides."

I stood up. "Come on, Jake. He's setting a trap for you. A nighttime meet on a lonely deserted beach? *Jake*. He's afraid of what Newman might have told you, and now he's coming after you."

Jake nodded.

"You know that. So…call the cops."

Nothing.

I sat down again. I felt winded. "You're not going to call the cops."

"No."

"Great. Just fucking great." I scowled at him. "After all this, I'll be damned if you're not going to go out there and get yourself killed. *Why?* Because you feel loyalty, affection for this ex-cop you didn't even know two weeks ago?"

He let me come to a full stop before saying, "I can't explain why I feel like I need to do this, but I promise you I'm not going to get myself killed. Okay?"

"Not really." I eyed him narrowly. "But if I can't stop you, I'm sure as hell going with you."

♪ ♪ ♪

The tide pulsed against the naked shingles of bone white beach. The stark moon burned high above hanging from the rafters of clouds — an ugly, lightbulb moon casting harsh chiaroscuro shadows on the sand dunes and crumbling, grassy hillside.

The café was dark and silent, like a black cardboard cutout silhouetted against a big paper moon. The nearby pier gleamed skeletal in the bright moonlight as the midnight water rushed around its pylons.

I watched Jake stride down toward the rickety structure, and I steadied the pistol on my forearm and watched the shadows.

We had argued a lot about this, Jake and I, and the compromise had been that he was going to meet Argyle whether I liked it or not — and whether he liked it or not, I was going too. The first compromise of this new life together — and hopefully not the last.

Something moved in the deep shade at the end of the pier. My gaze sharpened. My heart thumped hard against my breastbone, but that was okay. It was a normal scared-shitless heartbeat.

We were a couple of hours early, but I didn't trust that. However wily we thought we were, Argyle was the fox and we were the hounds.

"Nick?" Jake called.

Nothing moved, nothing but the tide soughing against the shore. Was there a more desolate sound?

"Okay, Nick," Jake said. "We both know why I'm here."

There was a slide of sand and pebbles to the right of me, and Argyle came down the slope at a half run.

I nearly shot him then and there. Partly because I'd thought he was under the pier and he startled the hell out of me, and partly because I wasn't sure whether Jake's affection for the old man might prove hazardous to his own health.

I didn't shoot. Well concealed in the rocks, I waited, and Argyle strolled past me, lean and easy moving like a much-younger man, like the man he'd once been. Steady and purposeful.

Jake turned to face him, his hand resting on his hip, where he was wearing his pistol beneath the open jacket.

I didn't think Argyle missed the significance of that, though his voice was almost friendly. "I didn't think you'd come, son."

"Sure you did."

Sure he did. Jake identified with old Wyatt Earp there, and I was pretty sure the feeling was reciprocated.

Our agreement, such as it was, was that if Argyle shot Jake — if Jake went down — I would empty my gun into Argyle. I had promised I would not hesitate. I wouldn't. My only hesitation was the terrible temptation to shoot Argyle now — in the back — before he ever had a chance to kill Jake. In one corner of my brain, I was horrified at myself. And in the other, I was judging whether, as easy a target as he made in the moonlight, I was a good-enough shot. The last time I'd been target shooting was with Jake. That had been over two years ago.

Besides, I wasn't sure whether Jake would forgive me.

"So you want me to tell you where the Cross of Rouen is?" Argyle said. "That it?"

"You sound like you think you know."

"I don't know for sure," Argyle said. "The tide has probably moved it quite a bit in half a century. I threw it off the edge of the pier."

Jake had known the truth, had hours to come to terms with it, and yet I could hear in the flatness of his voice that he had still hoped… "You threw it in the ocean."

"Wasn't any good to me. Near as I could figure, it wasn't any particular good to anyone in five centuries. And my fingerprints were on it. And Jay's blood."

"You're confessing to killing Jay Stevens?"

"I think you already figured that out, son. You've got your pal hiding in the rocks back there. I guess you know most of it by now."

The hair on the back of my neck stood up. I couldn't believe how calm Jake sounded. "I don't know why you killed Stevens. It obviously wasn't for the cross."

"Now that, I think, is the one thing you *do* know absolutely for sure. I think you know exactly why I killed Jay."

The ocean filled in the silence.

"Because you were — because you loved him."

"I don't know if I'd call it love," Argyle said wearily. "Maybe. I wouldn't have called it love back then, that's for damn sure. But I wanted him, all right. I wanted him so bad, I'd have let him go and take the damn cross with him, if he'd just have…"

He stopped.

Jake said, working his way through it, trying to understand, "You couldn't afford for anyone to know." And then, astonishingly, "Things were different in those days."

"That's true, but that wasn't why. That was why I couldn't come forward. Not ever. But believe it or not, I didn't intend to kill Jay. He was so...shocked, so...repulsed. I saw myself through his eyes. And what I saw there —" Time had not dulled that anguish, that fury. It still burned bright. "I hated him. Hated what I was. I never hated anything so much. I grabbed the cross off the bed, and I hit him with it. Once. Only once. He folded up like a house of cards. He died right there in my arms."

Even over the tide I could hear his hard, labored breaths — as though he'd been running all his life to reach this rendezvous.

"Then what?" Jake's voice sounded thick.

It seemed to take Argyle time to find the words. "Then I put him in the floor right where he'd hidden the cross. Him and his clarinet. I nailed it up again. I took the cross. It was wet with his blood. And put it under my jacket, and I walked out of the hotel and drove down to the beach — drove here — walked out on the pier and threw it into the water. And that was that."

When Jake didn't respond, he said, "No one saw me. No one...questioned it. Until you. Until you came along asking about Jay. Digging up the past."

"And Harry Newman?"

"It took fifty years for Harry Newman to figure out what was underneath his nose the whole time. When he did finally figure it out, he thought he'd found a way to fund his retirement. Don't waste your time feeling bad about Harry Newman."

"Why kill him if you were just going to turn around and confess?" Jake's voice was hard, but I heard the undernote of pain.

"Because I didn't plan on confessing."

I stared at the tense outline of Jake's silhouette. He *had* to know. Even I knew.

I saw Argyle shake his head. "I'm seventy-nine years old. I can't go to prison. I didn't stay silent fifty years to blab my story in a court of law now. I thought if I got rid of Newman, that would be the end of it. It was already too late. He'd already told you too much, and you were connecting the dots to the rest. You're good, Jake. You remind me of myself at your age."

I saw his shoulders move, saw him reach up to his shoulder holster. Jake drew his pistol, stepped into firing stance, and shot him in the chest. The blast echoed off the sandstone cliffs, seemed to reverberate forever.

Argyle stood there, weaving. He dropped the pistol. His knees gave, and he crashed to the sand.

Jake was beside him in three long strides. He turned him over gently. I scrambled out of my hiding place in the rocks and knelt beside them.

"Nick?"

Argyle's eyes showed white. His bloody mouth moved. He stopped breathing.

"Oh Christ," Jake whispered. He looked at me.

"Don't, Jake." I gripped his arm. "Don't you see? He planned this."

I don't know if he even heard me, but I knew I was right. Argyle had seen me in the rocks. The only reason I wasn't dead was he'd known at that point it was all over. He couldn't have shot me without Jake taking him out, and he was too good an old lawman to kill me if there wasn't a good reason.

But if Jake had come alone?

I said, "He knew exactly how this would play out. He knew you were armed. He knew how you'd react because — he said it — you reminded him of himself."

He was still shaking his head. For a time we stayed like that, with the distant sigh and rush of the ink black ocean. The surf pounded the shore in its heavy, ceaseless heartbeat.

Argyle's dead, glazed eyes stared up at the moon cresting the billowing white clouds like a silver galleon. I watched Jake and waited.

At last, he said, "I need to call this in."

We rose and started back across the white wash of sand. Behind us, Argyle's body looked no more substantial than a shadow.

As we reached the rocks, the strength went out of me, and I sat down on the nearest flat-topped boulder, leaning forward, resting my face in my hands.

Chandler said it. "I was as empty and hollow as the spaces between the stars."

Jake dropped down beside me. He put a hand on my shoulder, and I started to tremble. "Are you okay?" His voice was gruff.

I nodded.

"What's wrong? Adrien?"

I shook my head. I didn't dare try to speak. The realization of how close Jake and I had come loomed up before me.

For forty years, Jake had tried to force himself into being something he wasn't, and the fact that he wasn't crazy or a murderer was probably a miracle. If things had played out differently a few weeks ago…

I fought it, but the dam was breaking. I could feel the stone and mortar crumbling away and all the emotion, all the grief and fear and anger rushing out in a torrent. Two years, maybe even three years, of trying to hold it back.

I tried. The raw sound tore out of my throat, and even the pain of my healing bones and muscles couldn't stop those ragged sobs. Not for myself really. Or not only for myself. What were those three lonely years compared to the forty Jake had lost? Forty years of believing he wasn't good enough, wasn't worthy, wasn't even normal. Maybe half his life, if he lived to be as old as Nick Argyle. And Nick Argyle? His entire life. And all the other Nick Argyles…past and present?

It could have been us. It nearly was.

"Don't. Don't, baby."

I nodded. Drew deep, shuddering breaths.

"I want to tell you something," Jake said against my ear. His face was wet.

I nodded.

"I've always been grateful — even when I was married, even when I thought it was over between us — that it was you I fell in love with."

His cold face rested against mine as I listened to the echo of his words. Maybe it was true. Maybe one person could make a difference. Maybe love could make a difference. It had made a difference to me.

Jake kissed my jaw, kissed the corner of my mouth. I pulled away, wiped my face.

"You want to catch your breath while I go call this in?"

"No." I stood up. Brushed the last of the tears away. "I'll go with you."

The long and melancholy sigh of the dark tide followed us as we walked up the sandy steps to the car.

ABOUT THE AUTHOR

A distinct voice in gay fiction, multi-award-winning author JOSH LANYON has been writing gay mystery, adventure and romance for over a decade. In addition to numerous short stories, novellas, and novels, Josh is the author of the critically acclaimed Adrien English series, including The Hell You Say, winner of the 2006 USABookNews awards for GLBT Fiction. Josh is a two-time Lambda Literary Award finalist. You can visit his websites at:

http://www.joshlanyon.com/

http://jgraeme2007.livejournal.com/

http://groups.yahoo.com/group/JoshLanyon

THE TREVOR PROJECT

The Trevor Project operates the only nationwide, around-the-clock crisis and suicide prevention helpline for lesbian, gay, bisexual, transgender and questioning youth. Every day, The Trevor Project saves lives though its free and confidential helpline, its website and its educational services. If you or a friend are feeling lost or alone call The Trevor Helpline. If you or a friend are feeling lost, alone, confused or in crisis, please call The Trevor Helpline. You'll be able to speak confidentially with a trained counselor 24/7.

The Trevor Helpline: 866-488-7386

On the Web: http://www.thetrevorproject.org/

THE GAY MEN'S DOMESTIC VIOLENCE PROJECT

Founded in 1994, The Gay Men's Domestic Violence Project is a grassroots, non-profit organization founded by a gay male survivor of domestic violence and developed through the strength, contributions and participation of the community. The Gay Men's Domestic Violence Project supports victims and survivors through education, advocacy and direct services. Understanding that the serious public health issue of domestic violence is not gender specific, we serve men in relationships with men, regardless of how they identify, and stand ready to assist them in navigating through abusive relationships.

GMDVP Helpline: 800.832.1901

On the Web: http://gmdvp.org/

THE GAY & LESBIAN ALLIANCE AGAINST DEFAMATION / GLAAD EN ESPAÑOL

The Gay & Lesbian Alliance Against Defamation (GLAAD) is dedicated to promoting and ensuring fair, accurate and inclusive representation of people and events in the media as a means of eliminating homophobia and discrimination based on gender identity and sexual orientation.

On the Web: http://www.glaad.org/

GLAAD en español:

   http://www.glaad.org/espanol/bienvenido.php

If you're a GLBT and questioning student heading off to university, should know that there are resources on campus for you. Here's just a sample:

US Local GLBT college campus organizations
    http://dv-8.com/resources/us/local/campus.html
GLBT Scholarship Resources
    http://tinyurl.com/6fx9v6
Syracuse University
    http://lgbt.syr.edu/
Texas A&M
    http://glbt.tamu.edu/
Tulane University
    http://www.oma.tulane.edu/LGBT/Default.htm
University of Alaska
    http://www.uaf.edu/agla/
University of California, Davis
    http://lgbtrc.ucdavis.edu/
University of California, San Francisco
    http://lgbt.ucsf.edu/
University of Colorado
    http://www.colorado.edu/glbtrc/
University of Florida
    http://www.dso.ufl.edu/multicultural/lgbt/
University of Hawai'i, Mānoa
    http://manoa.hawaii.edu/lgbt/
University of Utah
    http://www.sa.utah.edu/lgbt/
University of Virginia
    http://www.virginia.edu/deanofstudents/lgbt/
Vanderbilt University
    http://www.vanderbilt.edu/lgbtqi/

Stimulate yourself.
READ.
www.manloveromance.com
THE HOTTEST M/M EROTIC AUTHORS & WEBSITES ON THE NET